MACK DADDY

NEW YORK TIMES BESTSELLING AUTHOR

PENELOPE WARD

First Edition, February 2017
Copyright © 2016 by
Penelope Ward
ISBN-13: 978-1542365994
ISBN-10: 1542365996

Cover Model: Anthony Gomez/anthonygomez.net
Cover Photographer:
Duc Nguyen/ducphotography.com
Cover Design: Letitia Hasser, RBA Designs
Proofreading & Formatting by Elaine York,
Allusion Graphics, LLC/Publishing & Book Formatting
www.allusiongraphics.com

CHAPTER ONE

Francesca

"You should get a look at the DILF at the registration desk," Lorelai whispered as she entered my classroom. "Hottest dad I've ever seen in my five years here."

I loved her to death, but my teaching assistant was a total bimbo. She threw around the "DILF" term a lot. *Daddy I'd Like to Fuck.* I sometimes had to wonder whether she was here to shape children's lives by teaching them or to influence their lives by stealing one of their fathers. Not to mention, this was supposed to be an uptight, religious institution. Priests and nuns were always lurking around these halls, and she couldn't have cared less.

"I have better things to do than fawn over married men today, Lor. None of these tables are even configured right. We have ten minutes till doors open."

It was the first day of classes at the private Catholic school where I worked as a first-grade teacher. Located

1

on the outskirts of Boston, St. Matthew's was an exclusive educational institution that welcomed boys and girls from all over the state if their parents could afford the twenty-thousand dollars per year tuition. Unlike a certain co-worker, I took my job very seriously.

Whereas most of my friends who were teachers dreaded the end of summer, I loved everything about the first day of school: the crisp fall air, the smell of new clothes, getting into a routine again.

"Seriously, this dad was a different level of hot," Lorelai said, pushing one of the chairs into its rightful position. "You know that perfect hair that some movie stars have? Thick, lush, shiny hair you want to run your fingers through? Like the guy from *White Collar*? What's his name?"

Sliding a chair into place, I answered, "Matt Bomer."

"Yes! That kind of hair. This guy didn't look like him per se, but he was just that kind of handsome. Tall, muscular, smelled good. And he has the cutest little boy, too. Kid had glasses and curly hair. He might even be in this class, because he looks pretty young."

I hadn't met any of my new students yet. There was an orientation I had to miss due to a prescheduled trip for my mother's destination wedding in Antigua. Another colleague had filled in for me. So, I felt even more out of the loop than usual.

I tried to get Lorelai to focus on the task at hand. "Wanna put these welcome packets on each table, please?"

2

Nothing seemed to be going my way today. I'd spilled some white paint on my black skirt as I placed the individual containers at each station. I had the bright idea that we would start the day by having the kids try their hands at painting a portrait of a new friend. I figured it would be a good way for them to break the ice and get to know one another. All of this would happen after the morning prayer of course, which was mandated to be the very first order of business before the day started.

Once I opened the doors, parents started trickling in with their children. I spent more time than usual on introductions, since I hadn't had the opportunity to meet anyone at the orientation.

Getting to know each student's individual needs and personalities would take some time, but I was always eager to familiarize myself with each and every one as fast as possible.

When I finally had my first chance to breathe after the parents and children dispersed, I was just about to head over to my desk for a quick sip of water when a familiar voice seemed to vibrate against my back.

"Frankie."

The hairs behind my neck stiffened, and my body stilled. That familiar, baritone voice shook me to my core. There was only one person in the entire world who called me by that nickname—a name that hadn't been uttered in years.

3

There was no possible explanation for why he could have been here. He lived in D.C., or maybe it was Virginia now.

He couldn't be here.

I braced for the worst, forcing myself to turn and face him.

A sudden onslaught of heat permeated my face, and it felt like my legs were going to collapse out from under me.

Mack.

Not only was Mackenzie Morrison standing right in front of me, but he looked even more amazing than I could recall. He was everything I remembered, just magnified. His muscles were even more defined, and gritty stubble peppered his angular jaw.

His sparkling eyes were searing into mine with a determined look that made me a bit uneasy. Clearly, this reunion wasn't having the same effect on him as it was on me. While my mouth felt numb, unable to form words, he appeared ready for this moment.

"You look like you've just seen a ghost."

"You might as well be one," I muttered under my breath.

"I expected this reaction."

I whispered, "Jesus."

We weren't supposed to use the Lord's name in vain here. I couldn't remember my own name right now let alone a single one of the Ten Commandments.

Opting not to look him in the eyes any longer, my gaze travelled down to his large hands and the veins protruding from them. The recollection of what it had felt like to wrap my fingers in his was clear as day.

It suddenly hit me that Mack was the DILF Lorelai had been referring to. For the first and only time, she hadn't been exaggerating about how incredibly good-looking someone was.

His tone was demanding. "Look at me, Frankie." When I didn't listen, he repeated, "Look at me."

I lifted my head. To look him in the face was truly painful, triggering an onslaught of memories I preferred to keep at bay. One thing was for certain: the grown man standing before me was far more confident than the guy whom I'd last seen with tears in his eyes.

"I don't understand. How is this possible? What are you doing here at my school?"

He slowly approached me, causing my skin to heat. "We live here now—in Massachusetts."

We live here.

Who was 'we' exactly?

My heart was thumping out of my chest in a mix of fear and an oddly disconcerting excitement that I didn't quite understand.

The wheels were turning in my head. I remembered looking at the class list and noticing a Jonah Morrison. The last name freaked me out a little, but I never could have imagined in a million years that it was Mack's son.

"Moses never told me you were living here in Boston."

"I know. I told him I wanted to be the one to tell you about the move."

I stepped back a bit, too overwhelmed by the closeness of his body and the realization that he smelled the same, that his earthy scent still caused my body to have the same reaction it always had.

My eyes wandered to the corner of the room, where out of process of elimination I identified Mack's little boy.

His son.

Oh, my God.

Mack seemed to notice where I was looking and allowed me a moment to take it all in. I could feel him watching me watching his kid.

Jonah was a bit scrawny. Through his thick glasses, I could see that he had his father's hazel eyes but otherwise looked more like his mother. His head full of kinky curls was a darker shade of brown than Mack's.

My eyes returned to meet his when I asked, "How did your son end up in my class?"

"If I told you it was a coincidence, would you believe me?"

"No."

"Well, it's not," he was quick to admit.

"Why? Why are you doing this? Why didn't you warn me?"

"Would it have made it any easier?"

"No," I whispered.

"We came to the orientation. You weren't there. I was hoping to have this happen then, not on the first day of school."

I wasn't sure if by 'we' he meant him and Jonah or him and his wife. Or was it his girlfriend? Were they even still together? I had no clue.

My heart was pounding even harder at the thought of having to meet Jonah's mother, Torrie. "Where's his mother?"

"She has to be at work early in the morning. I'll be picking him up to take him to school every day since I work from home."

It was all too much. I started to walk away. "You'll have to excuse me. I have to attend to my students."

The kids were talking among themselves, making a racket, and oblivious to what was going on with Mack and me.

He followed close behind. "I know this is a shock."

"You think?" I quipped, before turning around to face him again.

"Let me just introduce you to Jonah. Then I'll leave." He walked over to the boy, who was seated and messing with his lunch box. Although I'd never met Torrie in person, I'd seen pictures and knew she was multi-racial, a beautiful mix of black and white. Jonah's skin was olive-toned, somewhere in between Torrie and Mack's complexions.

"Jonah, this is your teacher, Frankie."

"Miss O'Hara," I quickly corrected. "Francesca O'Hara. It's nice to meet you, Jonah."

The boy wouldn't look me in the eye and began to fidget.

Seemingly embarrassed by his son's behavior, Mack raised his voice. "Jonah! Frankie is talking to you," he said, clearly ignoring my request to be addressed more formally.

The kid's face turned beet red. "Hi," he finally said while reluctantly lifting his head to look at me.

"It's great to meet you. Welcome to St. Matthew's."

Actually, I'm terrified to meet you.

Mack was the only parent left in the room, and we were already behind schedule.

Lorelai's eyes were glued to the two of us. A smug grin spread across her face when she mouthed "DILF" as if I didn't know it was Mack she'd been referring to earlier. Then, her eyes landed on Mack's ass before she gave me a thumbs-up. His back was facing her, so he had no clue.

I addressed her, "Miss Brown, will you lead the class in the morning prayer, please, while I walk Mr. Morrison out?"

"Sure." She winked then mouthed, "Holy fucking shit."

My heart was pounding as Mack followed me out the door.

When I turned to him, I noticed that a look of worry on his face had replaced the confidence from earlier.

"So...my son...he gets... anxious—really nervous very easily. I worry about him."

I let him continue.

"You're the only one I trust with him, Frankie. His mother works all of the time. And I don't know what the

8

fuck I'm doing, in general. I know it may seem like eons ago that we were close, and I know you're confused right now. I know I fucked everything up between us, but I've never forgotten you. Not a single day. When Torrie was transferred to Boston, I knew it was a sign. Moses told me where you were teaching, and when I found out it was first grade, I took that as the *biggest* sign. I did everything I could to get him into this class."

Letting out a long, shaky breath, I just continued to look at him but said nothing.

Mack looked around to make sure no one was watching us then said, "I know we can't say everything that needs to be said right now. This is neither the time nor place. My intention certainly isn't to get you into trouble." His eyes trailed down to my black pencil skirt where I'd spilled the white paint earlier. He grinned. "I see you're still spilling suspicious, white substances on yourself."

I looked down, remembering how he'd teased me about the same thing the first time we met. My face felt hot. "I see you're a bit less crude in your terminology now. Must be the age."

"Not really. My humor is still pretty immature and crass. But this is not exactly the place to demonstrate that."

"No, it isn't." I cracked a reluctant smile.

He winked.

It was amazing how one simple movement of his eyelid could do a multitude of things to my entire body.

My physical reaction to him was certainly one thing that hadn't changed a bit. I had no clue how I was going to survive this year.

"I have to go," I said.

Ignoring my need to leave, he asked, "What happened to your glasses?"

"Lasik surgery. Don't need them anymore."

"Wow. I never thought you'd have the guts."

"Yeah. It was actually fairly seamless. I, uh, noticed Jonah's glasses are pretty thick."

"He has crappy eyesight like you did, so he needs to wear them. Of course, he doesn't wear funky turquoise or purple frames like you used to. Whenever I look at his glasses, they remind me of you, though." He smiled. "But a lot of things remind me of you."

His stare was once again making me uncomfortable, so I turned to open the door, pausing when he spoke from behind me in a thick voice.

"It's so good to see you again, Frankie."

Victor spoke with his mouth full. "Tell me all about your day, darling."

I lived with my boyfriend, Victor, in Boston's Beacon Hill. His two-story brownstone condo had more room than we knew what to do with.

Vic was an anthropology professor at Boston University, my alma mater. We'd met two years ago through mutual friends at B.U. Seventeen years my senior, he was the only older man I'd ever dated. He took care of me well, made me feel safe, and provided me with anything I needed. On the outside looking in, I was truly living the perfect life.

There was a light fall breeze coming in through the window as the sun set. The faint traffic noises from busy Cambridge Street below were the only sounds. I looked up at the dark wood molding surrounding the built-in shelves in our dining room and finally answered his question.

"Honestly, I felt very overwhelmed today. Missing that orientation was a mistake. They've stuck me with twenty-six kids, and a couple of them have some really significant needs."

"I'm sorry. That's really unfair of them to do." Victor picked the cauliflower out of his vegetable medley and took another bite. He always ate his mixed vegetables one kind at a time.

"Well, you know, each extra kid is a lot of additional revenue for the school. They just don't pay us teachers more to compensate for the extra work."

"You know you don't ever need to worry about money, right? So, don't let that stress you out."

"I know. It's not that. I just know it's going to be a challenging year."

He examined my face. "Something else is bothering you."

I couldn't tell him. I just couldn't tell him about Mack. I'd never mentioned Mack at all to Victor. What was the point? I'd been trying to forget what happened, and it was several years ago anyway. Despite the urge to blurt out, *"Oh, and the man who broke my heart showed up randomly, too,"* I chose to continue to keep that quiet.

"There's a student who has some pretty significant anxiety. He avoids the other kids, in general, and has these minor freak outs when he gets nervous, tries to leave the classroom."

My entire day had been consumed by my obsessive observation of Mack's son. Since his needs were not considered developmental, he didn't qualify for any special services. The school didn't specialize in anxiety disorders, and neither did I, aside from my own personal experience battling them. I understood why Mack felt that I was a good fit for Jonah. He'd seen me suffer my share of the same issues back when we knew each other.

I spent the remainder of dinner quietly obsessing. Seeing Mack today was a shock to the system, yet I couldn't stop thinking about him.

Victor had gone upstairs with a glass of Cognac to relax and correct some of his students' assignments. I planned to join him for the eleven o'clock news later. It was the same routine every night, for the most part.

When my cell phone rang at nine-thirty, my heart dropped. No one generally called me on a weeknight at that time. Even though I didn't recognize the number, my gut told me it was him.

CHAPTER TWO

Mack

She answered, "Hello?"

I closed my eyes at the sound of her voice, fighting the longing it triggered inside of me with every bit of energy I had left today.

"Frankie, it's Mack."

"You can't be calling me at home like this."

My stomach sank.

Great.

She fucking hates me.

"This is your cell phone, isn't it? It was in the email you sent to all of the parents. You said to call you anytime if we needed you."

I need you.

"I know, but...it's late."

"I needed to hear your voice, to know I didn't totally freak you out today."

She laughed a little. "Well, sorry, I can't say that, because you absolutely did."

"I know." After a long moment of silence, I said, "I can't stop thinking about you."

Whoa.

Back up.

I immediately regretted that admission, adding, "I mean...God, Frankie, to see you after all these years. For me, it was like no time had passed. I'm so fucking proud of you. You always said you wanted to be a teacher. You made it happen. What you do every day, it's the hardest job in the world."

"Exactly what do you need in regards to Jonah, Mack?"

Ouch.

"How was he today?"

"He seemed very nervous. My teacher's aide took him out of the classroom for a brief walk when he appeared to get anxious during a group discussion. But he seemed a bit calmer when they returned."

I was just about at my wit's end when it came to my son. I loved him so much, but his anxiety wasn't something I knew how to handle very well. It wasn't as easy as telling him to snap out of it, that was for damn sure.

"When he was younger, he was fine. Right around five years old, he started getting panic attacks, anxiety, you name it. My moving out hasn't helped the situation."

"What do you mean? You don't live with him?"

"No. Torrie and I aren't together anymore."

In her classroom today, I'd alluded to the fact that I'd be picking him up in the mornings, but she must not have put two and two together.

She didn't respond right away. Listening to the sound of her breaths, I let her process. I *knew* she needed to process that piece of information.

"When did that happen?"

"About a year ago. I tried to stick it out as long as I could for Jonah, but it was never gonna work. It wasn't an easy decision, but I was miserable for a very long time. I couldn't take it anymore."

"Moses never mentioned any of this."

"Yeah, well he and I haven't really had a chance to discuss it. He knows I'm back here, but he doesn't know the full details."

Moses Vasco was our only mutual friend. The three of us once lived together in an apartment above a strip of stores in Boston's Kenmore Square. After I left, I'd kept in touch with Moses mainly to get information on Frankie, but he and I had never been particularly close to begin with.

"Where are you living?" she asked.

"I bought a house in Framingham just off Route Nine. I wanted to make sure Jonah felt like he had a real home when he was with me, one with a yard and a nice bedroom."

"Where does his mother live?"

"Not far from the school in Newton. She commutes into Boston. Jonah's with her during the week, stays with a nanny after school while I'm working. I work from home."

"Am I going to meet her?"

The thought of my ex and Frankie coming face to face freaked me out. But I knew it was inevitable.

"She's planning on going in to meet with you soon."

"Does she know about us?"

"No. She doesn't have a clue that we used to know each other."

"Okay. I prefer it that way."

"Of course." Lying my head against the back of my bed, I sighed and asked the question that had been gnawing at me. "Are you happy, Frankie?"

After some silence, she said, "Yes."

"Tell me about the old guy you're living with."

"He's not that old."

"Fifty?"

"Forty-five."

"Old enough. His balls still in good shape? How low do they hang?"

"Oh, my God!"

I'd almost forgotten how much I loved embarrassing her.

"How low?" I was laughing and was relieved to get the sense that she was, too.

"I see you're still tactless."

"I see you still can't help but be amused by it." I let out a breath. "Seriously, does he treat you right?"

"Yes. He treats me like gold."

Why did hearing that hurt my chest? I wanted her to be happy. It shouldn't have hurt so goddamn much to hear that.

"Good. That's what you deserve."

"Do you have anything else you'd like to discuss?"

Do you still shave your pussy?

Trying to ignore the rumblings of my overly excited inner thoughts, I said, "Actually, I wanted to talk to you about volunteering. What can I do to help this year?"

That's better.

"Well, parents sometimes come in and read a book to the class or talk about their jobs. Teach some kind of lesson. You can really choose whatever you'd like."

"How about next Wednesday?"

"What did you have in mind?"

"I'd like to read a story to the class." I totally just pulled that out of my ass. But I'd figure something out.

"Okay, I'll schedule it in for one in the afternoon."

Her being so formal with me was weird. It was irking me a little. She was acting like we didn't know everything there was to know about each other at one time. I just wanted to virtually shake her and say, "*Hey, remember that time we got drunk and you begged me to fuck you?*" At the same time, her acting this way was a challenge to break down these new walls, a challenge I would gladly accept.

"Alright. Maybe I'll see you in the morning anyway at drop off," I said.

"Okay." After a long pause, she said, "Mack?"

"Yeah?"

"He'll be okay. We'll take care of him. Even when he's having a bad day, we'll do our best to make him feel safe."

"Thank you, Frankie. I knew you would. That's why I'm here."

For him.

And for me.

For you.

I'm here for you.

I want you in my life again.

Even if all you'll give me is your friendship.

Fuck that. That will never be enough for me.

Not with you.

There was so much I wanted to tell her but couldn't. She'd hung up without saying anything further.

Even though moving to Boston had been a huge adjustment for my son, for the first time in years, *I'd* felt like myself again. I'd only spent a few years here in my early twenties, but those were the best years of my life. I felt like I was finally home again. If only my feelings for Frankie didn't feel like they were stuck in a goddamn time machine. I feel no differently about her today than I did the day I left our apartment in Kenmore Square and never looked back.

She said she was happy with this guy, but I knew Frankie. She'd tell me that even if she wasn't. I needed to really know for sure that there was definitely no chance for us. The only way to do that was to earn her trust again, show her what kind of a man I was now since becoming Jonah's dad. Be her friend. Then she'd tell me the truth. I just didn't know if I could handle it. I didn't know if I could handle going back to being only friends with her if she ended up marrying this guy.

I loved her.

She just never knew that.

"Hey, Mrs. Migillicutty!" I said, waving as I rolled in my trash barrel from the curb.

My next-door neighbor was an eighty-year-old widow who lived alone in the house she'd owned for fifty years. She'd spent the better part of the past month trying to get me to date her divorced granddaughter despite my repeatedly turning down her offers to help set us up.

"Mack, why don't you come over for some Italian rum cake?"

"Thank you, but I'd better get back to work."

"Come on. You work from home. You're your own boss. Give yourself a break and have some goddamn cake."

Chuckling, I conceded. "Well, okay then. I guess there's always time for cake."

I followed her into the house, which was a dated, split-level design. It had the same layout as the house I'd bought, except mine was much more modern inside.

"I can save a piece of cake for Jonah when he comes this weekend. There's not really that much rum in it."

"He'd love that. Thank you."

I couldn't help the fleeting thought that a little rum might do some good for my son's mood.

"How's he been adjusting to the new school?"

"Whenever I ask, he tells me his day was okay, but he wouldn't tell me if it wasn't."

"Every day will get a little better."

"Thank you. I hope so."

"What is it you do for a living again?"

"I'm a business intelligence analyst."

"Sounds fancy."

"Yeah. Well, it's just a fancy way to describe someone who gathers data. It allows me to not have to go into an office, and since I work for myself, I can be there for my son when he needs me. His mother has a different kind of job. She travels a lot. So, it's more important for me to have flexibility so he never has two parents gone at once."

"What does she do?"

"Before we moved here, she was a political consultant in D.C. She started out working as an aide to my father."

"Who's your father?"

"Michael Morrison, the Virginia senator."

"Wow."

The last thing I wanted was to talk about my father. "We won't get started on him," I said. "Anyway, Torrie sort of moved her way up in the ranks over the years and was just recruited by a public affairs and advocacy firm in Boston, which is why we moved."

"Wow. Smart people, you folks are."

"Not really. It might sound like it, but no. Far from it. We've made a lot of mistakes," I said, playing with the whipped cream frosting on my cake.

"What's wrong, Mack?"

Her question caught me off guard. "What do you mean?"

"You seem to have something preoccupying you."

"Why do you say that?"

"Just a sense I get."

"It's nothing, Mrs. M."

She put her fork down, and it clanked against the table. "I've got the time, Mack. Does it look like I have anything better to do? I'm a lot cheaper than a shrink. I have no one to even tell your secrets to. Take advantage of me. Lord knows, if I were younger, those words might have meant something else. But I'm old enough to be your grandmother." Sliding a glass of milk toward me, she said, "I could use some drama."

She was making me laugh. "Alright. You ready for a doozy?"

"Shoot."

You asked for it.

"I'm in love with my son's teacher."

"Already? You move fast."

"It's not what you think. It's much more complicated than that."

"Lay it on me. I can take it."

"Frankie was my roommate back when we were both in school in Boston several years ago. I was in grad school studying political science. She was undergrad for teaching. We have a long history."

"You've already banged her."

I bent my head back in laughter.

She seemed surprised by my reaction to her bluntness. "What?"

"I just don't expect certain things to come out of your mouth."

"Like this?" She reached into her mouth, took out her teeth, and cackled.

I laughed even harder.

This woman was a trip.

She positioned her dentures back into place and said, "Look...I have grandchildren and cable. I know the terminology."

I wiped the tears of laughter from my eyes. "Gotcha."

"So, you banged your son's teacher."

"Actually, no."

"No?"

"No."

"We were just friends for a long time. Then things gradually changed. I never expected what happened between us to develop. But it never got to that point with Frankie."

"Why not?"

"That's a story for another day, Mrs. M."

"Maybe real rum instead of rum cake for that conversation?"

Taking a bite full of my cake, I said, "Without a freaking doubt."

CHAPTER THREE

Francesca

I was unable to concentrate. Mack was coming in this afternoon to read to the class, and that was preventing me from focusing.

The students were working on some math worksheets, and I looked over at Jonah who had finished before everyone else. That was typical; he was one of the smarter kids in the class. His social anxiety certainly had no bearing on his academic progress.

I walked over to him. "Your dad told you he's coming in today, right?"

"Yeah."

"That should be fun." I smiled.

He shrugged his shoulders.

"Does that make you nervous?"

He nodded his head yes.

"Don't be."

Jonah very rarely offered anything without being asked, so I was surprised when he said, "He's going to embarrass me."

I laughed inwardly at the fact that I was expecting him to be calm about Mack coming in when I was a nervous wreck about it myself—for totally different reasons, of course.

The firm knock made me jump.

Mack offered a smile and a wave through the narrow window of the classroom door.

Lorelai looked giddy when she spotted him there, which prompted me to roll my eyes at her.

It was show time.

When I let him in, the broad smile that spread across his face brought on a sudden feeling of nostalgia. So much had changed in our lives, but the intense emotions that pummeled through me whenever I looked at him were very much the same. They were just mixed with sadness, too, now.

"Sorry I'm a few minutes late. Lunch-time traffic on Route Nine."

"It's fine."

"No, it's not," he insisted.

His eyes lingered on mine, and suddenly I was back in college again, looking into the eyes of the first guy who'd ever broken through my walls, made me comfortable in my own skin, then broke my heart. Mack still had the ability to take my breath away. I'd missed looking into those gorgeous, hazel eyes that were a mix of green, gold, and caramel with brown borders. I had to look away because I sensed he wasn't going to be the first one to break the stare.

This was going to be the longest year of my life.

Turning my attention toward the students, I cleared my throat. "Class, this is Mr. Morrison, Jonah's dad. He's going to be reading to us today."

Knowing Jonah was embarrassed, Mack grinned sheepishly at his son. "Hi, Jonah."

The boy simply turned red but didn't say anything.

"What are you reading?" I asked.

"It's a children's story I wrote myself, actually."

"I didn't know you wrote children's books."

"Neither did I until this past week." He winked.

What?

Mack situated himself on the chair I'd set up in the middle of a circular rug. The children gathered on the ground around him. Lorelai grinned over at me. She still didn't know anything about us; she just thought he was hot.

"So, today, I'm going to tell you a little story I wrote and illustrated myself. It's called *Frankie Four Eyes and the Magic Night Stick.*"

My breathing stopped for a moment.

Frankie Four Eyes.

Great.

He'd made me into a book character.

He started, "Once upon a time, there was a little girl named Frankie Jane, but people called her Frankie Four Eyes because of her gigantic, purple glasses."

26

Giggles could be heard all around as I started to break out into a cold sweat. Of course, the kids had no clue it was based on me.

Mack continued, "Frankie was scared of other people and often hid behind her glasses. One night, she decided to take a walk in the dark without her spectacles."

"What are spectacles?" one of the girls interrupted.

"Spectacles are glasses. Just another word for them." He resumed reading. "But Frankie was blind as a bat. She couldn't see a thing. In the darkness of the night, it was even worse. Suddenly, a stranger crossed her path. At first, she was scared of this man. When he saw how frightened she was, he assured her that he wasn't dangerous. He even offered his nightstick for protection."

Nightstick. There was only one other time I could recall Mack using that term. This story sounded awfully familiar—vaguely like our first encounter. It occurred to me that this was just his own twist on it—one that was appropriate for children. *I have to give it to you, Mack. Very clever.* I couldn't help but laugh to myself.

Mack continued, "The man said the nightstick was magical and claimed it held the power to protect her from anything she was ever afraid of. The only thing was...she needed to hold onto it and never let go whenever she felt she needed it."

He looked at me. My face must have been turning red. I shook my head at him.

Seeming amused, he continued telling the story. "Frankie believed the man's tale and after that day carried the magic nightstick around with her almost everywhere she went. That is, until she spotted the man again in broad daylight, selling the nightsticks on a street corner for practically a dime a dozen. It was then that she realized her nightstick wasn't magical at all. It had all been an illusion. Frankie then realized that she never needed anything to protect herself other than a new point of view. She believed something, and therefore it was."

Wow.

Mack turned the page. "Frankie walked over to the man and gave him back her nightstick. She wasn't mad. She just didn't need it anymore. If anything, she was grateful. He'd given her a gift: the realization that she needed nothing but her own inner strength to be the person she wanted to be. Frankie now understood the power her own thoughts had over her. The magic wasn't in the nightstick. It was inside of her all along. The End."

In a way, I wanted to smack him, but honestly, it was brilliant. He'd completely morphed tidbits of our history in with Jonah's situation. And the kids, who were clapping, loved the story and the funny illustrations that he'd drawn in crayon. They weren't half-bad, although he'd made me look sort of like Peg from that PBS show, *Peg and Cat.*

Mack spent the next several minutes answering some questions and interacting with the kids about the meaning behind the story. Jonah remained quiet the entire time but seemed calm overall.

When his time was up, Mack closed the book and walked over to me.

"That was *really* interesting," I said. "I have to give you credit. Nightstick? Pretty clever."

"You liked that, huh? He smiled mischievously. "Well, I figured I might as well have a little fun with you while I'm here. The kids don't know the difference anyway. They enjoyed the story. At least, I think they did."

"They did. How long did it take you to come up with it?"

"Practically the entire week." He laughed.

"Don't you work?" I joked.

"I do, but I make time for things that are important to me."

"Taunting me in cryptic ways is important to you?"

"The overall message was a positive one. No one knows you're my Frankie."

His Frankie.

"Your son knows you call me that."

"I guess that's true, but he doesn't know the story. He's never asked about it."

Mack was giving me an intense look. I needed to get him out of here before he could see the effect he was having on me. He looked so sexy in jeans and a fitted, cable-knit sweater that hugged his chest. He smelled so effing good, too. I think it was exactly the same mix of

29

cologne and body wash I remembered. Whatever it was, it emitted the same pheromones that always managed to drive me absolutely crazy. It had been a long time since I'd felt this kind of physical attraction toward someone.

"Well, thank you for coming in."

Seeming to ignore my hint that he should leave, he continued staring into my eyes with that determined look and said, "Have coffee with me some afternoon this week."

"I don't know if that's a good idea, Mack."

"What's your hesitation?"

"I'm not sure."

"I know you're with someone. This isn't a date I'm asking you for. I just want to talk to you face to face... without children around."

I wanted to say yes, but the words just wouldn't come out. There were too many reasons why going out with him even just for coffee would have been a bad idea.

"I don't know. It just somehow seems inappropriate."

"You're making it out to seem like that, yes. It would only be coffee. Maybe a cookie if you're nice." He winked.

There it was again. That stupid shiver that ran through me anytime he winked.

I flinched when he reached out to move a stray hair out of my eyes. Just that simple grazing of his fingertip across my forehead made my pulse react.

"Just coffee, Frankie. We got off to a weird start, and I feel like I owe you more of an explanation of how we got to this place."

As much as it felt wrong to be meeting him, a part of me couldn't resist.

"When?"

"You tell me."

"Thursday at four. The Gourmet Bean in Chestnut Hill," I quickly said before I could change my mind.

He was beaming. "I'll be there."

After I agreed, Mack walked over to Jonah and mussed his son's hair before saying goodbye. Jonah didn't look amused, although he'd handled Mack's storytelling without needing to flee the room; I was really proud of him for that.

Later that afternoon, once the students cleared out, Lorelai snuck up on me as I was getting my things ready to leave.

She crossed her arms. "You need to spill. Right now."

"What?"

"What's going on between you and Mack Daddy? I was watching you two interact. I nearly had an orgasm."

"What did you say? Mack Daddy?"

"Yes. Mack Daddy. It's what everyone calls him around here. You didn't know that?"

"I guess it fits."

"He's the talk of all the moms at drop-off. There are quite a few looking to dig their nasty, gel-manicured paws into him, including me, if I'm being honest. His voice alone is enough to make me come. I swear, if I had one of those little tape machines reporters use, I'd record him reading and play it at night." She tilted her head, examining my expression. "That bothers you."

Shaking my head dismissively, I said, "No, it doesn't."

"Yes, it does. You're hiding something." She squinted. "Are you seeing him?"

"No."

"But something is going on. You guys know each other."

"We used to."

"I knew it! You used to date him?"

"We were roommates years ago."

"You fucked him."

"No."

"Damn. No? Really?"

"Really."

"That's a shame. But something happened..."

"Our relationship was very complex. When we first met, we couldn't have been more opposite from each other."

"But you know what they say about opposites?" She flashed her teeth.

"That they attract?"

"That they have amazing sex. And with him...I bet it would've been more than amazing."

Yes. I'm sure it would have been.

"Well, again, I wouldn't know. And you need to lower your voice."

"I think you're lying about the no sex thing."

"Why?"

"Because your face is totally red right now, Francesca. You look guilty."

"Like I said, we have a history. It wasn't exactly the stuff fairytales are made of, though."

"So, you wouldn't mind if I went after him? Because I think he's really hot and sweet, and I heard he's not with the mother anymore."

"I don't care what you do," I lied, despite burning up with a frantic jealousy. It felt more like panic.

"Great. Now your eye is twitching. You're so full of shit," she said.

"It's just been stressful seeing him again. What do you want from me?"

"I want to know what happened. Were you in love with him?"

I sat down and placed my hands on my forehead. "I thought I was. But it doesn't matter, because he didn't love me back. And honestly, I should be mature enough now to accept seeing him again. I'm really pissed at myself. I thought I'd done a good job over the years of moving on from this, but all of the feelings have come flooding back. Not to mention, I'm in a serious relationship."

"Maybe you just thought you were moving on, but maybe you were just blocking it out."

"You're not helping, Lor."

Lorelai took a few steps toward me. "We all have that one person. It's not necessarily someone we end up with. But it's that person who, for whatever reason, gets under your skin and stays there. You can move on, but parts of them are always with you. Sometimes, if things never had a chance to develop, if feelings are still unresolved, that person becomes an even more powerful force in your life, even in absentia."

"So, you're saying that because Mack and I have unfinished business, I can't let him go."

"Yes. Unfinished business between two people who are clearly attracted to each other is like an eternal case of blue balls."

"Ah, the things you can learn within the walls of a parochial school."

"Are you gonna tell me the story or what?"

"Now?"

"Well, it's almost time for happy hour at that bar in Brookline."

After this day, I could definitely use a drink.

I grabbed my purse. "What the hell. Let's go."

Lorelai teased, "Don't say hell. It's a Catholic school."

CHAPTER FOUR

Francesca

PAST

"I can't tell you how much this means to me. Are you sure your roommate won't mind me shacking up with you guys?"

"Nah. I spoke to Mack about it. He's cool with the whole thing. We needed another roommate anyway. Saved us the trouble of having to list the room online."

Moses showed me around the three-bedroom apartment. Through the window facing the street, I could see the famous illuminated CITGO sign in the distance.

He and I both went to Boston University, which was right down Commonwealth Avenue. Moses was a regular ball buster who hung out a lot at the student union. Since I worked at one of the cell phone stores right near there, we'd gotten to know each other. We'd shoot the shit, and when I happened to tell him my landlord was kicking me out of the small studio apartment I was renting, Moses offered me an empty bedroom in the apartment he shared with another guy.

"This is your room."

I looked around at the large open space with burgundy-colored walls. "It's nice, bigger than I expected." It was empty except for a lava lamp plugged into an outlet in the corner.

"Nice lamp."

"Yeah, Pat left that behind. It fits you, I think."

"It kind of does. Like a hot mess." I sat down on the bed and bounced on the spiny mattress. "This is really a lot of space for the city."

"Yeah. You lucked out. It's the biggest room. Neither of us felt like moving all of our shit into it when Pat moved out."

"I can't tell you enough how grateful I am."

"It'll be nice to have another nerd around."

Moses and I were a lot alike, actually. We both wore glasses and enjoyed comics, tech gadgets, and science fiction books, among other things. We definitely had a lot of similar interests. He was also one of the few people who knew about my social anxiety and OCD tendencies. It contributed to how we met.

Moses had been one of the unlucky visitors to the store on a day when one of the new Apple phones was introduced. It was my first time dealing with that kind of a crowd, and I had a minor freak out after my only co-worker bailed. Moses saved the day, pretending to be an employee and picked up the slack while I calmed my ass down in the stock room.

When I was closing down that night, he randomly came out to me; he basically just blurted out that he was gay. Moses admitted that he felt safe telling me once he'd realized there was no way I could be judgmental after the shit I'd just pulled. That was the day we became fast friends.

"So, what's Mack like? Is that his actual name?"

"It's short for Mackenzie. But he goes by Mack."

"Is he nice?"

"You'll find him intimidating," Moses said matter-of-factly.

"Great. Why do you say that? Is he an asshole?"

"He can be, depends on his mood. Sometimes he's cool. But mainly, he's just...easy on the eyes. And he knows it."

"You mean he's hot?"

"Yeah." He let out a breath. "Fucking amazing."

Shit.

I'm going to make a fool of myself.

"Does he know you appreciate...such things?" I asked.

"Does he know I'm gay?" Moses laughed. "I don't know. We don't talk about shit like that, but I'm pretty sure he caught me checking him out once when he whipped his dick out to take a piss in front of me."

"That sucks. I mean...that you got caught looking."

Moses winked. "It was worth it, though."

Lord.

"Is he a student? What does he do?"

"His father is a politician in Virginia. Mack is in grad school at Boston College—political science. He's doing some kind of paid internship at the State House. He's got a girlfriend in D.C., goes back there every so often, about twice a month."

"I see."

"He's not around much, which I like. Makes it seem like I live alone."

"How did you end up living with him?"

"Craigslist."

"Of course."

Moses grabbed his keys. "I gotta run."

Panic set in. "Where are you going? You're leaving me alone?"

"You live here, Francesca."

"I know, but what if Mack comes home?"

"What *IF* Mack comes home?"

"I don't want to meet him by myself. What if he thinks I'm an intruder? Does he even know I'm moving in today?"

"Yes. I told him this morning. You'll be fine."

Rubbing my temples, I sighed. "Jesus."

"Francesca...don't freak out while I'm gone."

"I'll try not to."

Despite Moses's assurances, I hid in my room the rest of that evening. To the best of my knowledge, Mack hadn't even come home, or at least he never bothered to introduce himself to me.

It was the middle of the night. I really had to pee but didn't feel like leaving my room. Lifting myself out of bed, I forced myself to walk down the hall. Without my glasses, I couldn't see much. The hallway was darker than I expected.

After feeling my way to the bathroom, I sat down on the toilet and let out a relieved breath. When trying not to wake anyone up while peeing, you have to push out at just the right speed so that it doesn't tinkle loudly when it hits the water. I discovered that if I pushed extra hard, the stream of urine would hit the water more quietly as opposed to a loud but slower tinkle. The only problem with this method was always the risk of flatulence. I found that out the hard way when I unexpectedly passed gas.

It was loud.

I froze. It was still quiet, and I prayed that I'd dodged a bullet—that no one had overheard me fart. I wiped and opted not to run the water, so I skipped washing my hands.

Back in the hallway, I started to make my way to my room by clinging to the wall and some furniture along the way in the pitch-black apartment.

The sound of something approaching startled me.

Then what felt like a man's rock hard torso knocked right into me.

I lost my balance then grabbed onto something for support.

"Fucking A. Get off my dick!"

That was when I realized that I'd grabbed onto *him* for support and was inadvertently holding his naked cock in my hand.

I whipped my hand back. "Oh, my God. I'm sorry!" I said, standing up.

"Are you alright?" he asked.

"I'm fine. I'm not hurt."

"No, I mean, are you alright in the head? Do you always grab onto people's junk like that?"

"No! No. It's dark, and I'm nearly blind without my glasses. I can't see you."

"That sounds like a cockamamie excuse to me. Pun intended."

I still couldn't make out his face when I stammered again, "I'm...I'm so sorry."

Before he could respond, I ran in the direction of my room, tripping over something before finally making my way inside and slamming the door.

The next morning, I wondered how long I could get away with staying in my room before I was forced to leave.

Moses had peeked in on me before leaving for class, and I pretended to be asleep. He likely didn't know what had transpired between Mack and me the night before.

All night I had tossed and turned, unable to get it out of my head.

I hadn't even met my roommate, yet I'd touched his cock. Not even touched—my hand was wrapped around it holding on for dear life!

I remembered how it felt vividly, thick and hot in my palm. I'd felt penises before. I wasn't a virgin or anything. I'd slept with only a couple of guys, stroked a few dicks in my life but honestly could say I had never felt one quite like *that* one. It felt like an arm for Christ's sake.

Oh, God.

The thought of facing him seemed unbearable. My heart was racing a mile a minute.

The clock showed nine-thirty. I was going to miss my class, which was two trolley stops away down Commonwealth Avenue. I really needed to get up.

Begrudgingly forcing my body out of bed, I rubbed my tired eyes and went in search of my purple-rimmed glasses. I threw on some clothes and made my way to the kitchen.

The house was completely quiet. I had no clue if I had missed him. If I was lucky, maybe he had already left for work or school.

After wolfing down a yogurt I'd found in the fridge, I noticed that there was some coffee left in a pot, so I decided to have some. Just as I was pouring it into a mug, the door to the kitchen swung open suddenly. Startled, I somehow let the carafe slip from my hands and shatter to the floor. Glass was everywhere.

"Shit!"

"God, you are a walking disaster!" I could hear him say behind me.

"I'll pay for it," I simply said without turning around to look at him. "You startled me, gave me butterfingers."

"I don't know. You seemed to have a pretty good handle on things last night," he scoffed.

Oh.

No.

Just kill me.

I can't believe he said that!

I turned around slowly to face him. "Did you have to bring—" I hesitated when I caught a look at the gorgeous face behind the voice...and his tall, muscular but lean body. My heart started to beat faster. Moses had said Mack was good-looking, but my entire body actually tensed upon the realization that he was *that* good-looking.

I cleared my throat. "Did you have to bring that up again? It was an accident."

Standing before me was probably the most attractive guy I'd ever been in such close proximity to. In Francesca O'Hara's life, guys like this didn't exist unless they were on the side of an Abercrombie and Fitch shopping bag.

His lustrous, chestnut brown hair was messy from sleep and slightly long around the ears. From his hazel eyes that glistened to the scruff on his chin, his face was simply gorgeous. His muscles were sculpted but not overly big and bulky. He was tall—bigger than life.

He was freaking perfect—like New York City billboard perfect—and I was screwed.

Mack was staring intently at me, probably picking up on my intense admiration. His expression was more amused than angry.

"Those are some funky glasses you have on."

"I told you. I'm blind as a bat. I didn't have my glasses on when I got up to use the bathroom last night. So, I didn't notice...you know...when I..." I lost my words.

"Practically jerked me off?"

My stomach sank. "Oh, my God," I muttered.

"Francesca, calm down. I'm just joking around with you." He looked down at the broken glass then back up at me.

After a moment of silence, I said, "I'm sorry. I don't do this very well."

"Do what very well?"

"Humans." It was the first thing that came to mind. Even though it sounded weird, it was technically true.

He suddenly bent his head back in laughter. "You don't do humans? Are you a simian or something?" He looked me up and down, and it gave me the chills. "I don't notice any fur on you."

"I don't do well with new people and new situations," I clarified. "Moving in here was hard enough and then to get off on the wrong foot..."

"So you *did* get off on it last night?"

"I didn't mean *get off* that way." Looking up at the light fixture, I whispered to myself, "Kill me now."

"Again…I'm just joking! Jesus Christ, you're breaking out in these weird blotches on your neck and chest."

Why was he looking at my chest?

"They're hives. I get them when I'm nervous."

"You might want to consider calming the fuck down. Stress isn't good for your health."

Neither are smoking hot, shirtless men whose boxers play hide and seek from the top of their pants.

Mack crouched down and began to silently pick up the shattered pieces of glass from the broken carafe. I watched his ab muscles flex as he moved. He then grabbed a dustpan and brush from under the sink. I just stood there observing all of this like an idiot.

"Thank you for doing that. You didn't have to."

"Well, I did if I didn't want to get shards of glass stuck in my foot later."

"I know. But I could've done it."

He ignored me and just kept cleaning it all up. He didn't stop until each and every shard was gone.

After he put everything away, he stood up and said, "Let's have a do-over, one that doesn't involve you grabbing my cock or suffering a nervous breakdown." He stuck out his hand. "Mackenzie Morrison. But call me Mack."

I accepted his handshake. Another chill shot down my back at the contact. My mind may have been terrified of interacting with him, but my body was experiencing an unwelcome arousal from the mere touch of his firm hand, which unfortunately reminded me of something else that was firm and warm. I cringed at the thought of last night.

"Francesca O'Hara."

"Why don't you do humans well, Francesca?"

"I've always suffered from a little social anxiety."

His brow lifted as if to challenge me. "A little?"

"A lot. It's just something that's in my nature."

"We're not born scared. Something must have made you this way."

"Nothing that I can pinpoint."

"Are you an only child?"

"Yes."

"That couldn't have helped. Siblings would've knocked you into shape, wouldn't have let you get away with that shit. Checks and balances."

"Do you have one...a sibling?"

"One sister...Michaela."

"Michaela and Mackenzie? That has a nice ring to it."

"Or it's annoying, depending on how you look at it. I tend to side with the latter. My parents are pretty vain people. My father is Michael—thus Michaela—and my mother's maiden name is Mackenzie."

"I see. What does Mackenzie mean?"

"What are you talking about?"

"Like what's the significance behind the name?"

"I told you. It was my mother's last name."

"No. Every name has a *meaning*. You can look it up. What you find is scarily accurate sometimes."

45

"I'm pretty sure that's bullshit." He took out his phone. "But let's look up yours."

"Mystical is one," I said. "For Francesca."

He nodded. "Yup. It says mystical here. But it also says—get this—eccentric and solitary." He laughed. "Holy crap. That's pretty funny. I barely know you, but that does seem to fit you." Looking back at the screen he added, "It also says imaginative and philosophical."

"Yes. I think that's right. Look up yours."

After he typed in his name, he squinted in confusion. "Mackenzie means comely. What the fuck does that mean?"

I could feel my face heat up. "Comely means..."

"What?"

"Pleasant to look at. But it's typically associated with a woman."

Grinning, he asked, "Am I comely?" He must have noticed my face growing redder and redder. "Jesus. You don't have to answer that."

I wiped the sweat off my forehead. "What else does it say?"

"It says, another meaning is 'son of a fair man.' I've been called a son of a something before, but never that." He put his phone down. "So, Miss Solitary, have you ever lived with roommates before?"

"No. This is my first time. I was living alone in a studio apartment off of Beacon Street in Brookline, near Coolidge Corner. It was in the basement of some guy's house."

He grimaced. "Sounds creepy."

"It was a little bit creepy, but no one ever bothered me."

"What happened? How did you end up here?"

"The place was foreclosed, and they had to kick me out. Moses happened to mention that you guys lost a roommate. So, that's how this came about. It's not really my first choice to have roommates. I prefer to live alone."

"You don't say," he said sarcastically. "You feel like you're allergic to other people or something?"

"I guess."

He sat down on one of the kitchen chairs and kicked his feet up on another. "Well, I'm allergic to bullshit. There's no such thing as this allergy you think you have. You're just shy, maybe a little insecure. It's as simple as that. There's only one cure for that shit and that's to say 'fuck it all' and stop caring about what other people think. Give zero fucks. Have no fucks left to give. Fuck it all until there's nothing left to fuck." He stopped himself, lifting his index finger and chuckled. "That last part didn't sound right."

"I understand what you meant. It's just easier said than done."

"Well, you know we can't live together if you get hives every time I'm around."

"I'll get used to you. I know you think I'm a weirdo."

"Who said that?"

"It's obvious what you're thinking."

"I would be willing to bet you have no clue what I'm actually thinking right now. Want to know the truth?"

"What?"

"It's refreshing to meet someone not so full of themself. I'm surrounded by people all day long who couldn't care less what other people think of them. I'm one of those people as well. So, the other extreme... we're not any better. But your scenario is a fuck of a lot more stressful on a daily basis."

"You got that right. I'd give anything to not care what people think."

He squinted his eyes and seemed to be examining my face. "I'll make a deal with you, Frankie."

What did he just call me?

"Frankie?"

"Yes. You look nothing like a Francesca. You look like a Frankie to me."

"What were you going to say?"

"I'll make a deal with you. I'm an asshole, right?"

"Okay..."

"You're a scaredy cat—a pussy."

"I'm a pussy..."

"I'll rub some of my asshole off on you if you rub some of your pussy off on me."

My eyes widened. "You'll rub your asshole on me?"

"Not literally. You've had enough of my *actual* private parts to last a year."

I smiled, stifling a laugh.

"Oh, shit. Is that a smile?" he asked.

"Maybe."

"Okay. Let me clarify. What I mean is…if I catch you acting like a nervous spaz, I'll call you out on it, remind you that it's not necessary. If you catch me acting like a dick—kind of like when I yelled at you last night after you accidentally tried to use my penis as a nightstick—you call me out on it. Can you do that?"

"I think so."

"Alright. And in the meantime, we just try to co-exist without accidentally touching each other's genitals, damaging household items, or breaking out into hives."

"I can't help the hives. They're a natural reaction to nerves."

"But you can help the nerves by learning to not give a shit."

"Okay. I'll try."

He chuckled. "I don't believe you."

"You can't just undo years of being a certain way overnight."

"That's true, I guess." He looked into my eyes, and I suddenly became uncomfortable again. "Why the glasses?"

"Because I told you, I'm nearly blind."

"Yeah, but why don't you get Lasik surgery?"

"I thought about that, but I'm scared they'll screw up, and I'll go blind."

"Aren't you already practically blind? I'd say it's worth the risk. Not that there's anything wrong with your glasses, but I get the impression you like to hide behind them. Am I right?"

Even though I'd never really thought of that before, there was something to it. I did always feel a sense of comfort with my glasses on. If the eyes were a window into someone's soul, then glasses were like a mini-shield.

I looked at the clock. "Shit!"

"What?"

"I missed my ten-thirty class. By the time I get there now, it'll be half over."

"So, skip class. I do it all the time."

"I have no choice now." I sighed. A moment of silence ensued until I attempted to find out more about him. "Moses said you're a poli-sci major?"

"Yeah. Grad school. It's the only thing my father would fund."

"Why?"

"My dad is Michael Morrison, the senator from Virginia. He's been grooming me for years to follow in his footsteps."

"Do you plan to?"

"Between you and me? He thinks I am, but the truth is that I don't know what the fuck I'm doing. I felt like I needed to get away from home for a while, so I took the opportunity he gave me once I got into the Boston College program." He pulled out a seat and nudged his head for me to sit in it. "What's your major?"

"Elementary education."

He raised his brow. "Education?"

"Yes. Why do you say it like that?"

"You're allergic to people, and you're studying to go into a field where you'll be in front of a bunch of snotty-nosed kids all day?"

"Actually, kids don't scare me."

"Really? They even scare the fuck out of *me*."

"Yeah. I don't really know why they don't bother me. I suppose it's because I perceive them as non-judgmental. They haven't been tainted by false ideals and expectations yet."

"That's a valid point, I guess."

I looked at the clock again then back at him. "Don't you have to be somewhere?"

"You trying to get rid of me, so you can go back to being a hermit?" He winked, and I swear, I felt it right between my legs.

"I'm just asking."

"I do have to head to class in a little while, so I'll be out of your monkey hair. Any other questions you want to ask me?"

"Why were you walking around naked in the middle of the night anyway? What happened could've been avoided if you'd just had some clothes on."

"I'm allergic to clothes like you're allergic to people."

"I highly doubt that."

"Actually, I just sleep better in the buff. You should try it sometime. Just put something on before you get up, because your blind ass could end up roaming the streets buck naked." He looked down at my chest. "You have a mysterious white substance that looks suspiciously like cum on your shirt, by the way."

Great.

I looked down. Apparently, I'd eaten the yogurt so fast earlier that I'd spilled some. "It's yogurt."

He laughed. "I know. Just trying to get a rise out of you, since you make it so easy. It's just...it looks very comely." He snorted.

We were both laughing now.

As nervous as he was making me, there was a growing part of me that was warming up to this guy. It was an odd contradiction to feel both nervous and comfortable at the same time. I guess the idea of him had been far more intimidating than the actual person.

I got up, opened the refrigerator, and noticed a full carton of eggs. "Whose eggs are these?"

"They belong to Moses. Nothing in there is mine. I never eat here."

"Why not?"

"For one, I don't cook."

"Your mom always did everything for you?"

"That's a joke and a half. No. My parents were too busy for family dinners. I don't think my mother ever cooked one meal. I did have some pretty nice nannies, though."

"That sucks."

"I don't mean to sound ungrateful," he said.

"At least you had both of your parents."

Mack cocked his head to the side. "You didn't?"

"No."

"Someone die?"

I really didn't want to talk about this.

"No...well...I don't know. It's possible. I never knew my father. He abandoned my mother when he found out she was pregnant with me. They were teenagers."

His expression darkened. "Oh. I'm sorry. That sucks."

"Well, you can't miss something you've never had, right? I don't know anything else, what it's like to have a dad."

"That's true, I guess."

Silence filled the air as Mack just continued to look at me. He never broke his stare.

I finally spoke. "Would you eat some eggs if I made some?"

"Hell, yeah. I'm starving."

"Do you think Moses would mind?"

"Go for it. If he gets mad, I'll let him touch my abs."

"So...you know that he's..."

"Gay. Yeah. Figured that out pretty quickly. It was the way he was watching me take a piss one day. His fucking pupils were dilating, wouldn't stop staring at my junk."

I couldn't help but laugh. "Oh, my God."

"I don't care. He's good people."

"He is." The fact that I was no longer freaking out around Mack wasn't lost on me. He was actually pretty easy to talk to. "How do you like your eggs?"

"Over hard." He had a smirk on his face when he said it.

"Is there a sexual joke there somewhere?"

"Let me think." He scratched his chin. "Over hard... kind of like your hand last night."

"You're gross."

"You asked."

I sighed. "Well, I like mine over easy. I'll make yours first. Hard eggs for a hard ass."

"Over easy. I'd call you easy, but I don't think you are. You'd have to like people to let them near you." He winked.

When I noticed him scrolling through his phone with a smirk, I asked, "What are you doing?"

"I'm looking up the meaning of Frankie."

"What does it say?"

Mack looked like he was trying to stifle a laugh when he said, "She who breaks wind in the night."

He was totally pulling my chain. He'd heard me pass gas! I wanted to die.

"You heard that?"

"Yes. It's what woke me up." He grinned. "It doesn't matter. We all do it. Maybe not as robustly as you." He looked down at his phone. "Hmm."

"What?"

"Honest. It says Frankie means *honest*."

"What do you make of that?"

"It's freaky, actually."

"How so?"

"I think if there was one word I had to pick to describe you based on first impression, it would be that.

You're a little different but you own up to it all. Just like you didn't even try to pretend that it wasn't you who cut the cheese. You could've pinned it on Moses or denied it. But it's not in your nature. What you see is what you get. You're a lot of things, but ultimately, you're honest about it all. See...I knew the name Frankie fit you."

Mack ended up devouring his eggs. That was the first of several morning classes I'd "accidentally" skip in order to have breakfast with him.

And he never referred to me by my real name again.

CHAPTER FIVE

Mack

She was late. Either that, or I was being stood up.

On my second cup of coffee, the caffeine was starting to give me the jitters. I wasn't nervous so much as energized and determined.

When Frankie finally walked through the door of The Gourmet Bean, my heart started to beat faster as I stood up to greet her.

She unraveled her scarf then settled into the chair across from me. I took a moment to just take her in as I sat back down.

Fuck, she looked beautiful.

Static from the cold outside had caused pieces of her pin-straight, red hair to stick up in the air. Her pudgy little nose was red, too. She was so freaking cute, still Frankie in every way despite everything that had happened. An ache developed in my chest because there was just so much I wanted to say.

"Sorry, I'm late. I got caught up talking to the principal after school."

"It's okay. I've just been meditating."

Ruminating. Same thing.

"What can I get you?" I asked.

"Oh, I'm just going to have coffee. I'll go up and order."

I held out my palm. "I insist. Stay here. Take a load off. You've had a long day. You still like hazelnut with extra cream?"

"Yes." Her smile was hesitant. "I'm surprised you remember."

I remember a lot of things you probably wish I would forget.

"I'll be right back."

In line, I would turn around from time to time to sneak peeks at her. Her back was to me, but I could see she was rubbing her palms together nervously. I hated that she was uncomfortable, hated the idea that she might have been dreading this.

When I returned to our table with the coffee, she took it but stayed looking down into the steaming cup. I couldn't take it anymore.

"Look at me, Frankie."

Her tone was curt. "What do you want to talk about, Mack?"

"I have to explain more about why I'm here...on your turf."

"You're here for Jonah. You think I would be a good fit for him. You already said that."

"No, Frankie. It's not *just* that."

"What is it, then?"

I let out a slow breath to gear myself up and vowed not to be a pussy.

"I've never stopped thinking about you. All of these years, they feel like a blur. I look at you sitting in front of me right now, and I'm feeling all of the same things I did when we were together."

"We were never together."

Hearing her say that caused me to snap a little, because there was no way she could deny what we had.

"The hell we weren't together. We never fucked, maybe, but we were connected in every other way that two people could be. You can't deny that. I hurt you. I know that. But deep down, I know you understand why I did it."

"That didn't make it hurt any less when you left."

"God, don't you think I know that?" I had raised my voice a little too much and made a conscious effort to lighten my tone when I asked, "This guy you're with… what's his name?"

"Victor."

"He takes good care of you?"

"Yes."

"Do you love him?"

"Yes."

"Do you really love him, or is it that you feel safe with him, because he's older and kind of like a—"

"Don't say it."

"Well, I *have* to say it. You have a daddy complex, Frankie. You're living with a man old enough to be your father because you have abandonment issues."

"I don't remember my father abandoning me." She raised her voice. "I *do*, however, remember the day you left very clearly."

Her words felt like a slice to my throat. She was right, though. For the first time since reconnecting with her, she had managed to silence me. It was also the first time I realized just how badly my leaving hurt her.

She must have sensed what I was thinking when she said, "I'm sorry, Mack. That was unfair. I shouldn't have said it like that. This is just really hard for me."

"I know it is. That's why I'm trying to talk to you. I don't want things to be weird between us. I miss you. There hasn't been a day that's gone by when I wasn't wondering what you were doing, what you were thinking about, whether you were hating me for leaving. When most people say stuff like that, it's an exaggeration. In my case, it's not. Every single day, Frankie."

"I assumed we would never see each other again. You being back here has turned my world upside down."

Hearing the pain in her voice made me take a deep breath before attempting to explain things to her.

"When Torrie got the job in Boston...knowing that I could move closer to you again—to have you meet my son—it seemed like a gift. Everything just fell into place. It felt like oxygen had returned to my body for the first time in years. This was an opportunity I couldn't let pass me by. I know what I did by getting him into your class was extreme."

"You think?" she said sarcastically.

"I just want to know you again, Frankie. I want *him* to know you. I swear to God, I didn't mean to turn your world upside down. If you're happy, I swear on my son's life, that makes *me* happy. I just don't want you to spend another day hating me for leaving."

"I don't hate you, Mack. I may have been very upset for a long time, but I never hated you."

It was such a relief to hear her say that, because I'd often wondered.

I reached over and took her hand in mine. I didn't care if it was a bold move. I needed to touch her. Then, I moved her hand and placed it over my heart. "You feel that?" I asked. "Feel how it's beating for you right now. Every time I even allow myself to think about you, it beats like this. And I don't know how to make it stop."

She kept her hand over it for at least a full minute. My heart continued to beat even faster into her palm the longer she kept it on me.

"What am I supposed to do with this?" she whispered.

There was only one answer.

"Just believe what it's telling you."

She stayed silent and eventually pulled her hand away. I knew I was having an effect on her. I knew she still had feelings for me, but I also knew that I wasn't going to be able to convince her with words to give me a second chance. It would have to be done through actions. And it was going to take time. But nothing was guaranteed.

"I didn't come to mess up your life, but you asked why I'm here. Here's the honest answer: I'm here for *you*, Frankie. I'm here to finish what I started years ago. If you honestly love him, then I promise I will accept that. I'll try to move on. But until you look me in the eyes and tell me there's no chance, I'm gonna hold out hope."

"I don't know what to say."

"You don't have to say anything. Just have this coffee with me. Talk to me. Be my friend again, even if it's nothing more. We'll just take this one moment at a time."

Taking a deep breath, she nodded. "Okay."

It felt like a massive weight lifted when she agreed.

Despite the tense start to our coffee date, the rest of the time spent at the café was pretty stress free. Frankie updated me on Jonah's progress in class, and I filled her in on my job. She and I even managed to laugh a little and reminisce. We also made plans to have me come in and volunteer in the classroom again soon, since the last time seemed to be a big hit. The coffee date that had started out as an emotional mess ended on a fairly calm note.

She eventually left to go home to her boyfriend, taking an even bigger chunk of my heart with her this time.

The following Sunday, I was driving Jonah back to his mother's after the weekend at my place. As usual, he'd been pretty quiet during his stay with me, wanting mostly to stay home and play with some new apps I'd put on his tablet.

I'd forced him to go out to eat and to read with me at night, but he never seemed fully happy with anything. He didn't want friends over, and that made it even harder to occupy his time.

I found myself giving into him more and more lately to compensate for my not being there every day. Between my moving out and then our moving out of state, it was a lot for him to handle.

It seemed that no matter how confident of a person I'd always thought I was, when it came to my son, I often felt helpless, like I didn't know shit and couldn't do anything right.

We were driving down Route Nine when I noticed him looking pretty sullen as he gazed out the window of the backseat.

"Jonah...everything okay? Aren't you looking forward to seeing your mother?"

As was typical, when I asked him anything about his feelings, he just shrugged his shoulders.

Looking at him through the rearview mirror, I said, "Well, I know she missed you. She always does."

My chest felt tight during the rest of the ride. My son was a way more sensitive kid than I ever was. Even though my parents didn't have the best marriage and were rarely around my sister and me, I somehow just accepted it. Jonah knew better, and more than that, he deserved better. I wanted to give him a better childhood than I'd had. Lately, it seemed like I'd failed miserably at that, even though I was trying my ass off to make him happy.

When we pulled up to Torrie's brick-faced house, I happened to notice a second car parked in her driveway.

After she opened the door, I could smell a hint of wine on her breath as she said, "You weren't supposed to be here for another half-hour."

"Well, Jonah left his Kindle charger here. He asked me if we could leave a little early. Is that a problem?"

"No, of course not. Why would it be a problem?"

As Jonah ran up the stairs to his room, I glanced over at a tall dude with a beard. He was standing in the corner holding a beer.

"Who's this?" I asked as I continued to stare him down.

He approached me, offering his hand, which I didn't take. "I'm Gerard Lockhart. Nice to meet you."

"Gerard works with me."

"I see." I nudged my head back toward the front door. "Can I talk to you outside for a minute?"

She followed me and asked, "What is it?"

"What are you doing bringing strange men around my son?"

"You don't have a say in whom I invite over to *my* house."

"He's not emotionally ready to have other men around. He's still getting over my not living with him."

"Whose fault is that? Someday when he asks why we aren't together, I'll tell him the truth, that you told me you didn't love me, that you never loved me. Don't blame me for all of this. Don't blame me for trying to find someone to give me what you never did. It's your fault we're in this place, and you need to accept it. You're the one who left."

Fuck. To be honest, it was the truth. Not wanting my son to overhear anything, I simply lowered my voice and said, "In the future, you really need to discuss these things with me first."

"Whatever, Mack," Torrie said before shutting the door.

Getting back in my car, I was too exhausted to start the engine. I leaned my head against the seat and closed my eyes before eventually garnering the energy to drive away.

Once I arrived home, I stayed in the car for a bit, staring at my phone. My finger hovered over Frankie's name. I wanted to text her so badly but decided against it. In my current mood, I might have gone overboard and said something I would've regretted, like how badly at the café I'd wanted to lick a line from her chest up to her neck to her bottom lip before sucking on it. We'd ended that meeting on a good note, and I needed to continue to take it slow.

Mrs. Migillicutty opened her window when she caught me walking into my house.

"Evening, Mack."

"Evening, Mrs. M."

"You look like shit."

I started to laugh. "Well, thank you. Tell me how you really feel."

"You know what the great thing about having me for a neighbor is?"

"What's that?"

"I double as a bartender."

"Is that so? I like that idea. We can call it Migillicutty's Pub."

"How about some of that rum I promised you? I make a mean rum and Coke."

God, I could use a drink tonight.

I threw my keys up in the air and caught them. "Serve me up!"

Once inside, she prepared my drink at the table. The Coke fizzed as she poured it over the liquor. She slid the glass over to me.

"Thank you."

"Are you kidding? I'm totally living vicariously through you, Mack." She crossed her arms and leaned in. "What's wrong?"

"What's *right* would be a more appropriate question."

"Talk."

"Let's see. Where to start? I'm angry at my ex for bringing a new man around my son without checking with me first. Speaking of my son, I'm pretty sure he hates me and blames me for his unhappiness. God knows what kind of false information his mother's feeding him."

"Anyone who sees you in action with that boy would never doubt the kind of father you are. The fact that you're not with his mother doesn't change that. As for this new man, be happy someone's filling her love tank so that you don't have to anymore."

"I guess that's one way of looking at it."

"Speaking of which, didn't you have a date with Miss Frankie?"

"It was hardly a date, but yeah. It started out a little rocky, but it ended up okay. We just talked."

"You never told me the story of how you met her. I know she was your roommate."

"You really want to hear it?"

"Fuck, yes."

I couldn't help but crack up any time she said something I didn't expect to come out of her mouth.

She looked confused. "What's so funny?"

"Nothing."

"So, tell me the story!"

"Okay...well, the thing with Frankie didn't start out romantic or anything. She was—for lack of a better word—odd, even a little geeky. At least, that was my impression of her when she first moved in. But there was something really endearing about her at the same time. I guess I liked the fact that she wasn't egotistical or intimidating like most of the other people I'd been associating with up until that point."

"I bet a lot of people find *you* intimidating, Mack."

"Maybe." I grinned. "Anyway, I'd been surrounded by people my whole life who I felt like I had to compete with. I was brought up to find value in shallow and unimportant things. Frankie, on the other hand, never made me feel anything but comfortable in my own skin. I never felt like she was judging me. She used to have this terrible social anxiety. I used to tell her she shouldn't give a fuck what people thought of her. Meanwhile, that was a little hypocritical because deep down, I definitely struggled with that a little, too, particularly when it came to my father. Anyway, those months of getting to know her as a friend were like a breath of fresh air that I didn't know I needed. It was like I'd been suffocating and didn't realize it. Frankie was sweet and caring. She'd cook for me—no one had ever cooked for me in my life unless they were getting paid to do it. But more than anything, being around her just...felt good."

"She made you happy. It's not always easy to understand why that happens with certain people. It's cosmic or something."

"Right. It's not always logical, either. It was definitely unexpected with her."

"So, what was the problem?"

"I was with Torrie when I met Frankie."

Mrs. Migillicutty smacked the table. "Ah. See, now this story is getting fucking good."

I laughed. "Frankie had basically been like one of the guys at first. But later, I began to realize that I was going out less. I'd be in work or class and thinking about how I couldn't wait to get home. I'd think of something funny and have to stop everything I was doing to text her. Or the worst part, I'd be visiting Torrie in D.C. and counting the minutes until I could catch my Sunday night flight back to Boston. But even still, I was in denial for a very long time. I'd never had feelings for someone that didn't start out as pure physical attraction. With Frankie, it was the opposite. I was extremely attracted to her brain, to her heart, to just being with her, to how she made me feel. Then over time, I'd started to look at her differently. I'm not even sure exactly when it changed, but my admiration for her definitely extended to the physical. I'd notice the way she bit her lip, and I'd find myself wishing I could be the one biting it. I'd count the tiny freckles over her nose and wish I could trace a line over them with my tongue. I'd notice when her nipples were peeking through her shirt…"

She grabbed a napkin and began fanning herself. "This is better than my online porn."

Taken aback, I chuckled. "Ohhhh-kay."

"Go on."

"Anyway, the physical part took a long time to develop, but once it did, it was so strong that I almost couldn't handle it. And basically, I knew I was in trouble because I'd been knee-deep in this relationship with Torrie for years."

"How young were you when you started dating Torrie?"

"Torrie is the daughter of my father's closest aide, Burton Hightower. She worked in public relations for my father for a long time. It was why she stayed behind in D.C. when I moved to Boston for grad school. She'd just started working for Dad at that time. From a very young age, my parents had been pushing me to date her. Torrie is very driven. She was always pursuing me from the time we were in middle school. My father had it all planned out. I'd follow in his footsteps career-wise and marry Torrie. It seemed like a done deal. Don't get me wrong...she was beautiful and smart—what many would think was the whole package. I was attracted to her for a long time and finally gave in and started dating her exclusively in college after playing the field in high school. I really thought maybe I could grow to love her someday, that things would work out."

"That didn't happen."

"No, it never really did."

She poured me another drink as she said, "Then along came Frankie."

"Yup. I didn't see that coming at all. I guess you don't really understand what it feels like to truly connect with someone until it happens. You think what you've experienced up until a certain point is all there is. Then, someone comes along and rocks your world, and you realize you didn't know shit about shit."

CHAPTER SIX

Mack

PAST

It was my Sunday night ritual. The D.C. to Boston shuttle would land at eight. Then, I'd hop the train and be back at the apartment by nine, just in time to catch Frankie doing laundry in the basement of our building.

She was always afraid to leave her stuff, so she'd lean against the washer and read until I inevitably joined her to keep her company. I'd always bring my own laundry down to throw into the other machine if it was empty. We'd stay there late into the night until we finished washing and folding all of our clothes.

It seemed crazy, but the laundry ritual was the one thing I looked forward to most after a hectic weekend. Something about the smell of the detergent, the soothing sounds of the machines, the mellow lighting in that room and—most of all—Frankie's company calmed me down after the stress of D.C. A part of me also worried about her being alone down in that dingy basement without me.

"Hey," I said, standing in the doorway.

Frankie, who'd been deep into reading, put her book down and smiled. "Hi."

"Any freaks come bother you?"

"Not until you showed up, Morrison." She winked.

"You're hysterical," I threw one of my shirts at her and watched as she proceeded to smell it. "Did you just smell my dirty shirt? I worked out in that."

"It's morbid curiosity."

"You like to smell things that might not emit a favorable outcome? Like that old *Saturday Night Live* character who loved to sniff her own armpits. What was her name?"

Frankie smiled. "Mary Katherine Gallagher."

"Yup. I'm gonna start calling you Mary Katherine."

She giggled. "Seriously, though, you've never done that? It's like...you know something may potentially smell bad, but you sniff it anyway? I sort of get a sick pleasure from it."

I bet you're a little freak in bed.

I couldn't help my thoughts toward her lately.

"Oh, right," I said. "I did that to your dirty underwear once. First and last time I smelled them. Learned my lesson the hard way."

"You're lying."

I threw another shirt at her. "I am."

Although, I'd definitely fantasized about that— among other things.

71

She sniffed the second shirt, too.

"What does that one smell like?"

"Like your cologne mixed with tacos."

Shaking my head, I said, "You never cease to puzzle me, Frankie Jane."

"Why do you call me that? My middle name isn't even Jane."

"I don't know. The two names seem to go together."

"You just call me whatever you want, don't you?"

"I'm sure you call me a lot of things under your breath." I picked up the book she'd been reading from atop the dryer. "What weird shit are you reading this time?" I looked down at the title. *"The Man Who Folded Himself?* What the hell?"

"It's a time travel novel."

"What's the gist?"

"The main character encounters various versions of himself in different time periods. He even has sex with some of them. He just got someone pregnant. I'm trying to figure out if he's carrying his own child."

"What in the ever-living fuck, Frankie? That shit is so twisted."

"I know. That's why I like it. The author's imagination is endless. There are no boundaries when it comes to the human mind and what it can conjure up."

"You find everything fascinating."

That's one of the things I love about her.

Frankie always found something interesting in everything. It was a testament to how much our attitudes shape our life experiences. The more I hung out with her, the more I realized what a miserable fuck I really had been all my life.

"I do have a pretty big imagination myself, which is probably why I appreciate books like this. But the imaginative mind can be a curse," she said.

"What do you mean?"

"My imagination is too active sometimes and because I have an obsessive mind on top of that, it can cause problems for me. For instance, I'll get a bizarre thought, and I'm able to visualize it so clearly that it feels like it could be true. But then I start to obsess over the thought, trying to find the meaning behind it."

"Give me an example."

"Well, like you might be talking to me, and I'll have a random thought about stabbing you. The average person would just dismiss it as a fleeting thought. But someone with an obsessive mind like me would perform mental rituals in order to determine if there's any validity to it. It's a form of OCD. They call it Pure O. It's like my mind never stops. It was worse when I was younger. I've learned to deal with it."

"What did you do to make it better?"

"I read some self-help books and saw an OCD specialist. Basically, it all comes down to accepting uncertainty. Rather than freaking out about your thoughts—like the possibility of being a murderer— you just have to accept them for what they are: just thoughts. I used to try to mentally prove them wrong by ruminating, but it's like an endless cycle. Instead, you have to tell yourself that the doubt you feel is just your OCD. The key is to accept the uncertainty that you *might* be a murderer and go on with your life. Anyway, how was your birthday weekend?"

"Only you would confess that you might be a murderer and ask about my birthday in the same breath."

"I'm not a murderer. But I can't actually *say* that... it's reassurance. My OCD will just try to prove me wrong. So, let's just assume I *might* be a murderer and move on."

"Fine by me. I'll hide the knives." I smiled. "Kidding. Thank you for sharing that with me. I bet it's more common than you think."

An image of fucking her while she stabbed me in the back flashed before my eyes. Speaking of fleeting thoughts.

"Do you think I'm nuts?" she asked.

"I thought you were nuts way before you confessed your OCD. But it's all good. I like your brand of nuts— not that hard to crack."

"So...the birthday...how was it?"

Truthfully, being down in that basement with her *was* the best part of my birthday weekend. Being able to just relax...talk about anything...even weird shit...I would have chosen laundry with Frankie over most things lately.

"It was alright."

"Just alright?"

"Torrie had a little party for me, surprised me with some of my friends."

"That's nice."

"Yeah."

I could always sense her jealousy whenever the subject of my girlfriend came up. I could feel it, even though she obviously didn't express it. I'd always suspected that Frankie liked me more than just as a friend, but recently, Moses had let it slip that she'd actually said something to him. Even though I wished he'd never said anything to me, deep down, that news wasn't anything I didn't already know. He'd said he wasn't happy about going behind her back but felt it was necessary to make me aware of it so that I would back off a little. It was basically a warning to check myself before I ended up hurting her. But the problem was, I didn't *want* to stay away from her. Moreover, I didn't know *how* to stay away from her as long as we were living under the same roof.

"That reminds me. I got you a present." She reached into her laundry basket, picking up a wrapped box.

"Is it Anthrax? After all, you *might* be a murderer."

"Not this time."

I looked at her suspiciously as I ripped the paper. *"Buffy the Vampire Slayer*, the entire series...holy shit."

Her face was turning red. "Yup. Thirty-nine discs. Seasons one through seven."

"You look embarrassed. Were you nervous to give this to me?"

"I didn't know if you were gonna like it. I remember once you said you used to watch that show when you were younger. At the time, I thought it was pretty much the one thing we had in common. I figured maybe you'd want to take a trip down memory lane."

"Are you kidding me? This show was the best. When Willow and Oz broke up? I mean, come on!"

"Right?" She beamed.

"Seriously. This was sweet as hell. You didn't have to do that. Thank you."

My body stiffened, because I got the urge to hug her but thought better of it. I was afraid of what it would do to me to feel her body against mine. So, I restrained myself. More and more lately, my body was reacting to Frankie without even having to touch her. The physical feelings had been slowly getting stronger over the past month, and even though I knew it was wrong to feel that way, fuck if I knew how to stop it.

"One night this week we should watch an episode," she said.

"You know, I probably wouldn't have admitted my addiction to that show to anyone else."

"But because I'm weird, you know I won't judge."

"I used to find you a little weird, yeah, but your quirks have definitely grown on me. In fact, normal things are starting to seem boring in comparison."

"Welcome to my world."

"It's a compliment."

She blushed as she often did whenever I said anything nice to her. I wondered if she could sense how badly I wished I could kiss her.

Frankie cleared her throat. "So, did you get any other surprises for your birthday?"

"Dad decided to stop by the party for like a half-hour."

"Was he at least being nicer to you for the occasion?"

"That would've been too much to ask, so no, not really. He gave me a pen with Morrison engraved on it, though."

"Sounds kind of formal."

"Yup. Typical Dad gift—cold and boring."

"Well, you're his only son. I suppose he knows you're his only chance to carry on the family name. So, the pen was representative of that."

"I'm painfully aware that he considers me his only hope to carry on his legacy. The problem is, I'm pretty sure he's going to end up gravely disappointed. The more time that passes, the more I just don't see myself following in his footsteps or even working for his administration at all. I haven't had the balls to really break the news. I'm just glad I had the good sense to major in business undergrad, so I have something to fall back on when he cuts ties."

"Well, if he truly loves you, he'll end up supporting your decisions in the end."

"You hit the nail on the head. I'm not so sure he does...truly love me. I think he cares more about himself and his political endeavors, to be honest."

"You don't mean that."

"The verdict is still out. Honestly."

Her expression darkened a bit, and it hit me that she might have been thinking about the fact that I shouldn't have been constantly complaining about my father when she didn't have one in the picture at all.

I suddenly felt like an ass.

"I'm sorry, Frankie. I'm complaining about my dad again when—"

"I told you not to worry about that."

"You say it doesn't matter, but I don't really believe you. You seem to get sad whenever I bring up my father or ask you about your childhood. It's not anything you say. It's just the look on your face. I can see through you."

She adjusted her purple glasses then looked away from me. "It is what it is. Maybe it does make me a little sad. I just try not to dwell on it." After a long pause, she added, "It wouldn't be so difficult if I weren't reminded of him every time I look in the mirror."

"You look like him? You never told me that. I thought you said you didn't know what he looked like."

"By process of elimination. My mother has dark hair and dark eyes. She once confirmed that he was a ginger like me, had blue eyes like me, too. I look nothing like her, so I just know when I look at myself, that in a way, I'm looking at him. I used to try to find him in my reflection when I was younger. But now that I'm older and know better than to glorify a man who abandoned his own child...I just resent the resemblance. It sucks."

I wished she could see what I saw whenever I looked at her face: eyes equally full of wonder and humility and a beautiful smile that seemed to be the only medicine I needed lately.

"As someone who's had the pleasure of knowing you, it's his loss, Frankie. He just can't imagine what he's missing."

I meant that. She was an extraordinary person. I didn't think she had too many people in her life ever tell her that.

Her eyes were starting to water. "Great. You just made me cry."

"I'm sorry. I didn't mean to."

"You're not supposed to say things like that. You're supposed to be an asshole, Mack Morrison."

"Oh, yeah. Thanks for reminding me." I wiped her tears with my thumb. "Maybe you're rubbing off on me."

"That was the deal when we first met, wasn't it? I'd rub my pussy on you?"

Fuck. Why did she have to say that? The image that it conjured up made my dick twitch.

I looked away and pondered what the fuck I was doing, letting myself fall for her when I had a girlfriend I wasn't planning on breaking up with. I couldn't have it both ways.

Frankie was taking her first load of laundry out of the dryer and stopped to bury her nose in a towel. "When I was younger, I would wait for my mother to throw the warm laundry on the bed. I'd jump in the pile and sometimes fall asleep in it."

I'd love to fall asleep with you tonight, bury my nose in your chest, bury my dick in your—.

There came another inappropriate fleeting thought.

I felt like such a fucking scumbag lately. But how was I supposed to stop my innermost thoughts? It was impossible to control where my mind went when it came to Frankie. Unlike her OCD, these thoughts *were* based in reality. I told myself that I just needed to accept that these feelings would be there and that it was okay to have them as long as I didn't act on them.

Frankie lifted a black shirt from her pile. "What do you think of this with some dark jeans for Friday night?"

"What's Friday night?"

"I thought Moses said he told you."

"Told me what?"

"He and I are going on a double date."

Thinking she was making a joke about dating Moses, I said, "I hate to break it to you, but I'm pretty sure Moses is not interested in vagina."

"He's not my date. You know the guy he's seeing?"

"Yeah, Brad or something?"

"Yes. Well, apparently, he has a brother who's straight. He's coming along to meet me."

My stomach sank.

I swallowed. "Where are you guys going?"

"Not sure."

My heart felt like it was pounding through my chest. I hadn't realized how bad I had it for Frankie until that moment. I didn't even know what to say, because I was afraid my jealousy would be obvious.

"I thought you were allergic to people."

"Honestly, I'm not really looking forward to it, but I really need to start forcing myself. I haven't been with anyone in a long time, and the longer I wait, the harder it's going to be to get back in the game."

"Do you even know what he looks like?"

"Nope."

"It's a blind date?"

"Yup."

"When you say you haven't 'been with someone,' you mean gone out on a date or had sex?" I cringed at the thought of her letting some guy take advantage of her.

"Both. I miss both."

Hearing her say that she was essentially longing to be fucked made me ache.

Unsure of what to say, I asked, "When is this date taking place?"

"I already said...Friday."

I'd lost my ability to think straight. She had already told me it was Friday.

"I'll get to meet him, then."

She looked alarmed. "You're not going to D.C.?"

"Not this weekend, no."

"Great."

"Are you nervous that I'm gonna be here or something?"

"Kind of, yeah. You're very intimidating."

"Good. He should be very worried if he plans on messing with you."

She was quiet for a while then surprised me when she suddenly changed the subject and asked, "Does Torrie know about me?"

"What do you mean?" I asked, only to buy myself some time. It truly amazed me that she hadn't inquired about that sooner.

"Does she know you have a female roommate and that we're friends?"

In hesitation, I bit my bottom lip. "Not exactly. She knows I have a second roommate named Frankie. She kind of assumed you were a guy. And I sort of...never corrected her."

"Are you kidding?"

"No."

"So, it *would* upset her if she knew you lived with a girl?"

"Upset isn't the right word. It's more like...she'd blow her lid."

"Why didn't you ever tell me that my being here could be a problem for you? I would've looked for another place."

"It's *not* a problem. I love having you here."

"Yeah, but when she finds out, she's gonna be pissed." She stared off in thought. "Is that why you always go there, and she never comes here?"

"No. She never used to come here even before you moved in. She's not crazy about flying, only does it when she absolutely has to. It would take too long for her to get here by train. So, I just go there. Makes it easier."

"Can't you just explain to her that she has nothing to worry about and that I'm here because Moses took me in? From the pictures I've seen of her, I don't think she'd be threatened by me."

"Why is that?"

"I mean...look at her. She's tall and gorgeous. Look at me."

It pissed me off to hear her say that.

"You think you're unattractive?"

"I can't really be the judge of that. I don't have a clear understanding of how people see me physically. But I'm certain I don't compare to her."

You're right. You don't.

My heart was pounding because I was dying to tell her what I really thought. I wished things were different, that for even one night I could've shown Frankie how attracted to her I was. She had no clue how badly I wanted to taste her lips. Just one taste. What would things have been like if I had been able to just let go of all of my inhibitions? I envisioned backing her up against the washing machine and pressing my erection into her so she could feel how much I wanted her. She'd never doubt my level of attraction to her again. I wished I could just make her feel good, take her body to places I bet it had never gone before.

Listen to yourself.

I needed to be realistic. I wasn't going to cheat on Torrie. And breaking up with her to somehow be with

Frankie would be a mess. My family and Torrie's were too tied together. I was in too deep and pretty sure my father and her father would make my life a living hell—maybe even make Frankie's a living hell, too. I couldn't let that happen. More than that, I didn't trust myself not to royally screw things up with Frankie, even if the other complications didn't exist. Her father abandoning her when she was a baby really fucked her up. I couldn't trust myself not to hurt her. As much as I knew this dilemma would be easier once grad school was over and I didn't see her every day, I also couldn't imagine never seeing her again. But that was what it would come to.

Despite everything, I wanted her to realize how beautiful she was, inside and out.

Her voice snapped me out of my thoughts. "Have I lost you?"

"Let me try something, okay?" I took hold of the side braid she was sporting.

"What are you doing?"

"I just want you to see something. Humor me."

I slowly undid her braid from bottom to top and could feel her breathing quicken the longer I was messing with her hair. When all of the tresses were loose, I ran my fingers repeatedly through her red strands.

Then, I slipped her glasses off and placed them on top of the dryer.

"You try to hide. You're far more beautiful on the inside than pretty much anyone I have ever met. I don't know if I even realized how much that mattered until I met you. But fuck, woman, you do everything in your power to hide everything else—the physical beauty God also gave you on the outside. I'm not gonna lie. I didn't see it clearly at first."

I turned the camera so she could use it like a mirror.

"Look at this. There is no way that someone wouldn't be threatened by you. This girl...she's fucking hot, Frankie."

She squinted. "I can't see. I don't have my glasses."

Shit.

I had forgotten how blind she was.

The sexual tension broke apart as Frankie and I both started to crack up. We got a good laugh out of that one.

CHAPTER SEVEN

Francesca

The moment I'd been dreading for years was about to happen.

While for everyone else, this was just another morning here at St. Matthew's, today was the day I was meeting Torrie Hightower for the first time.

Lorelai had agreed to man the class while I headed down the hall to the conference room. It was hard to believe after all these years, I was going to come face to face with her. It was even harder to believe that she'd have absolutely no clue how significantly she'd impacted my life.

I peeked through the door and saw her typing on her phone. She was almost exactly how I'd pictured her: a tall, commanding presence with perfect skin that was slightly lighter than the color of caramel. The curls of her shoulder-length, black hair were neatly sculpted. Donning a beige dress and matching Louboutins, she seemed way overdressed for this meeting. Torrie was even more beautiful in person than in the photos I'd seen years ago. That realization brought on unwanted images of Mack and her together. Exhaling, I vowed to brush off my jealousy.

I finally opened and forced the first words out. "Hello, Miss Hightower. It's nice to meet you."

She stood up and extended her long fingers toward me. "Miss O'Hara. Thank you for meeting with me. I'm sorry that it's taken me so long to come in."

"I understand. You're very busy."

Torrie sat back down in her seat before turning her phone on vibrate. "Let's cut to the chase. Jonah has had a very difficult year, for more reasons than just our move from Virginia. Things at home with him have been very difficult, so I'm curious as to what you've noticed at school."

"Well, first of all, your son is very bright. He's probably one of the most intelligent students in my class. But, yes, it's clear that he suffers from a great deal of social anxiety. We used to remove him from those situations that seemed to bring him discomfort, but now we've been taking a bit of a different approach."

"How so?"

"Well, it's really not benefitting him to teach him to run from situations that make him uncomfortable. So, we've been trying to make him stick it out longer, to teach him to cope with those feelings."

"What's your take on the medicinal route?"

"Well, I'm not a doctor. So, I don't feel equipped to answer that, except to say that in my own experience, meds only help ease symptoms. They can't cure a way of thinking that leads to a cycle of anxiety."

"So, you think just trying to teach him to deal with it is the answer."

"I do. But it's also about teaching him that it's okay to feel fearful. Once you accept the feelings, often they lose their power over you. Training a way of thinking is more of a long-term tool. But your family doctor would have more information on the risks and benefits of supplemental medication."

"Is there a pill for a wrecked home life?" she asked sarcastically.

I had no clue what to even say.

"I'm afraid not."

Torrie crossed her legs and leaned back into her seat. "You've met Jonah's father..."

My throat suddenly felt extremely dry. "Mr. Morrison has volunteered a couple of times in our class, yes."

"He's trying to be as active as possible, to make up for the fact that he walked out on his son."

My heart started to beat faster in anger. Feeling the need to defend Mack, I said, "He seems very involved in his son's life, actually. We have a lot of students whose parents live in separate homes, and I can't say I see their fathers as much as I see Jonah's dad."

"Well, his moving out was the straw that broke the camel's back for Jonah. Things were bad for a very long time before that, though. My son has never really known what it's like to have two parents who get along. I often wonder how much our home life has impacted his lack of desire to be among people, in general...if it's why he shies away from everyone."

"Well, he's still too young to truly understand that divorce has nothing to do with him."

"Oh, we were never married."

What?

"Oh...I'm sorry. I just assumed..."

"No. I was never good enough for Jonah's father, apparently."

They were never married?

Come to think of it, Mack had never mentioned it one way or the other. I'd just assumed that Torrie had chosen to keep her maiden name.

"Anyway, I'd really like you to tell me if you notice things getting any worse with Jonah," she said.

"Well, we will do everything we can to make sure he's happy and thriving. But, of course, we'll notify you if anything out of the ordinary arises."

"You have all of my contact information?"

"Yes. I'll be sure to update you soon."

"Well, I can see he's in capable hands. I have to admit when Mack insisted on researching the schools in this area, I was so busy with the job transition and the move that I just let him handle it. I wasn't sure I should trust him to make a sound decision, but it seems that he has."

"Thank you. I appreciate the vote of confidence."

"Unfortunately, I'm late for a work meeting." She checked her phone before standing up. "It was nice meeting you."

"You, as well."

Listening to the sound of her heels echo in the hallway, I stayed in the empty conference room and let out a deep sigh of relief. That hadn't gone nearly as badly as I'd anticipated. Still, the fact that she knew nothing about my history with her ex made me very uncomfortable.

Reminding myself that I only had to deal with this situation until the end of the year, I put on my big girl panties, got up, and returned to the classroom.

The next afternoon, Mack had come to the school to read another one of his stories to the class. He had asked if he could meet with me first during my lunch break.

His hands were in his pockets as he stood waiting for me under a tree on the school grounds. The colorful leaves of fall were drying up and falling around him, a sign that the New England winter wasn't too far away.

I hadn't had a chance to speak to him in great detail since our coffee date, but honestly, not an hour of any day went by when he wasn't on my mind.

Mack looked beyond amazing in a black, ribbed sweater and knit hat. His unintentionally sexy look was in stark contrast to the conservative atmosphere.

He lifted his hand when he noticed me approaching. "Hey."

"What's up, Mack?"

Cutting right to the chase, he said, "I heard she came to see you yesterday."

"Yes."

He examined my eyes. "Are you okay?"

"Yes. I'm fine. The visit went better than I expected."

"Okay, just making sure."

"We mainly discussed Jonah's anxiety in light of all of the changes in his life."

"So, she didn't badmouth me?"

"I didn't say that."

His face turned red. "Fuck. I knew this would happen." He looked down at his shoes and shook his head in disgust before looking up at me again. "Frankie…"

"Mack, listen. You don't have to defend yourself. If there's one thing I know about you, it's that you're a good father. There is nothing that she can ever say to make me believe otherwise."

He blew out a breath that momentarily warmed the skin on my face. "Thank you. Some days I feel like a failure. But I swear, I'm trying my ass off."

"I can see that. I'm not blind."

"Not anymore, at least. You got Lasik."

"Yeah." I smiled.

My body suddenly became all too aware that he was only inches from me. Time seemed to stand still for a bit as the leaves rustled around us. He kept looking at me intensely, and I just stood there soaking him in.

"Thank you for always believing in me," he finally said.

Trying to fight the feelings of hurt that were also creeping in, I had to ask, "I don't know why, but I'd assumed you two had gotten married."

"No. We were engaged for a long time, but the wedding never happened...much to my father's dismay."

"I can imagine he gave you a lot of grief about that."

"I just couldn't go through with it. Ending it was not easy. I knew she wouldn't take it well. I put it off for so long because I didn't want her to taint Jonah's view of me. I worry about what she says to him."

"All you can do is your best to show him you love him. As he gets older, he'll see things for what they are."

"I hope so." He sighed. "She's bringing this new guy around lately. Never told me anything beforehand. I happened to accidentally find him there when I dropped Jonah off recently." He brought his hand to my forehead, removing a flyaway hair. "Anyway, I don't mean to vent to you like this. You need to get back to class."

My body shivered from the contact. Whenever he touched me, it felt like the world stopped.

Touch me again.

I cleared my throat. "It's okay. I'll see you in a bit. You're still coming in at one?"

"Yeah. I'm just gonna take a walk, kill some time. I'll see you soon."

We each walked away in separate directions. Almost at the front entrance, I turned back around to look at him in the distance. My heart clenched upon realizing he was staring back at me, too.

A couple of women who'd been volunteering elsewhere in the school weaseled their way into my classroom for Mack's story time that afternoon. Among them was Clarissa McIntyre, the mother of one of my students. She was single, and it was obvious she had her eye on Mack.

With her long, blonde hair and svelte figure, Clarissa was probably as attractive as the mothers at this school got. Her being here because of Mack definitely made me uneasy. The same thing had happened the last time he'd come in to assist with a Halloween art project. Random women seemed to just magically appear in the corner of the room. Whenever I would hear them whisper the nickname "Mack Daddy," it made me want to punch someone.

Mack took his spot in the chair at the center of the circular rug. He took out his book, and I immediately noticed a new drawing of the cartoon version of me on the front.

"I've brought Frankie Four Eyes back in today for a new adventure. This one is called *Frankie Four Eyes and the Boy Band Bathroom Conundrum*."

Oh goodness.

"Once upon a time, there was a little girl named Frankie Jane, but people called her Frankie Four Eyes because of her gigantic, purple glasses."

Apparently, all of his stories started out with the same sentence.

"One day, Frankie was at a concert seeing one of her favorite boy bands. She managed to sneak backstage and was so excited, she nearly peed herself."

Everyone got a kick out of that.

"Frankie found a private bathroom that was supposed to be for employees only. But before she could sit down, to her dismay, her glasses suddenly fell into the toilet bowl."

The kids thought that was hysterical.

"This was a conundrum because—"

"What's a con eardrum?" one of the students interrupted.

"Not con eardrum. A *conundrum*. And that's a very good question. A conundrum is like a difficult problem... hard to solve."

Mack repeated his previous line, "This was a conundrum...because Frankie was a germaphobe."

Mack looked out at his audience anticipating a question.

A boy named Cayden raised his hand. "What's a germaphobe?"

"Good question! A germaphobe is someone who is afraid of germs." Mack continued, "Frankie didn't know what to do. She didn't want to stick her hand down the dirty toilet to get the glasses, but if she didn't, she wouldn't be able to see. She was also embarrassed, so she chose not to yell for help. Frankie ended up keeping herself locked in the bathroom for several minutes. This was another conundrum. If she opened the door, someone would see her glasses in the toilet. If she didn't, she'd be stuck in that bathroom unable to see." He put the book down momentarily. "What do you think Frankie should do?"

"Call for help," someone yelled.

"Yes. Let's read on and find out what she does." Mack turned the page. "Frankie didn't have to decide, because there was a knock at the door. It was one of the singers from the band who needed to use the bathroom. She once again didn't know what to do. This was another..." He paused.

The class answered in unison. "Conundrum."

"That's right." He continued, "Before Frankie could open the door, a boy barged his way in. Frankie squinted to see who it was. Turned out, it was Mackenzie Magic, the lead singer of the band. Not only was Frankie embarrassed, but she was starstruck." He turned the page. "The boy noticed Frankie squinting then looked down and saw her glasses in the bowl. Without thinking twice about it, Mackenzie Magic reached into the toilet, retrieved the glasses, and cleaned them off with soap

95

and water. Not only that, he even joked about it, making Frankie laugh. She never expected that someone as famous as Mackenzie could be so nice. Later that night, he even ended up calling Frankie up on stage during the evening performance. Frankie realized that sometimes help comes from the least likely of places and sometimes—with the right person—a conundrum can turn into something great. The End."

As the children clapped, Mack's eyes darted toward me to gauge my reaction. He chuckled when he realized I was smiling. He knew he'd once again brought back a memory for me.

Mack spent the next several minutes discussing the theme of the book with the children.

While he was wrapping up, the mother I'd had my eye on waltzed her way over to him. Clarissa was going in for the kill. Straining my ears through the noise of the class, I struggled to hear what they were saying.

She held out her hand. "Clarissa McIntyre, Ethan's mom."

"Mack Morrison, Jonah's dad. Pleasure to meet you."

Just seeing her hand in his made my skin crawl.

"I've been meaning to look you up in the directory. Ethan's been telling me how much he'd love a playdate with Jonah sometime."

"Really? That's interesting, considering my son generally keeps to himself."

"They have similar personalities. I think that's what appeals to Ethan, actually."

Sure, it does.

She continued, "You'll have to give me your number. I'll program it into my phone. Maybe sometime later this week?"

"I'm actually only with Jonah on the weekends. His mother has a nanny who's with him after school."

"The weekend would actually work better for us."

I bet it would. Much better for your purposes.

Mack was non-committal. "Alright, well, maybe."

"Okay, I'm ready for your number whenever you are."

She was so pushy. I watched as she entered his digits into her phone.

Mack then walked toward me without saying anything further to her.

"Sorry about that," he said.

"No, it's fine. Clearly she's eager for a *playdate.*"

He'd picked up on my sarcasm. "I won't be playing in the sandbox with Clarissa, Frankie."

"I'm sure she'd love for you to play in her box."

He seemed amused by my apparent jealousy. "Yeah, well, I won't be."

"Thanks for coming in."

I shivered when he leaned in and whispered in my ear, "When can I spend some time with you again?"

"I don't know, Mack."

We just stood there staring at each other for a bit. The look in his eyes this time was different from the other times we had silently connected recently. His eyes were telling me he had a lot of fight left in him. In fact, they were telling me that he hadn't even begun to fight. He looked like he wanted to say something, but instead, he just turned away, grabbed his coat, and left.

For some reason that night, I just couldn't stop thinking about him. Well, more so than usual.

While Victor wrapped his arm around me as he drifted off to sleep, something in my bones told me that things in my life were about to get very complicated.

CHAPTER EIGHT

Francesca

PAST

Mack was leaning against my bureau as I was putting on my earrings. He had his arms crossed and looked preoccupied.

"So, what do you really know about this Emmett?"

"He's a car dealer now, but he used to be in a Boston-based boy band when he was younger."

"Are you kidding me? He sounds shady. And cheesy."

"You don't even know him. Don't judge him based on something he used to do. That's like me judging you for ever thinking about going into politics."

"I wouldn't blame you one bit if you did. Politicians are the shadiest—my father included." Mack let out a deep breath. "Well, at least you'll be with Moses."

"Even if I wasn't, I can take care of myself."

I didn't really understand what was happening between Mack and me. All I knew was that with each week that passed, I felt more physically ill each time he'd go home to D.C. to be with Torrie. The jealousy monster had fully overtaken me. Yet, sometimes it was even harder having him around on the weekends, because it would give us more time together. My feelings for him had torpedoed into something that was seriously dangerous for my well-being.

The whole purpose of this date was to break the cycle—a cycle which mostly consisted of obsessing over Mack, fantasizing about Mack, longing for someone I couldn't have.

At the same time, I cherished his friendship. That made the situation complicated, because I couldn't seem to give him up.

I truly didn't know how he really felt about me, but I suspected based on how he was acting tonight, that he was a little jealous. That gave me a thrill and confused me at the same time.

Moses walked in. He looked at Mack and then at me. There was an awkward silence. He knew about my true feelings for Mack. That was one of the reasons he was pushing me to go on this date.

"They should be here any minute," Moses said before turning to Mack. "Don't you have somewhere to be?"

"Nope."

Moses glared at him. "Can I talk to you for a minute?"

Both guys then left the room.

What was that all about?

Before I knew it, the doorbell rang. With Moses and Mack still talking in private, I went to let our guests in.

Emmett had red hair like me, blue eyes, and a nice smile. In any other world, he might have even seemed handsome. But in *my* world, no one compared to Mack Morrison.

"You must be Francesca."

"Yes. Nice to meet you."

"Nice to meet you, too. Moses has told me so much about you."

"Likewise." I then turned to his brother, Moses's boyfriend. "Nice to see you again, Brad. Where are we headed tonight?"

Moses entered the room and answered my question. "I was thinking we'd go to Dick's Last Resort."

Dick's was a gimmicky restaurant in the city known for its whacky décor and intentionally obnoxious staff.

"Speaking of dicks..." Moses said, looking over at Mack, who'd just emerged from his bedroom.

Mack headed straight for my date. "Emmett! What's up, bro? How ya doin'?" He spun around in a Justin Bieber-like dance move then extended his hand.

Oh, God.

In an apparent attempt to mock Emmett's former boy band stint, Mack had changed into low-slung jeans that were hanging halfway down his ass. His boxers were pretty much on full display. He'd also put on a white, wife beater tank and was wearing a baseball cap sideways. Despite my embarrassment, I couldn't help but notice how good his muscles looked in that shirt. *Damn.*

Moses chose to ignore Mack's little show and headed to the kitchen to grab a couple of beers for our dates.

Feeling anxious, I took the time to use the bathroom.

That was when things literally went down the toilet.

I'd stupidly flushed a tampon, resulting in the toilet clogging. It came right back up along with a deluge of water that gathered at the top of the bowl. With no plunger in sight, I truly didn't know what to do. The thought of sticking my hand in the toilet skeeved me out beyond belief. Yet, there was no way I could have just left it there and gone out. One of the guys would have seen it. I knew that one of them would be using the bathroom before we left for the night, especially since they'd been drinking. Worse, if they didn't, then Mack would be the one to see my floating tampon after we left.

After I'd been hiding in the bathroom for upwards of a half-hour, there was a light knock on the door.

"Frankie, what the hell? Are you okay?"

Shit. It was Mack.

"No."

"What's wrong? You sound weird."

"Do we have a plunger somewhere that you could hand to me?"

He laughed. "What did you get yourself into, Frankie Jane?"

"Just...do we have one or not?"

"Moses is a germaphobe. He took the plunger a while back and said he was going to replace it but never did."

"Well, I need one."

"We don't have one."

"Can you go get one for me?"

A few seconds passed before he said, "I'll be right back."

Mack disappeared for about five minutes before returning.

"Are you decent?"

"You can't come in here!"

He repeated, "Are you decent?"

"Yes, but—"

The door opened.

Mack was sporting rubber, dishwashing gloves and carrying a bucket.

"What are you doing?"

"Unclogging the mess you made."

"You can't."

"Watch me. How bad could it be anyway?" He had to eat his words when he looked down at my bloody tampon that had now expanded in the water. "Oh."

I cringed. "Yeah."

"Apparently, you're not supposed to flush those."

"No shit, Sherlock," I snapped.

"I'd ask you why you're cranky, but obviously it's that time of the month."

Despite my mortification, I couldn't help but laugh a little. Mack grinned and winked at me, causing my heart to flutter. How this guy could have me swooning at a time like this was pretty unbelievable.

Mack geared himself up. "Alright, here goes."

Without delay, he reached into the toilet to extract the tampon. After dumping it into the trash, he then proceeded to squirt copious amounts of shampoo into the toilet bowl. Then, he headed over to the sink where he filled the large bucket. After pouring the scalding water down the bowl, he was able to get things moving again. He finished it off with a successful flush.

"How did you learn how to do that?"

"It's Mackenzie magic." He winked then said, "Actually, Google. Looked up remedies for unclogging a toilet without a plunger."

"Thank you for coming to my rescue. That was beyond your duty as a friend."

"You're lucky I like you, Frankie Jane. I think that was proof I'd do just about anything for you."

His words gave me serious butterflies. He always made me feel like he *would* do anything for me.

"Thank you."

"You know what I think?"

"What?"

"I think subconsciously you're just trying to avoid going out with him."

"Why do you say that?"

"Because no one stays locked up in a bathroom because of a floating tampon." He took his gloves off and discarded them in the trash. "Why don't you just tell them you're sick or something? Stay home."

"That would be rude at this point."

"And disappearing into the bathroom isn't?"

I changed the subject off of me. "What was with the boy band act? You're such an attention whore."

"Only when it comes to your attention."

My heart started to beat faster. I was a lost cause.

"Well, next time you're tantruming for my attention, try not to be so insulting to other people."

"You're right. It was immature."

"You did make me laugh, though."

"That's because you have the same sense of humor I do. And neither of us is that nice, which is why we get along so well."

"Maybe."

Our eyes locked, and the tension in the air was transparent. His hair was messed up from the hat he'd been wearing, but in a way, that made him look even more handsome. I wanted so badly to run my fingers through that hair, to tug on it, pull him into my mouth and just suck on his lips. If he only knew that just thinking about that was making me wet.

Could he tell how badly I wanted him?

When he reached his hand over to my waist, I flinched. For a split second, I'd thought he was going to pull me into him or something. It turned out he was just fixing my shirt.

"It was halfway untucked," he said. "You're a bit of a mess."

My pulse was still recovering from the excitement of that brief contact when Moses entered without knocking.

"What the fuck is going on?" he spewed.

"Nothing. Mack was just helping me with a toilet mishap."

"Whatever. You're being fucking rude, Frankie."

"You're right. I'll be right there."

Moses exited the bathroom, slamming the door behind him.

"He hates me right now," Mack joked. He and I continued to stare at each other for a few seconds before he said, "I should let you go." Grabbing the bucket, he started to leave before stopping at the door one last time to say, "I really need to learn how to be better at that—letting you go."

It was the first real implication of his jealousy. Why did I feel badly that my going out with Emmett was upsetting him? Mack had a girlfriend! God, our relationship was so fucked-up.

The school year was coming to an end. I knew Mack would be heading home to D.C. soon for the summer. He was supposed to be home from his weekend away any minute. On this particular Sunday night, though,

I decided to forego meeting him down in the laundry room. Instead, I made my way up to the rooftop of our building.

Lights from nearby Fenway Park lit up the night sky. A Red Sox game against the Orioles had gone into overtime, and the cheers from the crowd could be heard. Feeling super emotional tonight, I let the sounds from the park serve as the backdrop to the multitude of thoughts going through my head.

After about an hour alone up there, Mack's voice startled me. "Frankie?"

Shit.

I turned around. "Hi."

"You threw me off. I was expecting you to be down in the basement. I don't know what made me decide to check up here, but I had a feeling."

"I wasn't in the mood for laundry tonight, for some reason."

He sat down next to me as we both gazed out at Fenway.

"Nothing like baseball on a balmy night in Boston," I said.

"You don't normally come up here alone. Something's up. Did that fucking Emmett do something?"

I shook my head. "No. I'm not even seeing him anymore."

"Why not?"

"Nothing. It just fizzled away."

"Well, I couldn't see you with him anyway."

"Yeah," I whispered.

His tone became more insistent. "Something is bothering you. Talk to me."

I looked up at the stars. How could I tell him what was really eating away at me? That I felt like I was falling in love with him. That I wasn't sure I could handle my jealousy anymore. That I was miserable at the thought of him leaving for the entire summer. That I feared he might decide not to come back and that I'd never see him again. That in some ways, I feared him coming back again even more. That I'd never been more confused in my entire life.

Probably sensing my inner turmoil, he said, "You know you can talk to me about anything, right?"

"I don't know how to talk to you about *you*."

He simply nodded. He knew exactly what was wrong.

Mack shocked me when he reached over and grabbed my hand, firmly locking my fingers into his. He stared down at our hands for a while. "This conversation has been a long time coming, hasn't it?"

"Yes."

"It's not one-sided, Frankie. I know you can feel that from me, because I don't hide my jealousy very well."

"You know, it's pretty pathetic that the best part of my weekend is always when you come home. You asked me why I wasn't downstairs...I was kind of hoping you didn't find me."

"Damn, it's come to that, huh?" He smiled.

"I need to break the pattern, get used to you not being around, not just for the summer but the long term. This is not healthy."

He gripped my hand tighter and just continued to look at me as I continued.

"I've gotten attached to you, Mack—way more than a friend should."

"I know it's fucked-up, Frankie. This whole experience in Boston was just supposed to be a temporary reprieve for me, to figure out my future, to get away from home. I wasn't expecting that being here would *feel* more like home. That's because of you. You weren't part of the plan. At all."

"I don't want to have these feelings for you."

"I used to tell myself I'd eventually tell Torrie about you. But the longer I put it off, the harder it's become, because my feelings for you now are more complicated than they used to be in the beginning. I'm afraid she'll see through me. It's not fair to her, and it's not fair to you. I'm just so fucking confused about everything. All I know is...I don't ever want to hurt you."

"I know that." I nodded. "This summer apart might be a good thing."

"Yeah. I think you're right."

We sat in silence for a while after that, staring at the Fenway lights and listening to the sounds of the cheering baseball fans.

I looked down again at our interlocked fingers, knowing that I could count on one hand the number of days left before he would be gone.

CHAPTER NINE

Francesca

The students had been assigned to draw a picture of their families before recess. It was part of a lesson on the diversity of the family structure in America. As I was looking through the kids' submissions, I stopped upon Jonah's, which was very telling.

Three harsh lines were drawn in thick black crayon between the images of his mother, father, and him. Oddly, Jonah had drawn Torrie with a smile on her face but had drawn Mack and himself with frowns. The drawing clearly depicted how he viewed his current family situation along with his emotional state.

While it wasn't my place to analyze the boy's artistic interpretation of his home life, I couldn't help but want to talk to him. Maybe it was inappropriate to be giving his drawing any special attention over the others, but I couldn't seem to ignore it. The truth was, he reminded me a lot of myself when I was younger.

As was typical, Jonah was playing off to the side of the schoolyard, kicking around a ball, separated from the other students. I took the opportunity to try to talk to him before recess ended.

"Hey, Jonah. Can I speak to you for a minute?"

He simply nodded and followed me inside and down the corridor.

Back in the classroom, I took a seat next to him. "So, I was looking at your drawing here, and it sort of caught my eye because of how different it was. There's nothing wrong with that. I just wanted to talk to you about it."

Jonah continued to remain quiet but attentive.

"First off, I want to make sure you understand that there are all sorts of families. Families with parents who are together, families with two mothers, two fathers, families with one parent. Let me show you a picture of my family."

I walked over to my desk and grabbed a drawing that I had quickly put together myself right before. It showed my mother and me on one side and a cut out piece of black construction paper pasted onto the other side of the page.

"So, this is my family. It looks different than yours but nevertheless, still a family. I never got to meet my dad. So, he's sort of like a mystery to me. That's why he's represented in black."

"Where is he?"

"I don't know, Jonah. He decided he didn't want to be a father before I was born. But you know what? I had a great mother. And she took really good care of me. But see…I wanted to share my story with you so that you understand that not everyone has a storybook family. That was my reason for this project, to demonstrate that. If your mom and dad aren't living together, you're not alone. It's okay to be upset about that, because emotions are natural. We can't help them. But you have two parents who love you. I can assure you of that. They will always love you, even if they aren't together."

"Your dad didn't love you?"

"He didn't know me. And he was very young."

"Do you forgive him?"

The kid had totally stumped me, because that was a question I truly didn't know the answer to.

I hesitated before answering, "That's a tough question." I rustled his curls playfully. "Can I come back to you on that?"

"Yeah," he said, cracking a slight smile that was reminiscent of Mack.

"Just remember it's okay to be different. That goes for when you start to feel like you're not blending in with the other kids. You remind me a lot of myself when I was younger. I used to wear glasses just like you, too."

He surprised me when he said, "I know, you're Frankie Four Eyes."

"You do, huh?"

"I won't say anything."

"Okay." I smiled. "You know what else, Jonah? I was also really shy around people, too. Just like you."

"How did you get to become a teacher, then?"

"Well, for me, I tend to get nervous around other *grown ups*. Even still to this day, sometimes."

"What do you do when that happens?"

"I deal with it until the funny feelings pass. They always do. And I never run from things that make me uncomfortable. Kind of like how we've been having you stay in the class when you ask to leave. Have you noticed you haven't been asking to leave as often?"

He nodded.

"That's because you've stuck it out enough times now that you've learned there's really nothing to be afraid of."

Jonah seemed to ponder that.

"Anyway, the lesson here is that it's okay to be different, and it's okay to not love being around people all of the time. What's important is that you try—not for them—but for yourself."

"Okay."

"Thanks for the talk." I smiled. "You still have a few minutes of recess left if you want to go back outside, or you can stay and hang in here with me."

He decided to stay. I'd left Jonah's family portrait on his desk. I watched as he sat down, stared at it for a while then picked up his crayon and altered it somehow.

I'd notice later that he'd switched his frown to a smile.

I don't know what finally possessed me that particular night to tell Victor about Mack. But it was time.

The guilt had finally worn me down. Even though I hadn't technically done anything wrong, I'd been so preoccupied over the past several weeks. It's not easy to hide an obsession from someone you live with day in and day out. Every night, he'd ask me whether something was bothering me, and I'd always tell him it was school-related and nothing more. Victor was probably the person I respected most in the entire world; he deserved better than to be lied to.

After I'd given him the full story of my history with Mack, my boyfriend's reaction further proved why I'd fallen for him in the first place.

"You still have feelings for him."

"I don't exactly understand what they mean. They could just be feelings of nostalgia."

"But you're confused."

"Yes."

"You know your happiness means everything to me, right?"

"I know you really mean that. I'm just not sure if I deserve it."

"Francesca, I don't think I've ever really felt that I deserve *you*. You're young and beautiful...nurturing and intelligent. I go to sleep every night feeling like the luckiest man alive to be sleeping next to you." He smiled. "And when your mood allows, getting to make love to you. But I wake up every morning unsure of whether that day will be the day you figure out that you could do better. Or that maybe you'd prefer being with someone closer to your own age. The one thing I *am* sure of is that I don't want you here if you don't want to be. I love you enough to let you work this out if that's what you need."

The only man who'd ever really made me feel safe was offering to distance himself from me. That didn't exactly sit well.

"I don't want to go anywhere, Vic."

"I'll always take care of you if that's what you want. I'll always want you in my life, but only as long as I can make you happy. Do you understand what I'm saying?"

"Yes. You do make me happy. You always have."

That was the truth.

"Since we're being honest with each other tonight, I actually have something I need to talk to you about."

My heart began to race. "Okay..."

"You remember that program that B.U. was trying to get going with Oxford?"

"Yes?"

"Well, last week, they offered me the opportunity to spearhead it in London for the first year."

"Oh."

"I turned them down, Francesca."

"Why didn't you tell me?"

"I didn't think it would be possible for you to leave your job and come with me. So, it wasn't an option for me to leave you. If, by some chance, you don't plan on being around next year, I would take the position. But in case there's any question, I'd rather have you. Nothing is more important to me. I just thought you should know about the offer."

Knowing that he so readily gave up a dream position for me made me feel horrible given the fact that I was basically hung up on another man.

"I love you, Francesca. I hope that's enough for you."

"I love you, Vic." I truly did love him. My feelings for him may not have been fueled by the same crazy passion I'd once felt toward Mack, but they were real just the same.

Victor's eyes were sincere. "Thank you for being honest with me."

Nothing got resolved that night. If anything, I was more confused as to why I was still pining over a man who'd left me years ago when I had one who worshipped me right under my nose.

It was the evening of our monthly PTO meeting. On the agenda was to designate the volunteers for several fundraisers that would take place in the spring.

Setting up the refreshments and a coffee urn in the hallway outside of the classroom, I couldn't wait to get this over with so that I could go home, get into my pajamas, and relax. It was always exhausting to have evening commitments when the workday ran so late to begin with.

A deep voice from behind startled me. "A keg would be much more fun, wouldn't it?"

I turned around to find Mack standing there, holding a box of chocolate chip cookies from the supermarket.

"What are you doing here?"

He placed the cookies on the table. "This is the parent and teachers meeting, isn't it?"

"Yes, but..." I hesitated, not even knowing what to say.

He finished my sentence. "But I'm not supposed to be included in that group?" Mack snapped his finger. "Oh, I'm sorry. I thought PTO stood for 'pissing teacher off.' My bad."

"Well, if that were the case, you might be in the right place."

"This *is* the right place for me tonight."

"This meeting is for serious participants."

"I'm serious about the teacher. Does that count?"

"No."

"Actually, in all *seriousness*, I'd also like to help. It's the least I can do after crashing your school year. I really would like to be as involved as I can in Jonah's education. That's the truth, okay? Getting to spend time with you is an added benefit."

What could I say? He had just as much right to be here as anyone else.

"Just be aware that this isn't the right place to be joking around or distracting the other attendees, for that matter."

"I don't plan on distracting anyone but you."

"Yeah, well you have quite the fan base here. We have a very strict agenda to adhere to."

He moved in closer and just stared me down for a bit. The contact caused my skin to prickle and my nipples to harden. "Don't worry," he said as he looked down, seeming to notice that my nipples were piercing through the fabric of my shirt. "Your points are well noted, Miss O'Hara." He wriggled his brows. "I'll see you inside."

I hated that he knew he was having an effect on me. If my body had this kind of response now, what would have happened if he'd actually done more? Spontaneous impregnation? Some things just never change, and my reaction to this man was an example of that.

A long table sat in the middle of the spare classroom where we held the meeting. There wasn't a single man in the room besides Mack. He was like the centerpiece.

I took my seat at the end of the table. "So, shall we get started?" Looking down at my list, I said, "First on the agenda is the book fair. We need to elect someone to be in charge of it and coordinate the volunteers."

Mack raised his hand.

"Yes?" I asked.

"That sounds like it's right down my alley. I'd like to volunteer to run the book fair."

"What makes you want that task? It's a lot of responsibility."

He thought about it for a moment then said, "I write children's books. I think I'd be a perfect fit."

"That's a good point," one of the women said. "He might be the *perfect* fit."

I'm sure you're thinking he'd be the perfect fit, alright...in your vagina.

"Okay...but I hope you know that there is a tremendous amount of work that goes into organizing that particular event. It takes place over the course of an entire weekend. You have to place orders with the bookseller, do inventory, delegate tasks, and arrange for an onsite food vendor because many people just come for the food. Ultimately, the food is the bait."

"I can bait people. I'm a master baiter." He paused. "I mean...I can handle it. I'll get a shitload of people to sign up."

An attending nun gave him a dirty look for his use of foul language.

He cleared his throat, seeming to regret his choice of terminology. "I'll get people to attend. Don't worry."

"I'll put your name down as a possibility. We'll take a vote at the end."

"Thank you."

Looking around the room, I asked, "Is there anyone else here who is interested in taking the reigns on the book fair?"

Not a single person budged.

One woman said, "No, but I'll be happy to help Mack with whatever he needs."

I'm sure you will.

Mack nodded then offered a smug smile. "Thank you." He then took a bite of his cookie and winked at me.

I was sure my cheeks were turning crimson. "Okay, then. Moving on."

By the end of the meeting, the votes for Mack to head the book fair were unanimous. That event also had the most volunteers out of every other, especially once he offered to hold the planning meetings at his house. A vision of Mack in a Hugh Hefner-like bathrobe, smoking a cigar, surrounded by swarms of horny mothers flashed through my mind. I shrugged it off.

For the most part, Mack was on his best behavior for the remainder of the meeting.

Once everyone dispersed, he lingered until it was just the two of us alone in the classroom.

He was leaning back into his chair, swiveling back and forth slightly as he just looked at me with a mischievous smile.

I began to pack up my things. Without looking him in the eyes, I said, "You've never run a school event before. Don't you think you're going to be in a little over your head?"

"Not when I have you to help me."

"Isn't it typical to ask someone first before assuming they'll help you?"

"Frankie...can you help me run the book fair?" He joked.

"You have more than enough volunteers, actually." I held up a piece of paper. "Look at this list."

"Yeah, but none of them are as smart and resourceful as you. As an example, none of those women would know to use their boogers as glue."

I couldn't believe he remembered that. I'd once confessed to him that as a kid, I'd run out of glue during an art project and used some of my own snot to hold some construction paper together. It was an absolutely disgusting thought now. Nevertheless, I couldn't deny it.

"How do you even remember that?"

"I know everything about you, Frankie Jane. Well, up until a certain point."

"Anyway, there are easier ways to spend time with me than hijacking a school fundraiser, you know."

"Really? Because you don't make it easy at all. Every time I mention getting together, you change the subject. Is it because you truly don't want to spend time with me, or are you just afraid of what you might feel if you do? Personally, I think it's the latter. You think I can't read you, but I can."

"Is that so?"

"Yes. It's one of my many talents."

Holding out my hand, I said, "Stop."

"What?"

"I know you're about to go on about your other talents, and you're gonna say something suggestive. Don't forget where we are."

"Jesus...you're no fun."

"Don't use the Lord's name in vain, either," I whispered. "Sister Theresa is right outside that door. She'll come in here and hit you with her famous stick." When he smirked, I held out my index finger. "I know you want to say something right now about *your* famous stick."

"God, Frankie...what kind of a pig do you think I am?" he teased.

"Don't say God."

"You are totally putting words in my mouth, trying to predict what I'm going to say next. Although, words are not what I fucking want in my mouth right now."

Jesus Christ.

Don't use the Lord's name in vain.

I tightened the muscles between my legs.

"See?" I spewed.

"See what? That I'm a crass king of sexual innuendos who'll use any opportunity he can get to make you blush? Yes. Then I am completely guilty. Forgive me, Father, for I have sinned."

"Shh. Don't say that!"

"Maybe that's what I need, to go to confession."

"You have issues."

"You're absolutely right. I think I'm gonna go this week, in fact. I'll tell Father Louis about my coveting the beautiful, young teacher who used to be my best friend. I'll tell him how I fantasize about what my hand print would look like on your ass. Maybe he can splash some holy water on me, cool me down. I hope to God he can help me get over you, because nothing else has ever worked."

"Stop."

"You're not even enjoying this a little bit?"

I was enjoying it a lot...a little too much to the point where my panties were now drenched.

Lifting my bag over my shoulder, I said, "We should get out of here. They need to lock up the building."

He stood up and gestured his hand toward the door. "After you..."

The air was cold outside, and it was foggy. Mack quietly walked me to my car.

As we stopped in front of my vehicle, we just looked at each other for a few moments.

His expression turned serious. "I thought I saw you once."

"What?"

His breath was visible as he spoke. "Jonah was about six months old. Torrie and I had taken him to the mall. He was in one of those carriers on my chest. She'd gone off to shop in one of the stores, and I was standing there in the middle of the mall carrying the baby. There was this girl. She looked just like you from the back, same straight, red hair that was exactly the length it was the last time I'd seen you. Same posture, too."

"You really thought she was me?"

He nodded, looking sullen. "I was sure of it. My heart was pounding out of my chest. I was so caught up in the idea that it was you, I couldn't even rationalize in my brain that your being in Virginia at that time probably wouldn't have made any sense. I guess that was because I wanted so badly to believe that it was you. And I did. I truly believed it."

"What did you do?"

"I stood there for the longest time working up the nerve to go up to you. Jonah was crying, but it was like I'd forgotten he was even there attached to me. Nothing else mattered in that moment as I began to gear myself up to tell you how much I missed you, to tell you all of the things that had been building inside of me in the time we'd been apart. In my delusional state, I didn't even doubt for one second that it was you. I remember my chest feeling so heavy. One step at a time, I moved closer and closer to where you were standing in the food court, checking out a menu. I don't know what I was thinking would happen. It wasn't like I could have run away with you or something. I just remember feeling like I'd been given a second chance, that somehow, some way, God had brought you to where I was in that exact moment."

"You went up to me? To her?"

"Yeah." He let out a slight, unamused laugh and shook his head. "I called out, 'Frankie.' When she turned around, obviously it wasn't you. I felt like such a fucking fool."

"You didn't know."

"I should've known you wouldn't have been all the way in Virginia. But I just wanted to believe it was you so badly."

"What did the girl say to you?"

"Nothing. I apologized, letting her know I thought she was someone else then walked away in a daze. Torrie came back soon after carrying some bags. She kept asking me what was wrong that night. I guess I must have looked as spent as I'd felt. In some ways, it was harder than anything that had happened up until then. It was like I'd lost you all over again. It made me realize just how filled with regret I was, how much had been left unsaid."

"What were you going to say to me? You know...if it were really me at that mall?"

"That's the thing...I didn't even know what I was going to say, but I'm pretty sure I would've made an absolute ass of myself, standing there blubbering away with a baby hanging off of me. It wasn't meant to be that day. I made a vow in that moment, though, that if I ever did get the chance to see you again, that I wouldn't fuck it up, that I would come prepared. I promised myself that I would make my intentions crystal clear to you and wouldn't waste the opportunity that the universe granted me."

"Have you ever heard that song '*Pictures of You*' by The Cure?"

"I think so, yeah."

"Every time I hear it, I think of you."

"I'll have to listen to it tonight." Mack reached his hand toward my neck and removed my loose scarf, repositioning it around my neck. "Anyway, it's cold. You'd better get into the car and blast the heat."

Suddenly not wanting to leave him, I wasn't sure what to say, so I simply responded with, "I'll help you with the book fair stuff if you want. I've been involved with it before."

"I would really appreciate that."

Later that night, I was in bed when a text message lit up my phone.

Mack: That freaking song. Wow. I'd never listened to the words.

I typed.

Francesca: I know.

Mack: Now I can't stop playing it.

I didn't know what had compelled me earlier to admit that song reminded me of him. He'd shared the mall story with me. I guess I wanted him to know that he wasn't alone in having feelings of regret and sadness over the years.

Mack: It always killed me that all I had left of you were the pictures I'd stashed away. How was it even possible that we never took one together, though?

Francesca: I know. I've wondered the same thing.

Mack: Anyway...I just wanted to let you know I love the song. Thank you for sharing that with me.

Francesca: You're welcome.

Mack: By the way, I started looking at this catalog of children's books for the book fair. I know which one I'm gonna order first.

Francesca: Which one?

Mack: It's called Do You Want To Play With My Balls?

He sent me a picture of what looked like a children's book featuring that same title.

Francesca: This can't be real!

Mack: LOL. No, it's not. It's for adults. Did I just give you a heart attack?

It was one of many mini heart attacks he'd given me lately.

Francesca: This is totally something you would have given me as a gag gift back in college.

Mack: Back in college? It's been ordered and is being shipped to you. Estimated delivery is Monday.

Francesca: Are you kidding?

Mack: Nope. Just don't let the old man see. He might get excited and give himself a real heart attack.

Francesca: You're crazy.

Mack: Goodnight, Frankie Jane.

Francesca: Goodnight, Mack.

CHAPTER TEN

Mack

It wasn't a typical Saturday at all. I'd woken up determined to get Jonah out of the house and away from his electronic devices.

We drove into the city and got breakfast in the North End. The plan was that later we would go to the Museum of Science. At least there, if he didn't feel like talking to me, there would be plenty for us to focus our attention on.

Deciding to kill some time after breakfast, we hit the farmer's market. I'd promised Mrs. Migillicutty I'd bring her back some corn. Handing Jonah a bag, I told him to pick out any amount of fruit he wanted.

Almost immediately after that, I noticed a familiar, dainty hand squeezing an avocado. Another hand—not so familiar—was squeezing Frankie's ass. I swallowed, taking in the sight of her and her boyfriend standing right in front of me. A cocktail of jealousy and adrenaline coursed through me.

Say something.

She hadn't noticed me yet when I leaned in and said the first thing I could think of. "How the heck do you even know if they're ripe anyway?"

She jumped at the sound of my voice.

"Mack. What are you doing here?"

"Same thing as you. Squeezing things?"

Frankie's cheeks turned red.

Her man faced me then turned to her. "This is Mack?"

She simply nodded.

Wow. She'd told him about me.

I wasn't sure whether that gave me satisfaction or disturbed me.

He held out his hand. "Victor Owens."

I took it. "Mack Morrison." It was a bizarre feeling to only now be coming face to face with someone who'd been my number one adversary for a long time.

He'd kept a firm grip around her waist with his other hand. Much to my dismay, Frankie's boyfriend was actually a decently good-looking, older man. Despite the salt and pepper hair, he was in good shape and what most women of any age would probably deem attractive.

Jonah appeared by my side with a plastic bag full of apples and pomegranates.

Frankie forced a smile. "Hey, Jonah."

He looked uncomfortable to have run into his teacher. "Hi."

"We're heading to the Science Museum in a little bit," I said.

"Oh, he'll love that." She smiled.

Victor turned to my son. "I used to love going there when I was a kid, although it's way better now. Make sure you visit the Colossal Fossil."

"What's that?" Jonah asked.

"It's a sixty-five million-year-old dinosaur skeleton, discovered in the Dakota Badlands about a decade ago. Really neat if you're into dinosaurs."

While my jealous and immature ego wished it could make a joke about *Frankie* being into dinosaurs, it was hard to take my inner thoughts seriously right now. In reality, this guy came across as younger than I'd imagined him. For the first time, I realized I had some serious competition if I ever dreamt of stealing Frankie away from him. A sinking feeling developed in the pit of my stomach as I looked back over at his hand that was planted just above her ass.

"Well, have a nice time," she said.

Fumbling my words, I said, "Yeah. You too. I mean...a nice weekend."

"Thank you," she said.

Frankie's eyes locked with mine in a silent acknowledgement of how awkward this encounter was.

Victor briefly patted my son on the shoulder. "Nice meeting you, Jonah."

My chest felt tight as we walked away.

That afternoon, while Jonah and I gazed up at the stars atop the ceiling of the museum's planetarium, my mind was elsewhere. I couldn't get the encounter out of my head. More than ever, it felt like I was running out of time.

Sunday night, I pulled up to Torrie's with Jonah. I was feeling particularly emotional between the run-in with Frankie the day before and having tried my ass off to bond with my son all weekend.

I looked behind me at Jonah who was hugging his backpack. "I hope you had a good time this weekend. I know I had fun spending it with you."

Instead of answering me, he floored me with a question. "Are you sad?"

My heart felt like it stopped beating for a moment. "What do you mean?"

"You smile to my face, but sometimes, you seem sad when you don't think I'm looking."

My boy was apparently more perceptive than I'd given him credit for. I stopped to think about how I could explain it to him.

"We all have our moments. There are some things in life I wish I could change. And those things make me sad sometimes. But you're not one of them. You're the best thing that ever happened to me. If you ever think I don't look happy, it has nothing to do with you. You're the one thing that brings me the most happiness. You're my home, Jonah. We're a team. I go where you go. Even if I'm not under the same roof at night, I'm still with you...just a phone call or a quick drive away. Whenever you need me, I'm there. Got it?"

"Okay."

"Good." I turned to reach into the backseat. "Now, give your old man a hug."

After we embraced, I was just about to exit the car when he said, "Miss O'Hara doesn't have a dad."

"She told you that?"

"Yeah. I feel bad for her."

I simply nodded, making a note to ask her what prompted her to admit that to him.

With Jonah back at his mother's for the night, the urgent need to see Frankie that had followed me around that entire weekend was at full force.

I picked up my phone and called her from the road.

She knew it was me when she answered, "Mack..."

"Frankie..."

"What's up?"

I got right to the point. "Can you meet me somewhere? I'd come pick you up at home, but I'm not sure if he'd appreciate that."

"Is everything okay?"

"Yes. Everything's fine, but I really need to see you. I'm in my car. Just tell me where to go. As long as it's not to hell."

After some hesitation, she agreed to meet me. Frankie had me pick her up outside of the Massachusetts statehouse, which wasn't too far from where she lived.

Waiting on the steps, she was dressed in a fitted, beige blazer and jeans. A bright-colored scarf was wrapped around her neck. Looking sexy as hell, she was also wearing tall, black, leather boots. Her style had definitely evolved for the better over the years.

She opened the door and got in.

I turned to her. "Where did you tell him you were going?"

"I told him I was meeting you. I don't want to lie to him."

"He's okay with that? Is he nuts?"

"He appreciates my honesty."

"I was surprised he knew who I was at the farmer's market. What exactly does he know?"

"Everything. I told him the whole story last week."

"Well, it takes a pretty confident guy to let his woman go out with another man."

"You said you wanted to talk. It's not a date. He knows that."

Her words were a harsh reality check. As much as I'd wanted it to be, it wasn't a date.

"Of course."

As I was approaching the onramp to I-93, she asked, "Where are we going?"

"I don't know."

"You don't know?"

"No. I just wanted to steal you away. I don't know where the fuck I'm going, Frankie. Don't know what the fuck I'm doing, either. I just needed to see you."

She leaned her head back against the seat, turning to me but stayed silent.

"Have you eaten?" I asked.

She smiled. "I could eat."

I smiled back at her. She knew that whenever I used to ask her that question, she would always respond with, "I could eat." Eating together had always been one of our favorite pastimes.

An idea popped into my head. "You think Sullivan's is open this time of year?"

"I know they're open," she said.

"Have you been back there?"

"I've gone a few times."

"With him or alone?"

"Alone."

That was our place.

Twenty minutes later, we pulled into a parking spot at our old stomping grounds. Sullivan's was a small, takeout joint by the water on Castle Island in South Boston. It wasn't a great beach for swimming, but we used to like to sit overlooking water, watching the planes flying low as they landed into nearby Logan Airport.

The mid-November ocean was choppy, and it was freezing near the water, but I barely noticed those things.

Looking up at a 747 coming in, I spoke louder over the engine noise. "This feels so good, being here with you, watching the planes land. I've fantasized a lot about coming back to this place with you."

Frankie quietly ate her grilled hot dog as she gazed out toward the water, the wind blowing her hair around erratically.

"Will you tell me how you met him?"

She wiped her mouth before clearing her throat. "I was taking a graduate class at B.U. He's a professor there."

"He was your teacher?"

"No. But we met there. I didn't know he was a professor, at first."

"How long after I left Boston did you start dating him?"

"A while after. We've been together two years now."

"Were you with anyone before him?"

"I dated here and there, but Vic was the first serious relationship. I had a hard time connecting with anyone for a long time after you left."

That was hard to hear. But it didn't surprise me. I knew she cared deeply about me, and to this day, our chemistry was like nothing I had ever experienced. While it satisfied me somewhat to know she'd felt that way, it also hurt to hear that it took her a while to move on after my leaving. I never expected otherwise, though.

"What was different about him?"

"Everything. He respects me, appreciates all of my quirks—kind of like you did. And he takes care of me, makes me feel safe. I've never had anyone take care of me before. I'd always had to take care of myself. It was a nice change."

"I promise I won't joke about the daddy complex."

"Look, you're not totally wrong there. He's been able to fill a void for sure. But I don't like to think of it that way."

I really didn't want to envision him filling any of her voids.

"Does he want to marry you? I mean, he's getting up there."

"He says he wants spend the rest of his life with me, but he doesn't place a lot of value in the institution of marriage. He says he'd do it if I wanted it. Same with kids. But he doesn't need them to be happy, either. I know he enjoys his freedom."

"Was he ever married before?"

"No."

"Do you want to get married?"

"Right now? No."

"Are you still sexually attracted to him?"

"My God, Mack, this is like the third degree. Why do you want to know that?"

I was done beating around the bush.

"I need to know where any points of weakness are."

"Because you plan to try to steal me from him?"

"If you're meant to be with him, I won't be able to do that no matter how hard I try."

"But you *do* plan to try."

I plan to try like fucking hell.

"I know I might be too late. I'm not stupid. But I would never forgive myself if I didn't at least try."

"What exactly do you plan to try?"

"I won't be in Boston forever. I don't suspect that Torrie's job here will last. It's just a contract position. And I have to go wherever Jonah is. So, this is a window of opportunity that I can't waste. You asked what I plan to try? Everything. Every goddamn thing, Frankie—until you tell me to stop. Until you look me in the eyes and tell me there's no point in continuing."

"You have to go where your son is. I get that. Your hands are tied. I can imagine that the past several years have not been easy for you."

"They haven't. But my biggest regret is hurting you. I don't regret my son. I may not know what I'm doing all of the time, but that boy means the world to me."

"I know he does."

"I used to think staying with his mother was the best thing I could do for him. I was wrong. Having two parents who are constantly fighting was never gonna make his life better. I've finally realized that if I'm not happy, I can't truly be the kind of father my son deserves. He can see right through me."

"He keeps to himself, but he's very aware."

"You talked to him about your father."

"He told you that?"

"Yeah."

"I did. We had a lesson about diverse families. He'd drawn a picture of you, Torrie, and him with thick lines separating each of you."

Wow. That broke my heart.

"No shit, huh?"

"Yes. I wanted him to know that many people have different family structures and that it's okay. That was why I shared that piece of info with him."

"Thank you for doing that. I know it's not easy for you to talk about it."

"He asked me if I forgave my dad...for abandoning me."

"Really?"

"I thought that was a good question and answered him honestly. I told him I wasn't sure, but that I would get back to him on it. He seemed to accept that." She gazed out toward the water then back at me. "Are things better with him at home?"

"I think we're slowly getting to a better place. This was a good weekend."

"I'm glad to hear that. What about *your* father? How's your relationship with him now?"

"Same as it always was. He's not happy with me—from my career choice to my refusal to marry Torrie. But his opinion doesn't matter to me at this stage in my life. He can't change my decisions. And more than that, I don't allow him power over my thoughts anymore. That's been the biggest change. But Dad's been good to Jonah. I have to give him that. Otherwise, he's the same miserable prick he's always been, concerned more with his public reputation than anything else."

Our conversation was interrupted when Frankie's phone chimed. She looked down at it.

"Is that Victor?"

"Yeah. He just wants to make sure I'm okay."

"Does he think I'm gonna hurt you or something?"

That wouldn't have been off base, considering I'd definitely already hurt her enough for one lifetime.

"No. He's just doing what any boyfriend would do in this scenario."

"I know. I don't blame him one bit."

She began to shiver, and I fought the urge to wrap my arms around her. As much as I wanted to do that, it wasn't my place.

Her eyes glowed in the moonlight. "It *is* getting late. I should get back."

"Let's get you home, then."

The ride back to her neighborhood went by way too quickly. My time with her was always limited; I hadn't even begun to scratch the surface of everything I needed to say.

When we pulled up around the corner from her house, I asked, "When can I see you again?"

"Victor is going to England in a couple of weeks to consult on a new anthropology program at Oxford."

"For how long?"

"For a week."

One week.

Despite all of the evil planning in my brain, I attempted to sound casual. "Dinner, then?"

"We'll talk," she said in a non-committal way.

My heart beat faster. I knew this was my one chance to really spend time with her, to have my Frankie back—even if just for a week.

CHAPTER ELEVEN

Francesca

Victor zipped his suitcase. He was being unusually quiet this morning as he prepared to leave for his trip. Seemingly lost in thought, at one point he paused then placed his hand on my forearm, pulling me into him.

Hugging me tightly, he whispered in my ear, "I wish you were coming with me."

I breathed in the scent of his signature Givenchy cologne and said, "Me too, but you didn't ask me. I didn't know that was even an option."

"I think we need this week apart. You need to figure some things out. I'm giving you the space to do that for a week. I won't question anything that happens while I'm gone. I don't want to know." He pulled back to look at me. "But, Francesca, I can't live like this forever. At some point, I'm going to need to know your heart is mine. I may come across as a very strong person, but lately, I'm realizing more and more that I may not be as strong as I thought I was. I love you so much. But I can't bear to be with you if your heart isn't in this with me."

His words were sobering. I stayed silent as he continued.

"These two years with you have been the best of my life. I never doubted that we would be together forever—until recently. And when I found out the reason why you've been acting strange, it was proof that my worries were warranted."

"I'm so sorry to have put this kind of stress on us."

"Don't be sorry. You were honest with me. I appreciate that more than you know. But I'm not going to lie. After seeing that the guy you're hung up on looked like a Calvin Klein model on top of everything, well, that didn't help."

I laughed slightly only because I didn't know how else to react or what to even say. Mack *did* look like a freaking model, but that had nothing to do with why we were in this predicament. "I'm not a superficial person. You know that. My connection with him was more than skin deep, just as my connection to you is."

"I know you think with your heart and mind. So, if at any point you decide that your heart isn't in this, I would prefer that you rip the Band-Aid off. That's all I ask. I don't want to be strung along."

"I promise never to do that to you, Vic. And I promise to work this out so that we can move on with our lives."

He looked down at his watch. "I'm going to be late, but one more thing before I go." He placed both of his hands around my face. "If you do determine that I'm the one, I've decided that I want to go all in. Because there is no halfway with how I feel about you, my love. And I'm not sure I realized it until losing you became a very real threat. I want to marry you. I want to have babies with you. I want to love you for the rest of my life and do nothing but make you happy. You just need to decide which road you want to take. If the journey is with me, I promise, you won't regret it."

Tears began to fill my eyes. Victor had never said anything quite like that to me before. "I love you, Vic. I do."

"I love you, too, Francesca. Take care of yourself this week, okay?"

"Okay."

Then, he was gone.

My head was pretty much in the clouds as I attempted to teach that morning. I couldn't stop thinking about Victor. He'd never bared his soul to me like that. It made me truly realize how much I stood to lose if I let my feelings for Mack get in the way of my relationship with the only man who'd ever claimed to love me.

Later in the day, my mood would change and not for the better. I was correcting papers while the students were completing a spelling test.

Lorelai came up behind me and spoke low. "I was talking to Clarissa this morning. She mentioned that Mack was at her house yesterday."

My stomach churned.

"What?"

"According to her, they spent the whole day together."

My blood was boiling. Here I was, putting my entire life on the line due to unresolved feelings for him, and he was canoodling with that whore?

I was angry.

I was confused.

I was missing Victor.

"Did she say anything else?"

"She just kept going on and on about him, how hot he is, how sweet he is, what a great dad he is. She has got her sights set on him hard, Francesca. I just thought you should know what she's been saying."

"Thank you."

I feigned calmness that entire afternoon, but as soon as the class was dismissed, the emotions I'd been harboring were about to explode. I had no right to even feel jealous or angry. But that didn't seem to make a difference.

Taking out my phone, I took a deep breath before texting him.

Francesca: Heard you had a nice time with Clarissa.

The three dots signaling that he was responding appeared almost immediately.

Mack: It was a playdate for Jonah. I wasn't going to entertain it, but he actually asked me for it. I couldn't say no. I wasn't going to just drop him off at a strange house, especially with his freakout tendencies.

Francesca: I don't think Clarissa saw it as just a playdate. She wants you.

Mack: It doesn't matter what she wants.

Francesca: Maybe you should go for it.

Mack: Where are you right now?

Francesca: I'm still at school.

Mack: Stay there. I'm coming to pick you up.

Francesca: I have a car.

Mack: Meet me out front in twenty minutes.

My heart was racing as I waited just inside the front door to the school. When I saw Mack's truck pull up, I looked behind my shoulders to make sure no one was around before heading toward him.

I opened the door and got in, slamming it shut.

Mack looked angry when he said, "Hi."

"Hi."

Letting out a deep breath, he put the vehicle in drive and took off. We must have driven in silence for the better part of a half-hour down Route Nine.

He suddenly drove onto a tree-lined, residential street. It seemed like a nice, middle-class neighborhood.

"Where are we going?"

"My house."

I swallowed, nervous at the prospect of being alone there with him. "Why?"

"We need to talk. I don't want to do it in front of people."

Mack pulled into what I assumed was his driveway and waved to an older woman who was outside getting her mail.

"Shit," he muttered.

"What?"

"That's Mrs. Migillicutty, my neighbor. I was hoping she wouldn't see me with you."

"Why?"

"She knows about you. This might get a little weird, okay?" Before I could respond, he opened his door then came around to let me out.

Mack nodded his head. "Hey, Mrs. M."

The woman placed her hand over her eyes to block out the sun as she approached, dragging her slippers along the concrete. "You must be Frankie."

"Yes. How did you know?"

"The red hair."

"Well, it's really nice to meet you," I said.

She winked at Mack.

"I'll talk to you later, Mrs. M."

"I fully expect that." She snickered. "Wonderful meeting you, Frankie Jane."

Frankie Jane? She knew about that name, too? What the hell?

"What was that all about?"

Mack looked amused. "She's sort of like my neighbor-slash-bartender-slash-psychologist."

"She knows everything?"

"Pretty much. Talking to her keeps me sane."

As weird as it was, I found Mack's friendship with the old lady quite endearing.

Mack lived in a large, split-level home. Just inside the front door, there was a small set of stairs leading up to his living area and another set of stairs off to the left leading down to the finished basement.

He threw his keys on a small table in the living room. "This is it...the house I bought for Jonah and me. It's definitely a lot of space for just the two of us, but I wanted to give him a real home."

It reminded me of the types of houses my friends' families had growing up. While my mother and I always lived in apartments just outside of Boston, many of my friends lived in houses on quiet streets with big backyards.

I walked around quietly, running my fingertips along the surprisingly homey furniture. Mack was always two steps behind me as he followed my path.

"Did you decorate this yourself?"

I could practically feel his voice vibrating against the skin of my back. "It was already furnished. The couple who sold me the house had just gotten a divorce. They went their separate ways and left everything here. They had a couple of kids. So, I'm basically living in the memory of someone else's shattered life. It's pretty ironic," he joked.

"That's kind of sad," I said, making my way to the large, bay window that was just behind the couch. As I gazed out of it, Mack stood behind me. The closeness of his body gave me goosebumps. He wasn't touching me, but I could still feel him as if he were.

The sound of his low voice gave me the shivers. "Did he leave this morning?"

"Yes. How did you remember?"

"I've had it marked on my calendar ever since we went to Castle Island."

I turned around to find his stare was burning into me. He leaned in, causing my heart to start beating rapidly. "What was up with that text from you, huh?

"What about it?"

"Do you really think I came to Boston to hurt you all over again?"

"I don't have a right to tell you who to fuck. I'm with someone."

"Do you have any clue what hearing you even say the word *fuck* does to me?" He moved in closer, causing my nipples to stand at attention. "I would never do anything to hurt you. Do you understand? I have no interest in that woman. Would she have let me fuck her in the pantry while the boys were playing? Yes. You don't think I know that? But do you really think I'm here to fucking hook up with the mothers at the school? Is that the kind of person you think I am? Because if it is, then I have a much bigger fight on my hands than I originally thought."

Closing my eyes to fend off my body's reaction to him, I whispered, "What do you want, Mack?"

"I want this week," he said without hesitation.

"This week..."

"I want you to give me this week. Every day after school, I pick you up. We spend time together, talk, work through what happened with us, maybe have a little fun in the process. We use this opportunity to get to know each other again. No expectations, except getting a little bit of the time we lost back. It's all I'll ever ask of you. Just give me this week."

Mack stopped speaking, but his eyes were still pleading with me.

My boyfriend's words from this morning rang through my head. Victor was giving me a one-time opportunity to figure things out, and Mack was offering me essentially the same. I needed to do this.

"Okay, Mack."

His eyes widened. "Yes?"

"Yes."

He let out a relieved breath that I felt against my lips. I couldn't deny that I wanted to taste him probably more than I craved anything. I'd never gotten a chance to do that. We came close to kissing once from what I could remember—the last evening we were together. We'd gotten drunk that night, so my memory of it was hazy.

Mack's voice interrupted my chain of thought. "There were days, Frankie, when I might have temporarily forgotten about some of the many conversations we've had. I might have even had trouble remembering exactly what you looked like at times. But not for one second, have I ever forgotten how you made me feel—that connection that we had. It's a feeling I have never been able to replicate. I miss it. I miss you. So fucking much."

Shutting my eyes again, I let those words sink in. "Where do we start?"

"We get the hard part over with. We start by talking about what happened the last night we were together. And what happened after."

CHAPTER TWELVE

Mack

PAST

The last few days of the end of the semester came way too quickly.

It was Friday, and my flight back to D.C. for the summer was scheduled for Saturday afternoon. Frankie and I had decided to blow off work, since it would be my last full day in Boston before we wouldn't see each other until fall. Even though we weren't talking about our impending separation, there was a certain melancholy in the air. We were both being fairly quiet during breakfast.

Moses had already left earlier in the morning to head back to Ohio for the summer. Tonight would be the first night that he'd ever left Frankie and me completely alone. I felt anxious, like we really needed to get the fuck out of the apartment before I said or did something stupid.

"I think we should go out and enjoy the city, stay out until late. Fuck everything we're supposed to be doing. It's my last day, and my flight isn't until mid-afternoon tomorrow."

"What did you want to do?"

"We could go down to Newbury Street, get something to eat, look around. Maybe we could hit one of the clubs on Lansdowne later."

"You're usually more of a homebody. I'm surprised you want to go clubbing."

"I used to go out all the freaking time until I started hanging out with my homebody roommate."

She threw her napkin at me. "Don't blame me for your lameness."

"Remember when you first moved in? I don't think I'd ever eaten a meal at the apartment until you started cooking for me."

"Is my cooking that good?"

"It's good, but I stick around for the company."

Frankie blushed like she often did whenever I complimented her. "Well, the economy will love you again someday when I'm not around anymore."

Things suddenly got quiet. *When I'm not around anymore.* Frankie's assumption was valid. I'd never given her any indication that I would leave Torrie. But a lot had changed recently, and honestly, I could no longer envision a scenario where Frankie ever disappeared altogether from my life. I couldn't stomach the thought of her dating other guys anymore, either. I'd lucked out that after Emmett disappeared, there hadn't been anyone else. If I could barely hide my jealousy then, it would have been impossible now.

I banged my mug down on the table. "Come on...it's my last day. I don't want to waste it at home. I feel like doing something crazy."

Her face perked up. "You know what I've wanted to do for a very long time?"

"What?"

"I want to get a tattoo."

I laughed. "You want a tat? Where?"

"Well, it would be small and something I could easily hide. I was thinking either my ankle or my lower back."

Fuck. Her lower back. The thought of that was so sexy to me that I could feel myself getting hard just thinking about it. She looked so innocent, but Frankie definitely had a wild side.

"Your lower back?"

"Yeah. Why?"

Biting my bottom lip, I grinned. "You're gonna get a tramp stamp, Frankie Jane?"

"You think it's slutty to get one there?"

"I think it's hot, actually. I think something subtle would look nice against your skin."

"Maybe I'll get one while we're out. I'm feeling oddly impulsive today."

"Why do you think that is?"

"Maybe because you're leaving," she said. "It's putting me in a weird mood."

"Me, too. I've been in a funk all week."

She looked hesitant to say something else.

"What, Frankie?"

"It's gonna be really weird not having you here."

"I know."

"It's so strange when I think back to when I first moved in. I used to prefer living alone. Now, I'm not sure how I'm going to go back to that."

"It's only a couple of months. It'll fly by," I said, even though I was probably even more freaked out about my leaving than she was.

"A lot can happen in a couple of months," she said.

She was right. An unwelcome thought entered my mind. What if Frankie met someone this summer? She didn't want to be alone; she'd likely seek out company so she didn't have to be. What if I came back and had to see her with some guy? What if nothing was ever the same again? A summer was only two months, but two months could change the course of an entire lifetime. What if today was the last day that things would be like this between us? My pulse was starting to race.

We ended up heading down to Newbury Street that afternoon and planting ourselves at an outdoor bar. The sun was hitting Frankie's hair just right, making it look more like the color of fire than normal. I didn't know what it was about that moment, but something told me I would remember it forever, just sitting here watching the sunlight hit her hair.

Frankie was working through her burger and fries, seemingly unaware that I was staring at her. I was feeling happy to be out with her, but sad at the same time, because I still couldn't stop thinking about having to leave her for the summer. The fact that she'd be totally alone worried me, especially knowing she'd be doing laundry by herself down in that dingy basement.

Oblivious to the thoughts circulating around in my head, she looked at me. "I'm tipsy. Maybe now would be a good time for me to go get that tattoo before I change my mind."

I scratched my chin. "Are you sure you want to do it?"

"Yes."

Nudging my head toward the street, I said, "Let's go, then."

A few blocks down, we came across an underground place that doubled as a tattoo shop and bar. It was aptly named, DrINK. Frankie had to put her name on a waitlist, which was just as well, since she still had no freaking clue what she was getting.

I went and got us a couple of drinks while she looked through a catalog of designs. When I returned with two Long Island Iced Teas, she still seemed unsure of which tattoo to choose.

She handed me the book. "You pick one for me. Surprise me."

"Are you serious? You trust me enough to let me do that? What if I pick something you hate, and you're stuck with it for the rest of your life?"

"You won't."

"What if I decide that you should have a big hairy ass on your back? How can you be so sure I wouldn't do that?"

She sipped her drink and smiled from behind the straw. "Because in all of the time I've known you, you've never said or done anything intentionally hurtful to me. I don't think you would randomly start tonight. You come across as a tough guy at first, but, in reality, you're very considerate and protective. You care about my happiness. And I think you know branding me with a hairy ass would *not* make me happy."

"You're no fun," I teased.

"Pick something I can be proud of, Morrison."

I came across a section on meaningful tattoos; one of the tats resonated with me. I decided that was the one because its supposed significance reminded me of her. And I was pretty sure she was going to love it. Not only because it couldn't have been further from a hairy ass but because it was really beautiful.

Like she was.

There was no denying how I felt anymore.

A heavily inked dude dressed in all black led us into a back room that smelled of incense. Frankie maintained that she wanted to be surprised, so I discreetly showed the tattoo artist the design I had selected from the book. She looked at me curiously and smiled.

My breath caught for a moment when she began to undo her jeans in order to lower them slightly off her hips. I felt my dick stiffen. One look at her creamy skin and the slope of her back that lead down to her taut little ass was all it took.

Lying flat on her stomach, Frankie cringed as the needle began to dig into her. Her skin was like porcelain. I couldn't even recall ever seeing her lower back bare before. If her pants had been a half-inch lower, her ass would have been showing. It was really easy to imagine what it looked like naked.

The tattoo artist rested the hand he wasn't using on her hip. I was getting palpitations. Flexing my fingers, I squelched the urge to knock his hand off of her body. *What the fuck was wrong with me?* I was getting jealous that he was touching her; he was only doing his job. My reaction to this was really telling.

Well over an hour later, he finally finished. "All set. Wanna take a look?"

She looked over at me and smiled. "I want to keep it a surprise. I like the mystery."

Tattoo Dude laughed. "I can't say this has ever happened before."

I chuckled. "Only her."

The man placed a clear bandage over the area before Frankie hopped off the table.

"What about you, Mack? Are you gonna let me pick one for you, too?"

"I'll take a rain check on that. You're a little too tipsy right now to be making smart decisions. I don't want to end up with a hairy bush on me."

She turned to the artist. "He wouldn't get one anyway. He doesn't want to ruin his gorgeous body and that flawless skin."

Frankie was totally buzzed and loose with her words. I knew she was attracted to me, but she never really said stuff like that. Her talking about my body wasn't exactly helping my predicament.

The two of us left the tattoo place a tad drunker than when we'd walked in. After wandering the streets of Copley Square for a while, we'd made our way toward the clubs on Lansdowne Street by nightfall.

We decided on Club Punk, and it was there that the mood of the night took a turn into territory I'd never ventured into with her before. That was due mainly to the fact that we continued to get inebriated. While Frankie and I would occasionally drink together, we had never gotten drunk until that night. I should've limited her alcohol, but honestly, we were having a damn good time. It seemed like a fitting end to a hectic semester. And more than that, it kept me from stressing over leaving the next day.

Even though Frankie stood out with her purple glasses, she looked sexier than I'd ever seen her. She had on a black halter-top and no bra, which easily displayed the exact silhouette of her pear-shaped breasts. Her nipples were peeking through the fabric. That also meant my eyes were wandering in their direction all night.

On our way to the club, she'd stopped in the drug store and bought some body glitter that she'd rubbed all over her chest and arms. Under the lights, you could really see it shine.

"You're sparkling."

"That was the point. I'm trying to stand out."

"I'm pretty sure you're the only chick here with purple glasses. Believe me, Frankie. You stand out."

She closed her eyes momentarily then said, "I need to get laid."

Her comment had come out of left field. But she was drunk, so it shouldn't have surprised me. Still, hearing her say that physically hurt. Maybe she'd done it intentionally to test my reaction because she knew I was confused, but in any case, it fucking stung. I guess that was a normal thing for a chick to admit to her "friend." The problem was, I didn't see myself as only that anymore. But she had every right to want something more. She also had no clue just how much things had changed for me when it came to her, because I hadn't told her.

I took a sip of my beer and changed the subject, opting not to want to delve further into Frankie's quest to be fucked by someone other than me.

"When are you gonna look at your tattoo?"

She shouted through the music, "I don't know. I'm still liking the excitement of not knowing what it is."

"You're nuts. That curiosity would be killing me."

"Good call on not letting me tattoo you, by the way."

"Why's that?"

"I was gonna choose one that said *Porn Star*."

"I'd own that," I joked.

Poking my finger into her rib playfully, I tickled her in response. Then, I took her by the hand and dragged her over to the dance floor.

After a couple more drinks, you could pretty much say my inhibitions were gone. Even though I knew I couldn't take things past a certain point, I was enjoying the close contact way too much. My dick was straining through my jeans as we danced close. I had no clue if she could feel it against her. The hint of alcohol on her breath mixed with the sweet smell of her body was driving me absolutely insane. My conscience remained the one roadblock. But Lord knows, I wanted to suck every drop of alcohol off her tongue.

I didn't want to leave her alone, but I was going to piss my pants. I spoke in her ear, "Are you gonna be okay if I go the bathroom?"

She nodded, and I left her on the dance floor despite my reservations. Weaving through the crowd, I headed toward the bathroom. After taking an extremely long leak, I checked my phone and saw that there were a few missed calls from Torrie.

The thought of talking to her right now while I was sporting a hard-on because of another woman made me ill. Guilt was consuming me, because what I needed to do when I got back to D.C. was becoming clearer by the minute.

My constant pining over the girl who'd become my best friend wasn't fair to my *actual* girlfriend. Torrie and I had a long history, and I cared about her very much—enough to not want to cheat on her despite these intense urges. Not to mention, Frankie deserved way better than to be caught in this limbo. I knew I had to end things with Torrie before taking things any further with Frankie. Making it through tonight without fucking up was going to be the challenge. But I had never cheated on anyone before and didn't want to start now.

Any remaining trace of normalcy to the evening ended the minute I made my way back to the dance floor.

A guy with sweat seeping through his white dress shirt was behind Frankie, grinding against her ass. She was wasted. I shouldn't have let her drink that much, and I most definitely shouldn't have left her alone for even a second.

The worst part? Her fucking glasses were gone. Given that she couldn't see shit without them, this was obviously a huge problem.

I wanted to kill the guy for taking advantage of her. "Get the fuck off of her," I said, pulling Frankie away from him.

"What happened to your glasses?"

"They fell. I can't find them."

A few seconds later, I felt pieces of plastic under my shoe. Her signature purple glasses had been crushed to smithereens.

Great.

Even though I knew she had a few spare pairs at home, those had to have cost a fortune, not to mention I would have to somehow lead her home blind.

"We'd better go," I said, guiding her off the dance floor.

She could hardly walk. I had no clue that she really couldn't handle her alcohol. We'd each drank about the same, but clearly my threshold was a lot higher. I felt guilty for not taking better care of her.

"Why were you letting that guy rub himself on you like that?"

"My back was turned. I thought he was you."

Well, shit. I didn't know if that made me happy or sick.

Frankie was practically tripping over her own feet. We didn't live far from the club, so I opted to just walk back to the apartment. We'd be able to get home faster than a cab would arrive anyway.

Since her legs were so wobbly, I decided to carry her home. Her arms were wrapped around my neck and as we made our way toward Kenmore Square. It must have rained while we were in the club because cars that were driving into puddles splashed us from time to time.

Frankie was quiet for a while during our walk until she suddenly spoke. "Don't come back."

"What?"

"I can't live with you anymore."

"Why are you saying that?"

Trashed or not, her bluntness shocked me.

"It hurts," she said.

"What hurts?"

"Knowing that I can't ever have you. You'll never break up with her. You're just biding your time here."

She may have been drunk as a fucking skunk, but I knew that the words pouring out of her were the absolute truth.

She looked up at me. Her eyelids were heavy. "God, if you didn't have a girlfriend right now, I'd..." She hesitated.

I needed to know what she was going to say. I needed more from inebriated Frankie.

"You'd what?" I prodded.

"Never mind."

The rest of the walk was quiet. My arms were killing me by the time we got back to the apartment.

When I put her down, she lost her balance, so I led her over to the couch.

We sat down, and Frankie ended up laying her head in my lap. The room was spinning a bit, but I was nowhere near as drunk as she was.

Carelessly running my fingers through her hair repeatedly, I bent my head back and stared at the ceiling. A part of me wished she'd just fall asleep while a bigger part of me wanted her to talk to me, to finish her sentence from earlier, to tell me what she would do if I didn't have a girlfriend. I looked down and could see her eyes were wide open.

"Are you okay, Frankie Jane?"

It was barely a whisper. "No."

She looked like she was about to cry. I nudged her up, mainly to get her face away from my dick. Moving her was a mistake because somehow she ended up straddling me. I looked up into her beautiful blue eyes and wondered what the fuck I was doing trying to deny my feelings. Her black mascara was smudged. Her hair was disheveled and yet, she was still the most beautiful girl in the world. I really wanted to know what she was thinking.

"Tell me everything that's on your mind," I said.

"I'm drunk. I can't be trusted."

"That makes two of us. We won't remember anything tomorrow. Tell me what you're thinking, and I'll tell you what I'm thinking. No one will ever know."

She leaned her forehead against mine, and it felt so good to feel her breath over my mouth as she panted. I wanted to kiss her more than I'd ever wanted to kiss anyone, but I still managed to hold back. My cock swelled beneath her. She might have been too drunk to notice.

"I want you, and it hurts so bad," she finally whispered.

This was killing me. Hearing her say that she wanted me caused my control to break.

"I want to fucking devour you right now, Frankie."

Her breathing became labored. "Do it." She laughed a little then said, "No, don't. I'm so drunk. I don't even know what I'm saying."

I groaned through my teeth. "I want to. Believe me."

I knew I wasn't going to let things go beyond this talking, but I wanted to hear her say it. The dirty, fucking bastard in me just couldn't help myself.

"If there were no consequences, tell me what you wish I could do to you," I asked.

She rested her face on the base of my neck and said nothing. I was expecting her to fall asleep until she said, "I wish that you could fuck me so hard that I'd feel you for days afterward."

Holy shit.

My cock was throbbing now. Aching.

Fisting her hair, I pulled her head back to look at her. "I would *love* to fuck you right now."

Even though I'd been encouraging her to tell me what she wanted, hearing those words come out of my own mouth was a reality check in the midst of a drunken fog. I wanted her, but it wasn't going to happen like this.

Needing relief like a motherfucker, I suddenly moved myself from under her, repositioning her to the corner of the couch.

Placing something beneath her head, I said, "I'll be right back."

Frankie curled into the pillow without saying anything further.

I went straight to the bathroom and shut the door before unzipping my pants. My boxers were wet from the precum that had seeped out of my cock. My dick was excruciatingly hard as I jerked it fast in a desperate attempt for relief. This was a hell of a lot safer than giving in to a drunk Frankie. Replaying her words, I pretended I was fucking her and not my hand.

"I wish that you could fuck me so hard that I'd feel you for days afterward."

After less than a minute, I banged my head against the back of the door as I came hard into my other hand. My palm was barely able to contain the load. Panting, I stayed at the door and closed my eyes, vowing never to drink like this again.

But coming didn't do shit to take away the longing. I knew it was still going to be a long night and no matter what happened at this point—an awkward morning.

After I cleaned up and returned to the living room, Frankie was passed out on the couch. I decided to carry her to bed. I was hoping she wouldn't wake up, but when I lifted her off the couch, she looked up at me in a haze.

"I don't feel so good."

"You gonna throw up?"

"I think I might."

Just as we'd made it past the threshold of the bathroom, she gagged and warm projectile vomit spewed everywhere.

I looked down at us. "Shit!"

It was all over her hair, my chest, her shirt. She was way too drunk to clean herself up. Covered in puke, I froze, not knowing how to handle it.

Placing her carefully down on her feet, I said the last thing I expected to actually be suggesting tonight. "We need to get you out of these clothes."

She simply nodded.

Running the shower to let the water warm, I could feel my heart beating out of my chest. I'd turned back around to find that she'd fully removed her pants and underwear, but still had her shirt on.

This was not good.

Frankie stepped into the tub and lost her balance. I ended up getting in with her to hold her up.

I tried like hell not to stare down at her pussy; I really did. Allowing myself one quick glance, I discovered that it was completely shaved.

Fuck. Me. This seemed like cruel and unusual punishment.

As the water poured down over us, I said, "I have to take your shirt off, okay?"

She closed her eyes and nodded.

This was not the time for me to be sobering up, but I was. After slipping the soaked shirt up in an attempt to get it over her head, I pretended not to notice the way her breasts bounced when they sprung free from the fabric. I tried not to look down, but I just couldn't help it. She had the most amazing tits. They weren't huge, but not small—way more than a handful each, like beautiful teardrops. Light pink areolas the size of half-dollars were perfectly centered on her creamy skin. Her nipples were extremely erect, as was my cock, which was bursting through my soaking wet jeans. I was still fully clothed under the water while she stood there buck-naked.

Turning her around so I wasn't tempted to ogle her bare mound, I poured some soap onto a loofah and handed it to her.

"Wash yourself, Frankie."

She took it from me and did a half-assed job rubbing it over her body.

I'd almost completely forgotten about the tattoo until it was staring me in the face through the clear bandage.

Fuck. Her ass.

Her ass was almost as amazing as her tits and pussy. It was so round, yet tight and blemish-free. I was seriously going to drop dead from blue balls on the shower floor.

Lathering some shampoo, I washed the vomit out of her hair, noticing how freaking long it was compared to when we'd first met. It was the most beautiful shade of ginger, shiny and straight like silk. I might have washed it a little longer than necessary.

She was clean, but I was still a mess. Frankie's back was still toward me when I slipped my wet Polo shirt over my head, letting it fall to the floor of the tub. I rubbed the loofah along my chest and neck and gave my hair a quick washing.

Frankie suddenly turned around and fell toward me, pressed her body against mine. That caused me to nearly fall back against the tile wall. With her tits plastered against my chest, she closed her eyes as I held her. I was pretty sure she was falling asleep on me.

The water continued to rain down on us. I stood there, holding her, unable to believe what was happening to me tonight. But being under that water with her, in that most intimate place—Frankie completely bare against me—made me realize more clearly than ever, that there was just no way to deny it.

She was the one.

Our time together seemed to flash before my eyes, all of our many conversations, ranging from our deepest thoughts and hang-ups to the strange and funny.

It was her.

It had always been her.

CHAPTER THIRTEEN

Francesca

PAST

The room was spinning when I opened my eyes the next morning and reached for one of the pairs of glasses stashed away in my nightstand.

All I remembered was that I'd gotten a tattoo and that I'd had way too much to drink at the club on Lansdowne Street. Everything else was a blur.

My heart nearly skipped a beat when I noticed Mack lying next to me in bed. He had no shirt on, although he never usually slept in a shirt. He'd also never slept *in my bed*.

Holy shit. Mack was in my bed. Next to me.

He had one arm over his head, showcasing his armpit. I'd never realized that I could find a man's underarm hair so sexy until this up-close look at Mack's. It was just another example of my unwavering attraction to his virile beauty.

I looked down at myself to find I was dressed in an oversized T-shirt I rarely wore. Where did he even find it? At least, it covered the tops of my thighs, seeing as though I wasn't wearing pants.

Where were my pants?

I was relieved to see I had underwear on, but it wasn't the pair I'd worn yesterday.

What happened last night?

I nudged his shoulder. "Mack?"

"Mmm," he moaned before turning around. His voice was groggy. "How are you feeling?"

My stomach ached, and my mouth was devoid of all moisture. "Like crap."

"I figured that."

"What are you doing in my bed?"

"You don't remember?"

"No."

"What's the last thing you remember from last night?"

"Being with you at the club."

Mack sat up and leaned back against the headboard. "I'm in bed because after the shower, you begged me to lie next to you. You said you were scared to be alone."

My stomach dropped. "The shower?"

He rubbed his eyes and laughed a little. "Nothing happened, Frankie. We both got pretty drunk last night. We danced a lot. I carried you home from the club, we talked candidly a little when we got home, and then you puked on both of us. So, I had to wash you off in the shower."

"What does 'talked candidly' mean exactly?"

"It doesn't matter. You were drunk. Anything you said...anything we both said...can be chalked up to that."

My mind was now backtracking through what he'd told me. "Wait. I was naked in the shower? I took off my clothes?"

"You sort of had to, because you were covered in vomit. We both were. You needed my help. You couldn't stand up straight. I was afraid you'd slip in the shower and crack your head open."

"You *saw* me naked?"

Mack hesitated. "Yes."

Covering my face, I said, "Oh, my God. I'm so embarrassed."

"Believe me, you have *nothing* to be embarrassed about."

"This is not how I wanted your last day to be, both of us hungover."

"Yesterday was the best day I could've ever asked for. It was like a hot mess I'll never forget." His words seemed sincere.

"Really?"

"Yes."

"I don't want you to leave."

"Believe me, I don't want to go. We overslept. Now, I only have like two hours before I have to leave for the airport."

I glanced over at the clock. "Shit. I wanted to make you breakfast, but I don't think I can stomach the smell of food."

"I'm not that hungry anyway. I'll grab something at Logan." Mack's eyes landed on my lower body. "You need to look at your tattoo. You still don't even know what you got."

"I guess I should, huh?" I laughed, lifting myself off the bed as a fresh wave of nausea hit me.

Mack followed me as I walked over to the oval, floor-length mirror in the corner of my room. He came up behind me and slowly lifted my T-shirt up to just above my belly button. His taking the initiative to partially undress me seemed like a brazen move. But it was certainly indicative of a shift in our relationship after last night.

The closeness of his body sent shivers down my spine. For a moment, I felt self-conscious that he'd see me in my underwear, but then it hit me that he'd seen a lot more of me last night.

Slowly ripping the bandage off, he said, "I hope you like it." The touch of his fingertips grazing over my lower back caused me to close my eyes momentarily.

I reluctantly turned my head around to look in the mirror. My mouth curved into a smile upon the sight of a beautiful blue flower about the size of a golf ball. It was better than anything I would have chosen for myself.

"It's beautiful. What kind of flower is that?"

"It's a lotus flower."

"I'm pretty sure I've seen it. I just didn't know what it was called. What made you pick this for me?"

"Well, that book I was reading said the lotus is a flower that's born from murky, slimy waters."

I raised my brows. "The slimy part reminded you of me?"

"No. Basically, the flower is considered pure because of its ability to emerge from the dark waters in the morning perfectly unscathed. What reminded me of you is the fact that from this murky water a beautiful blossom was made. You used to tell me you felt like a part of you just came from a black hole because of your father. And I know you walk around every day feeling like a part of you is missing. But whether or not you realize it, you're a light to those who know you—to me. Just like the lotus, you've risen above the darkness to become something beautiful—a beautiful human."

My eyes were starting to water. No one had ever said anything that poignant to me.

"Wow. I don't know what to say. Thank you." I wiped my eyes and asked, "What made you choose blue?"

"Actually, funny you should ask. There are different colored lotus flowers. And I read about each one. When I came to the blue...well, it was very symbolic of my experiences with you."

"How so?"

"The book said that the blue one also represents mind over matter, in particular, the spirit's control over one's physical senses or compulsions—which heightens one's spirituality by overcoming bodily temptations."

Oh.

We both knew exactly what he was getting at. He didn't need to explain further. Yet, he did anyway.

"The blue is my own personal badge of honor that I've basically stamped on you, Frankie."

"What?"

"I've done everything I thought I was supposed to be doing when it comes to you. I've been fighting everything that feels natural for a very long time. So, there really is something to that mind over matter mantra. But what they don't factor in is what happens when you *lose* your mind. I'm pretty sure I've just about lost mine. I've been trying to do the right thing, but it's fucking hard. And I realized last night that I don't want to go against what feels natural anymore." He placed both of his hands around my cheeks. "What would you think about my coming back sooner than the end of the summer, but staying for good?"

"What are you saying?"

"I'm saying I have to work some stuff out with Torrie and with my father when I get home. That's going to take time, but I don't want to be away from you all summer. I don't want to be away from you...ever, really."

Was this really happening?

"I don't want to be away from you, either."

"Things could've easily gotten out of hand last night. I'm pretty sure we would've fucked the shit out of each other if I'd let it happen. But I didn't want it to go down that way—drunken sex. When I finally kiss you, Frankie, when I finally make love to you...I want you to be able to know that I'm fully yours with nothing holding us back. And I want you to feel and remember everything. You deserve nothing less."

I wrapped my arms around his neck to embrace him. His heart was beating even faster than mine.

"Your heart is beating so fast right now, Mack."

"Just believe what it's telling you. Alright?"

The days after Mack left were tough. His promising words and the sound of his heartbeat were fading away with each passing day as worry began to consume me.

Left alone in the apartment, I spent my days waiting. Waiting for his calls. Waiting for him to show up at the door.

He'd called me a couple of times from D.C., but it didn't take a genius to know that something was really off in comparison to how we'd left things. The sullen tone of his voice whenever he would call, the brevity of our conversations, told me that something had changed. Something had happened in D.C.; I just didn't know what. And honestly, I was afraid to ask.

A surprise visit one Tuesday afternoon confirmed my suspicions were correct.

I would never forget that day. Having just started taking up running to combat my nervous energy with Mack gone, I'd come in from a jog down Beacon Street when there was a knock at the door.

When I opened, Mack was standing there carrying only a small bag and no suitcase.

"Mack. What are you doing here?"

When I hugged him, his body went rigid. His eyes were sunken in and tired. What happened to the charismatic, confident guy who'd left me with so much hope? He looked sadder than I'd ever seen him, like death warmed over.

An overwhelming feeling of dread washed over me.

Mack sat down and just shook his head without saying anything.

My chest tightened.

When he finally looked up at me, the hint of wetness forming in his eyes confirmed my worst fears.

CHAPTER FOURTEEN

Mack

"I remember not wanting you to even touch me that day. You hugged me, and I couldn't bear to let myself feel it. It was too fucking painful."

Frankie hadn't moved from her spot by my bay window. Leaning against the ledge beneath it, she seemed lost in thought before she said, "I swear to God, Mack. That was the last thing I ever expected you to tell me when you walked in the door that day."

My chest constricted just thinking about it. "You and me both. I didn't handle it well. I was still in such shock when I came to you. It was impossible to express how devastated I was. It seemed like a bad dream. I was just...numb."

"I remember. I'd never seen you like that."

"Torrie and I hadn't had sex in about two months by the time I went back to D.C. that summer. I'd made up excuses the last couple of trips before that. It was pathetic, but there came a certain point when it felt wrong. I knew in my heart that I was going to end things with her because my feelings for you were too strong to contain anymore. I just hadn't garnered the courage until the end of the semester came. By that time, I was more sure than ever of what I wanted."

"To be honest, I don't even clearly remember what you said to me that day. As soon as the word *pregnant* came out of your mouth, everything else just seemed like a blur."

"When she told me she was three months along... it just seemed impossible, even though it technically wasn't. She'd been on birth control, but I never should've trusted it."

"You don't think she planned it, do you?"

Shaking my head as I stared down at my rug, I said, "I honestly don't know. I know she sensed me changing. She likely sensed I was going to end it. I don't like to think that she would've done something like that on purpose, but honestly, Frankie, I'll never know, because she'd never admit to it if she did."

"I hope she didn't." Frankie stared out blankly at some kids riding their bikes on my street before she asked, "I can't even imagine what things were like for you during those months, Mack."

The fact that she was thinking about my feelings in that moment despite how much I'd hurt her really spoke to the type of person she was.

After I'd told Frankie about the pregnancy on that fateful day, I returned to D.C. and sent for the rest of my stuff. I'd also transferred to American University's graduate program soon after.

"I was basically just existing. I wasn't ready for a child. I wasn't in love with Torrie. It felt like all of the happiness had been drained from my life. All I wanted was to be back in Boston with you. But I just didn't see how that could've possibly worked. I knew my father would've made your life a living hell. In his eyes, my having an illegitimate child was bad enough, let alone abandoning the mother for another woman. His precious reputation would have been on the line, and Michael Morrison is not a good person, especially when his personal interests are being threatened. I didn't want him anywhere near you. But even knowing all of that, I still constantly second-guessed my decision to leave you behind."

Frankie appeared deep in thought then said, "I wouldn't have been able to be with you then. I wasn't strong enough. I couldn't have handled it. You made the right decision."

Hearing her say that meant more to me than she could have known.

"I also worried you would never respect me if I did anything other than own up to my responsibilities, especially given what happened with your father. So, I felt like I only had one option and that was to let you go."

She finally moved from her spot at the window to the couch. She placed her head in her hands, but she wasn't crying. She was processing. This conversation was eight years in the making and taking an emotional toll on us. But it needed to happen.

"What exactly happened that last night we were together, when we got drunk? I mean, you told me some vague stuff, but what exactly did I say to you?"

"You really want to know?" I laughed. "Let's put it this way, if you said the same stuff to me right now, we wouldn't be wasting time talking."

Her face pinked up. "Maybe I don't want to know. We never kissed?"

This was something I never told her.

"When I was helping you get dressed after the shower, you put your hand around the back of my head and tried to kiss me. I turned away—not because I didn't want to kiss you, because Lord knows I'd never wanted anything more than to taste you that night. I stopped it because I didn't want our first kiss to be a drunk one that you wouldn't remember. At that time, I was certain I'd have lots of opportunities to do it right. But I have to admit, if there was one thought that rang out in my head more than any other these past several years, it was that I wished I had taken that damn kiss when I had the chance."

"You didn't know."

"I lost all those years, only to end up in the same place, wanting you and wishing I hadn't ever let you go. In retrospect, I often doubt my decision, actually. But I can't control the past. All I can control is my life moving forward. I'm trying to take it back as much as possible while still being the kind of father Jonah needs. Having you here in my house is surreal. You're still my Frankie in some ways, and in other ways you've changed. "

"In what ways do you see that I've changed?"

"It's not a bad thing. I'm not sure I even know how to explain it. I wanna say it's like some of your quirkiness got swallowed up by a sophisticated maturity."

She laughed. "Believe me, the weirdness is still there. But you're right. I'm a bit different than I was back then, more guarded, maybe. What happened with us actually had a huge impact on my life."

"I need you to tell me what happened after I went back to D.C."

Frankie looked sad as she reluctantly remembered. "I was depressed and lonely for a long time. But I was still a better person for having experienced our relationship. You always made me feel special, and you helped me come out of my shell. I don't regret you, Mack. It's important that you know that. If there was a choice between erasing it or experiencing it all over again, I would choose the latter."

That was a relief to hear.

"I would never erase a second of it," I said.

"I don't think I ever really got over losing you. But I learned to put it away somewhere inside me because I had no choice. I knew lamenting about what I'd lost with you—what never had a chance to be—wasn't going to change anything. Don't get me wrong, thoughts of you always crept in no matter how hard I tried, especially on holidays and each year when I knew your son would be a year older. I'd wonder how you were handling it all and sometimes, I'd feel guilty, too."

"*You'd* feel guilty? Why?"

"Because first and foremost, I was your friend. Because I couldn't handle my own feelings, I wasn't there for you when you needed me. I knew that the pregnancy blindsided you. I knew that you weren't prepared. I knew that you needed support that you probably weren't getting from your family. Yet, I still couldn't be there for you, because I wasn't strong enough to handle what that would've meant for me."

"I never considered that you would ever feel guilty."

"I did."

"The moment Jonah was born was the first time I'd really let everything out. I remember bursting into tears, and it was this odd mix of emotions. It was amazing that I could feel instant love for this being that I'd never met. Before he was born, I'd been afraid that I would never feel it. I was terrified of what it would do to him as he got older if he sensed I didn't want him. So, knowing that the love came naturally was a relief. But I was also thinking of what I'd lost that day. Every moment, I was thinking of you, and I couldn't help it. A part of me wanted to call you and tell you."

"I would've listened if you did."

I'd had it with the tense conversation.

"Look, I think we've done enough talking for one night. It's getting dark. You must be hungry."

"I could eat."

When she smiled, I returned it. The mood had officially lightened. *Thank fuck.*

She followed me into the kitchen. "What are you gonna make me, Morrison?"

I didn't have to think too long about that one. "Spaghetti," I said proudly.

"Really?"

"Yup. Spaghetti. I'd love to make some for you."

"Since when do you cook?"

"Since I became responsible for nourishing another human being on weekends."

"I suppose that would warrant learning how to do it."

"Well, I learned to boil water, at least. And I can use a microwave. I can microwave a mean pile of bacon. Basically, if you can cook it by nuking it, I can make it."

"That's pretty sad but better than nothing."

"Well, I don't have Frankie O'Hara to cook for me anymore. It's a sad state of affairs in my kitchen."

"Torrie never cooked?"

"She's a better cook than I am, but that's not saying much. It's really not her thing, either. Her forte is working, not cooking. Jonah has had more than his share of takeout. So, I'm trying to change that."

"With spaghetti."

I nodded "With spaghetti."

"What kind of spaghetti do you make?"

"There's more than one kind?"

"I mean, how do you serve it?"

"With jarred sauce. Spaghetti a la Ragu."

Her laughter echoed throughout the kitchen. "How about this? We'll cook it together. You can boil the water, and I'll make the sauce from scratch."

"That sounds amazing, but I don't know that I would have the ingredients you need for your fancy sauce."

"You must have a grocery store nearby, right?"

We ended up taking a quick trip to the supermarket down the road. As we frolicked through the aisles with our cart, people must have assumed we were a married couple. In the midst of what most would consider a mundane task, I felt blessed to be spending time at the market with her. It was easy to imagine what a life with her would be like. People take so many things for granted, like sleeping next to the warm body of the person they love at night. For a few moments at the grocery store, I pretended that she was mine.

Back home, we were unloading the items when Frankie said, "Shit. The most important thing is missing."

Her words were ironic. That sort of felt like my life in general right now.

The most important thing was missing.

"What is it? "

"We forgot fresh garlic. I wasn't even thinking about it, since it's something I always have on hand."

"I bet Mrs. M. has some. She's always cooking." Taking out my phone, I said, "Let me call her."

My whacky but lovable neighbor answered, "Mack! Is Frankie still there? I'm dying to know what's going on."

"Yes, she's still here."

Frankie blushed when she realized we were talking about her.

"Very good," Mrs. M. said.

"We're about to cook dinner, and we need some fresh garlic. Do you have any?"

"Of course."

"I'll come by."

"Send Frankie," she insisted.

"No."

"That's the condition. I want to get a good look at her. Frankie or no garlic."

Crap.

I sighed. "Alright."

I hung up and looked over at Frankie. "She insists on you being the one to run over and get it. She's just being nosy. She's harmless. Do you mind?"

"No, not at all."

After Frankie ventured next door, she didn't immediately return. I then realized sending her over to my crazy neighbor's may have been a huge mistake.

CHAPTER FIFTEEN

Francesca

Mrs. Migillicutty pulled her long sweater closed to fend off the cold as she met me at the door.

"I didn't feel like putting on a bra just to give Mack some garlic. Didn't want to shock the poor guy with my waist warmers."

I laughed. "Ah. So, that's why you insisted I come?"

"Okay, not entirely." She waved me in. "I don't want to keep you. I know he values this time with you, but I need to tell you something real quick, Frankie."

"Okay..." I said, stepping inside her house.

"Just because he appears strong on the outside, doesn't mean his heart is indestructible."

Not expecting her to go there, I swallowed and said, "I know that."

"Now, I don't know anything about this man you're with, but that guy in the house next door to me? He thinks you're the one."

"He said that?"

"You can tell a lot about someone by what they say when they drink and let their guard down. You get to the bottom of their mind. You're all he talks about. And I'm pretty sure if he were taking his last breath, you'd be the last thing he thought about, too. Now, do what you want with the information. I've said my piece."

I didn't know what to say. "I appreciate your input."

She pointed to an old photo of a smiling man who looked to be in his seventies. "See this handsome man? Fifty-one years he called me the one. And thank God I don't have to live with any regrets, because when he died, he didn't have to wonder whether the person he'd chosen to give his heart to in this lifetime loved him back."

"I'm sorry for your loss."

"Don't be. No regrets. That's what it's all about, living with no regrets. If you truly love this other man you live with, just let Mack go. He'll move on eventually. Lord knows, there would be a line of women waiting for that day. But see...right now, he can't move on until he knows there's absolutely no chance with you. Whether you know it or not, you're carrying that man's heart around with you everyday. At some point, you either need to give it back and set him free...or give him yours. If it's him you want, don't let fear get in the way of a good thing."

Her words were hitting me hard.

"Okay, Mrs. M. I hear you."

"Have a good night, Frankie Jane. I can see why he thinks you're so adorable."

I couldn't help but smile as I walked back to Mack's house.

He was waiting at the door for me and must have noticed the look on my face. "Fuck. What did she say to you?"

"Nothing. We had a nice little conversation."

"Sure. Knowing her, that means she gave you the third degree."

Waving the head of garlic, I said, "I've got the magic ingredient."

"Nice change of subject. Seriously, did she say something to freak you out?"

Deciding to keep her advice private, I shook my head. "No, not at all. Come on, we have spaghetti to make."

Mack already had the water boiling as I began to chop the fresh basil.

The sound of a cork popping prompted me to look over at him. He'd taken two glasses out and was pouring red wine into each. There was something so sexy about watching him do it. Well, maybe it was just him that was sexy rather than the process of pouring the wine. It was then that I noticed that he'd taken off his shoes and made himself more comfortable. He'd also removed his sweater, and now I could see the outline of his sculpted chest through his T-shirt.

Handing me one of the goblets, he said, "Don't worry. I won't open more than one bottle. There's no fucking way I'm gonna spend any of this precious time too drunk to remember any of it."

"Given our track record, I think that's wise."

"Anyway, I don't need alcohol anymore to tell you how I really feel. I hope you don't mind if I'm direct from time to time. You don't have to say anything back, but I'm gonna tell you what's on my mind if the moment beckons. I don't really feel like I have anything to lose at this point."

"Thank you for the fair warning." Taking a sip, I said, "I didn't think you were a wine drinker."

"It's sort of a recent thing, maybe it's an acquired taste that comes with age. I've been pouring a glass or two every night to relax lately after a long day."

"It's hard to picture you all alone in this house during the week."

"You're telling me. I don't like it very much, but being alone is better than living with someone who makes you unhappy. I've learned that the hard way. I'm very much at peace here aside from the downside of having to live apart from Jonah."

Mack stood there swirling his drink around as he watched me prepare the sauce. My body was tingling, not from the wine, but from an awareness that his eyes were on me.

"Are you watching the pasta or me, Morrison?"

"Shit," he said as he realized he was about to overcook the spaghetti.

"You had one task," I joked. "One task..."

"Sorry, I was distracted. I love the sight of you in my kitchen too damn much."

We ended up having a really nice dinner. I was relieved that we'd gotten the tough conversation from earlier out of the way. I felt very comfortable in his house, and that was a little unnerving. It was very easy to get lost in Mack's magnetism. Guilt overtook me as Victor's face flashed through my mind, but it wasn't enough to keep me from enjoying being here.

"We got so caught up in talking, I didn't even show you the rest of the house. I'll have to give you the tour after dinner," he said.

"I'd like that."

"Then, I promise to get you home at a decent hour. I know you have to be up early—as do I—to get Jonah to school. You weren't exactly expecting me to kidnap you."

"I'm glad you did. We really needed that talk, and honestly, I love this house. Being here right now... sharing this meal...it's really nice."

"I love having you here."

During the second half of dinner, the conversation moved to even lighter topics, like Mack's volunteering at the school's winter carnival this coming weekend. It was an indoor festival, and the theme was summertime in the winter. Mack had volunteered to get dunked in the dunking booth to help the school raise money. I couldn't wait to try my hand at that game.

After we finished our pasta, Mack insisted on cleaning up while I polished off my glass of wine. It reminded me of the old days when I would cook, and he would do the dishes while we talked. A lot about the latter half of my time at his house tonight reminded me of old times. That feeling got even stronger as we made our way down to his basement.

"Holy man cave," I said as we stepped into the space.

A large, black leather sectional took up most of the room. There was a massive TV and really cool recessed lighting. Some abstract art hung on the wall. The décor was modern yet cozy.

"You like it?"

"We would've enjoyed this room back in the day."

"This is where Jonah and I watch movies when I can pull him away from his video games. And it's where I spend most of my time when I'm alone."

I wandered over to a bookshelf in the corner of the room. A few of the books were ones I recognized. One in particular shocked me.

"*The Man Who Folded Himself?* Didn't you make fun of me for reading this very book?"

"I didn't think I'd be bringing you here today, didn't have time to hide the evidence of my science fiction collection."

"Do you really read them?"

"I've read all of them. It's been sort of my little secret. At first, it was just a way of connecting with you all these years when I couldn't do it any other way. Over time, though, I found that I actually enjoyed them. I guess I was a latent geek all along."

The fact that he'd used books to remember me was very touching.

"I still read weird stuff," I admitted.

"I love to hear that. I figured you might."

In the corner of the same shelf sat the *Buffy the Vampire Slayer* boxset I'd bought him years ago. "You still have this, too?"

"Of course. It's my favorite gift that anyone's ever given me."

I smiled, remembering how excited and nervous I'd been to give him that present. "We had some really good times."

"We did." His gaze fell to my neck then met my eyes again. "Come on. I'll show you the rest of the upstairs.

A small hallway on the second level contained the bathroom and three rooms. The first room on the left was where Mack worked.

"This is my office."

A wooden desk sat in the corner. The apple at the back of his Mac laptop was illuminated. A small desk lamp provided the only other light.

"Nice laptop."

"Well, once you go Mac, you never go back." He winked.

"That was cheesy even for you, Morrison."

He snickered.

Running my fingers over his desk, I said, "It's nice that you can work from home."

"I'm usually cooped up in here most of the day. I get antsy for air sometimes, so I'll go get lunch and bring it over to Mrs. M.'s house."

"I love that."

He led me back out into the hall. "I'll show you Jonah's room."

His son's bedroom was sky blue with one solid red accent wall. There were toys everywhere in addition to lots of wires and game consoles. It was cluttered but seemed to be an organized mess.

"Wow. This room looks lived in for years."

"Yeah. He spends so much time in it when he's here. I filled it to the rim with everything he had back in Virginia and then some."

"You spoil him, don't you?"

"I do, but he doesn't act spoiled, if that makes sense."

"Oh, it does. I see that first hand. He's a good kid."

"I wish I could do more to make him happy. But I can only do so much. There are some things I just can't change."

A photo on the desk caught my eye. It was of Mack and Torrie with Jonah, looking like one big happy family on Christmas. An unwanted feeling of jealousy started to creep in. Mack noticed I was looking at it before I had a chance to say anything.

"That was taken a couple of years ago. I feel like it's important to keep stuff like that around for him, so that he doesn't think his parents were always miserable around him or with each other."

"You're right. It is important."

"I'm sorry. If I were more prepared, I would've put that picture away. You don't need to see that."

"Mack, please. Don't be silly. Hiding a photo doesn't change anything."

He nodded, seeming unsure as to whether my comment was meant to be simply factual or slightly bitter. I wasn't sure I even knew.

"Let me show you my room."

My heart beat a little faster as he led me across the hall into his bedroom.

Mack's room was everything I would have imagined it to be. I looked around, quietly absorbing its understated masculinity. His amazing smell filled the airspace. A navy comforter sat atop the king-sized, dark cherry wood bed that was fitting for a man of his size.

Sitting down on the edge, I bounced lightly on the bed and ran my palms across the plush fabric. Being alone with him in here was definitely making me tense.

He leaned against his bureau, crossing his arms and quietly observing me.

A thought crossed my mind. I wondered if he'd been with anyone else besides Torrie. Mack was definitely a sexual person. I wondered how he could have possibly stayed celibate even in the short time he'd been in Boston. I honestly didn't want to know if he hadn't and chose not to let my mind go there.

"This room is really nice."

He raised his brow. "Really? Then why do you look like you want to flee?"

"It does make me a little nervous being in your room."

"Do you want me to take you home?"

"No."

"Okay." He sat down next to me, leaving only a few inches between us. My body tensed up in an effort to fight my attraction to him.

He touched his index finger to a spot on my lower neck, sending chills down my spine. "What happened to the little mole that used to be there?"

"I got it removed years ago. I was afraid it was cancer. It wasn't. You know how paranoid I can get about things. I'm surprised you even remember that I had it."

He was looking into my eyes for a while before he said, "I remember everything, Frankie. I remember that you were wearing a *Punky Brewster* T-shirt the day we first met. I remember the way your hair always smelled. I fucking use the same shampoo—Finesse—just so I can smell you every day. Smelled every bottle in the store until I could remember which brand it was. I remember the last show we ever watched together—a rerun of *Friends*, the one where Phoebe found a human thumb floating around in her can of soda. You were laughing at the show, and I was just staring at you, wondering how the hell I was going to deal with not seeing you for an entire summer. I remember the way the sun caught the red in your hair at that outdoor bar during our last day together. And I'll never forget the look of sadness on your face when you knew I was leaving Boston and not coming back. I remember everything, and depending on the day, that's either a curse or a blessing."

My heart felt like it was ready to explode.

He placed his hand on mine. "I remember it all—the good and the bad—and I wouldn't trade any of it." Looking down at our fingers now wrapped together, he asked, "Is this okay? My holding your hand?"

Touching him felt really good. Even though it should have seemed like an innocent gesture, the contact was disconcertingly arousing.

I answered, "Yes."

We were quiet for a long while until he said, "No matter what happens, all of those memories will stay with me until the day I die. But I'd prefer to make new ones. It's fucked-up, but I didn't think I could want you more than I did back then. But now that you're with someone else, now that I may lose you a second time—forever—it's a whole different level of wanting you."

I broke the contact of our hands, stood up, and walked over to the window. It was foggy, preventing me from seeing outside.

"Before he left, Victor said he wants to marry me," I suddenly blurted out. "And have kids. He'd never said those words before, but I think he feels threatened by you."

"He does, does he? Are his feelings warranted?"

Did Victor have a reason to worry? The way my heart was beating, the fact that my panties were wet from the mere touch of Mack's hand, meant that Victor had *every* reason to worry. I still reacted to Mack the same way I had eight years ago. Nothing in that respect had changed. Every part of me that wasn't logical wanted Mack and only Mack. But this wasn't just a decision for my body and heart. My mind kept reminding me that there was a child and a bitter ex involved. Not to mention the fear that went along with giving someone a second chance when they'd already broken your heart.

But I answered him truthfully, "His feelings are warranted, yes. But I'm very confused."

He got up and walked slowly toward me. "It's weird how the roles have reversed. I used to want to be with you but stopped what felt natural because I didn't want to hurt Torrie. Nothing and no one is holding me back now. I don't care about him, but I respect that you do, because I care about *you*. I can relate to what you're going through. I'll do whatever you truly want. Your happiness is all that matters. You're holding all the cards, Frankie—every single, last one of them. But just be aware that I have no issue with showing you exactly how much I want you right now." He moved in closer, to the point where I could feel the heat from his body. "The next time you ask me to kiss you, I'm going to fucking kiss you." He pointed to the bed. "In fact, I'd love nothing more than to be making your eyes roll back right now."

I let out a slight audible gasp. The muscles between my legs instinctively tightened.

"Well, you said you weren't gonna hold back. I guess you weren't kidding."

"I'm not gonna pretend, no. I'm not gonna lie to you about my feelings. I'm not going to hide the fact that I want to make love to you more than anything."

His phone vibrated, disrupting the tension.

He looked down. "Shit. It's Torrie. I'd better take this in case it has to do with Jonah."

"No problem."

I listened as he spoke to her. His ex's calling in the middle of our moment was a timely reminder that being with Mack would always mean having to deal with Torrie being in the picture.

He put the phone back in his pocket. "I'm sorry about that."

"Everything okay?"

"Yeah. It had nothing to do with Jonah. She wanted to confirm what time the winter festival was this weekend."

I swallowed the lump in my throat. "She's gonna be there?"

"Yeah. She wants to go, apparently."

I tried to make light of it. "Well, that's one sure dunk in the tank for you."

He chuckled. "You can bet on that."

The following Thursday afternoon, Mack was parked outside of the school waiting for me at five; my staff meeting had run late.

He'd had to cancel seeing me the previous two days because Torrie got unexpectedly called out of town for a work-related emergency. Since Jonah had to stay with him, there was no way for us to spend time together after school. He'd been extremely apologetic, even though I'd told him it really wasn't necessary to be sorry about something he couldn't control.

When I entered the car, he looked morose. "I'm so fucking sorry, Frankie."

"I told you, it's fine."

He looked around to make sure no one had spotted us before driving off.

"No, it's not fine. We only have this week. This time has been like a gift, and I just lost two whole days with you. Now, we just have tonight."

Jonah's weekend with Mack started on Friday afternoons through Sunday evening. So, aside from the fact that I'd see him at the winter festival on Saturday, tonight would be it.

"We'll make the most of it." I smiled.

"I've been dying to see you," he said.

The words were at the tip of my tongue. I wanted to tell him that I'd thought of nothing but him for the past two days, but I needed to be careful. I didn't want to give him false hope, because admittedly, I was still torn about what was going to happen once Victor returned. This limbo wasn't really fair to either of them, but I vowed not to let my confusion ruin tonight. It was my one night with Mack, and I needed to focus on the moment.

I finally answered him, "You've been on my mind, too. A lot."

Mack was dressed to the nines in a fitted, collared shirt and formal trousers.

Looking him up and down, I said, "You're so dressed up."

"I have a surprise for you. But you need to stop at home and change into something nice."

"You're taking me to my condo?"

He sensed my apprehension. "Yes, but I'll wait in the car for you."

Once at my house and not wanting to waste time, I'd never gotten dressed so fast in my life. My pulse raced with excitement as I threw on a red dress and matching heels. Glancing over at a picture of Victor and me in our bedroom, I tried not to let the guilt seep in. I reminded myself that even Victor wanted me to use this time away to figure things out. Going out with Mack tonight was part of that process.

Mack's eyes widened when I returned to the car. "Fuck, you look gorgeous. I've always loved you in red. It accentuates your hair."

"Thank you." My skin felt hot from the compliment. "So, you won't tell me where we're going?"

"Like I said, it's a surprise."

Twenty minutes later, we pulled up to the Hyatt Regency hotel that overlooked the Charles River.

"We're going to The Spinnaker." He smiled.

The Spinnaker was a restaurant situated on the top floor of the hotel. It was known for its rotating floor, which spun around ever so slowly while patrons gazed out at different views of the city. Back in college, we'd gone there once to celebrate acing our respective final exams. Mack had racked up a huge bill on his father's credit card and vowed to deal with the repercussions later. We'd had so much fun that night.

We made our way to the top of the hotel, only— to our shock—there was nothing there anymore. A cleaning person was vacuuming a rug, but the doors that once led into the famous restaurant were locked.

"What happened to The Spinnaker?" Mack asked.

"Closed down several years ago," the woman said. "They just rent the space for private parties now."

"I didn't know," I whispered to him.

"Thank you," he told the worker before turning to me. "I feel so stupid."

Placing my hand on his shoulder, I said, "It's okay."

"It's not okay. It's not." He repeated, "None of this is okay. It's like I just expected everything to be exactly the same." I knew he was referring to more than just the restaurant being closed.

Mack was extremely quiet during the elevator ride back down to the lower level. Once outside of the hotel, instead of heading back toward the car, he stopped walking and stared out toward the river.

The wind caused by being so close to the water blew my hair around as I asked, "Mack, what's wrong?"

He looked up at the sky then over at me. "Am I delusional?"

"What do you mean?"

"Be honest. Am I grasping for something that's not there anymore?" He turned to me. "I wake up in the morning with hope, that every day I'm somehow closer to being with you. I still feel this bond between us. I feel it so strongly. But tonight is an example of how fucking clueless I apparently am. I just assumed...it would be here, just like I assumed that I could just come back into your life and somehow win you back after eight fucking years. The one chance I get to really be with you—this week—and my life gets in the way, once again demonstrating how I can never make you a priority like you deserve. Fuck, I don't even think I would choose me if I were you." He looked up at the sky then back at me. "I don't have all the time in the world to give you. I couldn't give you the perfect life even if I wanted to, because I am carrying so much baggage. Some days, I don't even know who I am anymore...Jonah's dad, Torrie's ex, Michael Morrison's estranged son. But when I'm with you...I'm *Mack*. I feel like myself. When you look at me, you remind me of who I am, who I want to be. I want to go back to being that man who was once happier than a pig in shit just from being around you every day. But it's not fair to steal away even an ounce of your happiness just so I can have mine."

As much as I'd wanted to avoid touching him, I couldn't help it. I pulled him into a tight embrace.

We just held each other for the longest time. His breath was shaky. I could feel his heart pounding faster than I could ever remember. For the first time, it hit me how vulnerable Mack really was. Even though he always seemed so confident and strong, he was letting his guard down completely in this moment. I still had no clue what the right choice was for me, but one thing I was sure of: I wanted to spend every minute of tonight with this man. The evening wasn't going to go to waste.

Breaking our long embrace, I asked, "Will you take me back to your house?"

He seemed surprised. "My house?"

"Yes. I want to cook for you and watch a movie on your big ass television. That's how I want to spend tonight, not in some fancy restaurant."

"But I'm supposed to be wining and dining you."

"What would make me happiest is to be able to cook us a nice meal and to just be with you. Can we go to your place?"

"Of course. Consider my house your house. I would love that more than anything."

"Okay...it's settled, then."

CHAPTER SIXTEEN

Mack

Frankie wanted to stop back at her condo to put on comfortable clothes and grab some food she had in her fridge so that she could prepare it over at my place.

Knowing I'd be stepping into *his* house made me a little ill, but he wasn't there, so that balanced it out a little. I was definitely eager for the rare opportunity to scope out where she lived.

This brownstone had to have cost in the millions.

"How did he afford this place?"

"It's been in his family for years."

"I was gonna say. A professor's salary alone wouldn't allow for this."

"It certainly wouldn't."

The décor was a combination of dark wood and interior brick with lots of built-in shelves and dark leather furniture. Books were everywhere. The ceilings were high, and there were lots of rooms; it was almost too much space for two people.

I followed her into the rustic-style kitchen. The cabinets were painted a light teal color and the island featured a butcher-block countertop. There was a small open pantry in the corner stacked with food items.

Frankie grabbed a canvas bag and began emptying some of the contents of her fridge into it. She eventually placed it down in a thud and said, "I'll be right back. I'm just gonna change into something more comfortable and then we can get out of here. Feel free to look around."

I made my way into the living room. My eyes landed on a picture of Frankie with Victor. I leaned in to examine it. The photo looked like it was taken on one of the swan boats on the Boston Common. His arm was wrapped around her. But that wasn't what filled me with jealousy. He was gently kissing her forehead while she shyly looked into the camera. His eyes were closed. I didn't have to imagine the thoughts going through his head in that moment because I knew full well what he was thinking; he was thinking what a lucky bastard he was. And that he didn't need anything beyond what was right in front of his nose. I wasn't gonna lie; seeing the picture upset me for more than one reason. It upset me because I was jealous, but it also upset me because it made me feel like Victor really cherished Frankie. And I knew she deserved that.

She appeared in the doorway and noticed me looking down at the photo. She was wearing sweats. It reminded me of something she would have worn around our apartment back in the day. Since reconnecting with her, she'd never looked more like the old Frankie than in that moment. There she was, right in front of me, yet so far away.

"There's the Frankie I remember."

"I'm sorry if I look like a bum, but it's been a long day. I wanted to just get comfortable."

My mouth curved into a smile as I took her in. "You've never looked more beautiful."

Her cheeks turned red. "You're a liar."

"I've never lied to you, Frankie. Not once."

She seemed to ponder that for a moment. "That's true. You never really have...that I know of."

I'd lost a little of my fight earlier tonight. It was back. Suddenly, as much as I'd felt badly for Victor after the realization that photo had brought to light, I transitioned back into fight mode. A voice inside me seemed to say, *"Fight harder."*

All is fair in love and war, Vic. Sorry, but I love her, too.

Frankie had made a tasty chicken and artichoke dish with sundried tomatoes in my kitchen. She'd also shown me how to make rice in a rice cooker I hadn't even realized I owned. It must have been left behind by the previous tenants.

After dinner, we retreated downstairs to my man cave. I turned on the pellet stove, and the blazing fire made the space nice and toasty.

Having her here with me was heaven and hell at the same time. It wasn't hard to imagine this being our life, getting to do this every night. But there was still the harsh realization that it could have been our very last time together like this. She'd given me no real indication of where her head was. And I was sure that was because she didn't fully know.

Frankie curled into the corner of my couch. Wearing fuzzy socks, she looked so comfortable. At one point, I took her feet, placed them on my lap and began massaging. In ecstasy, she closed her eyes and let me have my way with them. I could've done it all night long. The sounds of ecstasy coming out of her mouth were painful to listen to because they reminded me of what I wished I could have really been doing to give her pleasure tonight. I closed my eyes and imagined what it would be like to be inside of her. That was something I'd imagined a lot over the years, but it was far more frustrating to be doing it while listening to her little moans.

The television was turned to one of the cable movie channels, but neither of us was paying any attention to it. We were quiet for a while until an idea popped into my head.

"So, I was thinking..."

"That can be dangerous," she joked, her eyes still closed.

I squeezed her foot harder in response.

"Ow," she laughed.

"As I was saying...I think we need to write down a list of pros and cons."

"For what?"

"Me versus him."

She pulled her feet away from me and sat up. "Are you serious?"

"Yes. I know you're still confused about what's best for you long-term. Sometimes, it helps to write things down." I got up in search of paper. "Be right back."

I was certain she thought I was joking; I wasn't. We didn't have much time, and I needed to get a better feel for where things stood.

Returning to the couch, I moved in closer to her, relishing the smell of her hair. "Okay, let's start with him."

She shook her head. "I can't do this."

"Sure, you can." I drew a line down the middle of the yellow legal pad. "I'll start." I began writing. "Pros for Victor...he's safe. He adores you. He has a great job. Amazing house. No kids. No ex-wives. No baggage." I looked over at her. "You want to add some of your own?"

She responded with sarcasm, "Well, you seem to know everything about Victor, so..."

"I'm biased and can't be trusted. I'm about to go in for the kill on my side, so you'd better help out your friend."

She took the pen and wrote, "Honest. Caring. Protective. Ridiculously intelligent."

Swallowing my pride, I coughed. "Those are all good." I took the pen back. "Victor's cons...old as fuck."

She laughed. "He's not that old."

I continued listing things. "Let's you hang out with strange men."

"That's not a con. That means he trusts me."

"The fuck it isn't a con. If you were my woman, you would not be going out on my watch with some dude who's trying to get into your pants."

"That's a con in your corner then, Morrison. You're trying to get into my pants?"

"Frankie Jane, I have wanted in your pants since the night you made me stay up to watch that *Doctor Who* marathon."

She laughed. "That was when you decided you wanted to sleep with me?"

"I don't know if that was the exact moment, but I definitely remember wanting to suck on your neck really badly that night. There were many nights like that, but for some reason, that one sticks out." I pointed to the paper. "Stay focused. What are some of Victor's cons?"

Shrugging, she said, "Honestly, I can't really think of any."

"Are you kidding me?"

"Nothing is coming to mind."

"Everyone has faults. Even not having faults could be considered a con, because it makes him fucking boring." I wrote it down. "Boring."

She cackled. "In that case, you're very exciting, Morrison."

"Ouch."

"I'm just messing with you." In an effort to show me she was kidding, she ran her hand briefly through my hair. It was the first time she'd initiated any physical contact, and it made my pulse race. I wished I could pin her down and demonstrate what I was sure was a very big pro in my corner.

Shaking off the intense need to do just that, I said, "Okay, well since there are apparently no negatives for Victor, let's move onto to Mack's cons. I'd like to get those over with first. I'll start." Taking a deep breath, I started to write something, but my hand froze. Holy fuck, there were a shit ton of cons. I just couldn't get myself to write them down.

Got another woman pregnant.

Abandoned you.

Tons of baggage.

Corrupt family.

No time for you on weekends.

The list went on and on in my head. I let the pen drop and balled my hand into a fist.

"What's wrong?"

"I can't. There are too many. I'm gonna lose."

"Maybe start with the pros, then." She handed me the pen and smiled. That motivated me to continue.

I put pen to the paper again. "Funny...good-looking...well-endowed..."

"I can attest to that last one." She laughed. "From the brief and unintentional contact I had the night we first met."

"Unintentional is debatable." I winked. "Kidding. I'm glad I made a good first impression."

When I continue to stall, she grabbed the pen from me and wrote. "Great father."

"Thank you."

There weren't a lot of things that defined me; I truthfully didn't feel like I could go on and on about myself. But there was one thing—a major pro—that needed to be added. It was what mattered the most above all else when it came to her.

My hand shook a little as I took the pen back from her and wrote: *Loves you more than you'll ever know.*

She just stared down at the words, letting them sink in. I knew she wasn't expecting them to come at this very moment, but something told me that now was the most important time to say it.

I took her hand in mine. "You said earlier that I'd never lied to you. That still holds true. I have never loved anyone like I love you. From the moment we met, life just felt different. You brought color into my gray and dismal existence, made me realize what it means to have someone change your entire outlook on life, change your reason for living. I slowly fell in love with my best friend. You were my *first* love—my only love. I should've told you how I really felt back then. Even though life got in the way, even though everything changed in our worlds as we knew it, nothing could take the love I feel for you away. It's always been there all these years, even though I've never actually said those words until now. So, in case there was ever any doubt, I love you, Frankie. Maybe in the end, that's all I really have to give. Maybe that doesn't necessarily make me the best on paper. If you choose me, I'm just going to have to love you more, love you harder, so that my love for you trumps everything else. That's not gonna be hard for me, because I don't feel like there is a limit to how much I love you."

Even though she was apparently speechless, tears were forming in her eyes.

"You don't have to say anything," I said. "I just needed you to know."

Frankie looked like she wanted to say something, but things were quiet for a long time.

She finally admitted, "Victor said part of the purpose of his going away was to give me some space to figure things out. But I'm more confused and afraid than ever."

My heart nearly stopped in that moment.

"Wait...he actually said he was *giving you space*? I thought he was just going on a trip for work. He's actually *expecting* something to happen between us while he's gone?"

"He says he doesn't want to know what happens this week but that he hopes in the end, I choose him."

It felt like a vain had popped in my head. "Like 'don't ask, don't tell?' Holy shit." My voice grew louder. "He thinks we're *fucking* while he's away?"

"I'm not certain that he definitely thinks that. I think he might wonder if something happened, though. That's

214

not to say he wouldn't care. I think he'd be devastated if he believed that we crossed that line. But I got this vibe that he almost expected something to happen between us. But that doesn't make it okay. I wouldn't do that as long as I'm technically still with him."

I didn't know what to do with this information. I felt like I'd missed an opportunity I didn't even know I had. That made me furious.

"So, let me get this straight. He gave you a ticket to explore things with me? So, basically, we're *sitting* here talking when you could be *sitting* on my face instead?"

Frankie looked flustered. "Um…"

I was starting to lose it a little. My anger rose upon another realization. "You know what? The fact that he also mentioned wanting to marry you before he left means he thinks the likelihood of anything lasting between us is nil. Is he hoping that you would just be able to fuck me out of your system then go on your merry way with him?"

Her voice was basically a whimper. "I don't know."

"Any man who would let you out of his sight long enough to test the waters with someone else is a goddamn fool. He's hoping one good fuck might be all you need to get over me? Maybe we should test it."

She swallowed. "Test it?"

"Yes. Give me one night. We'll go up to my room right now and have hot, sweaty, amazing fucking sex. It will be the best of your life."

Her breathing quickened. "I'm pretty sure that wouldn't make my decision any easier."

"Well, *I'm* pretty sure there would be *no* decision anymore if that happened. I think that scares the hell out of you because you're afraid to want me even more than you already do." I placed my hand on her knee, causing her to flinch. "Do you want to know what you said to me the night you were drunk all those years ago?"

"What?"

"You said you wished I could fuck you so hard that you would feel me for days. It might have been the alcohol talking, but I got the impression that maybe that was always one of your fantasies. You like it rough? Is that what you prefer?" I raised my voice. "Does he give you what you want?"

Fuck. I was letting my anger show and needed to stop myself. Despite my rage, blood still rushed to my cock from the mere thought of getting to fuck her.

The news that Victor had basically given her permission to be with me had floored me. But that wasn't what upset me the most. I was angry because she chose not to take advantage of it, not to take the risk. That told me that whether she realized it yet or not, she probably planned on staying with him. Things weren't really in my favor like I'd hoped they were. In fact, I may have already lost her. Suddenly, the need to protect my heart from getting shattered seemed stronger than ever.

I stood up. "I'm sorry. This was supposed to be a low-key, relaxing night, and I've fucked it all up. It's late. I want you to take my bed upstairs. I'm gonna sleep down here."

"You're angry at me."

"Not angry at you. You didn't do anything wrong. You're trying to do the right thing. I'm just angry at life, in general, and I'm trying to stop myself from saying anything else tonight that I might regret."

Her eyes were glistening. "You regret telling me you love me?"

Yes.

I ignored her question. "Goodnight, Frankie."

CHAPTER SEVENTEEN

Francesca

I hadn't seen Mack since he dropped me off to pick up my car at the school in the wee hours of the morning that Friday. He'd continued to act guarded during the entire ride.

He also hadn't texted or called since. It was clear my admitting that I'd chosen not to take full advantage of the apparent pass Victor had given me really pissed him off.

Now, it was Saturday, and I was going to not only have to face him but also Torrie at the winter carnival. My stomach was churning just thinking about it.

As I sat alone in the kitchen sipping my morning coffee, the last thing I expected was the door to latch open suddenly. A cold burst of air entered the room as Victor walked in. He hadn't been expected back until late Sunday night.

"Francesca..." he simply said.

I put down my mug and lifted myself up. "What are you doing back?"

"I couldn't stay away any longer, caught an earlier flight home." He embraced me.

"How was Oxford?" I asked, my heart still pounding from the shock of his arrival.

"It was really great. They want me to go back again in the next few months." He paused and examined my face. Feigning a smile, he said, "You look shocked to see me."

"I am a little. I wasn't expecting you today. I have the winter carnival at school. I'm supposed to be volunteering all day. We won't get to spend time together."

"Well, I'll go with you. I'll be happy to help out." Placing his hand on my back, he drew me in close and gently kissed my forehead. When he pulled back to look me in the eyes, the worry was written all over his face.

I answered the question he seemed to silently be asking me.

"Nothing happened, Victor."

He gritted his teeth. "You didn't need to explain."

"But you were looking at me like you needed to know."

"Well, you can see through me, then. I *have* been worried." He let out a deep breath. "We don't need to talk about it now. I don't want to make you late."

Something felt vastly different between us. I couldn't put my finger on it, but suddenly it felt foreign to be standing in my own kitchen. As much as I'd told myself I was confused over the past week, it seemed something had shifted. My time with Mack had more of an effect on my feelings than I'd originally thought.

Victor rubbed my arm gently. "Do I have time to take a quick shower, or shall I meet you there?"

His accompanying me made me nervous, but I couldn't tell him not to go.

I looked at the clock. "You have about fifteen minutes. I'll wait for you, so we can drive together."

He gave me a peck on the cheek. "I'll be quick."

Panic started to build. Victor would come face to face with Mack today. And I still couldn't figure out why things suddenly felt really different. There was also a tremendous ache in my chest.

Taking advantage of the time that Victor was in the shower, I picked up the phone and called my mother. She was the only person I'd opened up to about my dilemma. We last spoke during my lunch break Friday, the same day Mack dropped me off after we'd left things on a sour note. So, she was up to speed.

Mom answered, "It's early. Something wrong?"

"I don't have a lot of time. I need your advice like I've never needed it before."

"What happened?"

"The shit's about to hit the fan. Victor came back early from his trip. He's coming with me to the winter carnival today. Mack will be there volunteering. I'm freaking out."

"You claim to be confused, Francesca, but you're freaking out because you know Victor has a reason to be uncomfortable. This situation is so obvious to me, sweetheart, and I just can't figure out why you can't see it. From the moment that man came back into your life, you've thought of nothing else. I know you value the time you've had with Victor, but it's clear to me that your heart is not in it anymore. It's with Mack."

"Why does it hurt so badly, then? Whenever I'm with Mack, it's like my heart physically hurts."

"You assume that pain is a bad sign. Sometimes, love expresses itself as pain. You're scared. That's all. You don't want to get hurt again. But your feelings are stronger for Mack. There's no disputing that. That's why it hurts."

I definitely hadn't looked at it that way, but I knew she was right. What my heart wanted—what it craved—wasn't the safest choice, but it was undeniable.

"I don't want to devastate Victor."

"Honey, you've already been doing that. The man came home early because he knows he's losing you. Don't you see that?"

She was right.

The pipes upstairs made a clanking sound, indicating that Victor had turned off the water. "Shit. I have to go. He'll be coming down any minute."

"Good luck today."

"Thanks, Mom."

I'm going to need it.

Mack was a rock star.

You would've thought that they were waiting to see someone famous. The line to his dunk tank was a mile long.

Victor and I were manning one of the pastry tables in the opposite corner of the large gymnasium. Mack had already been situated in the dunking area when we arrived, so he hadn't seen us yet. Relief washed over me. I was under the radar for now.

The winter carnival at St. Matthew's was the school's biggest fundraiser, featuring craft tables, games, auctions, and homemade foods. Held in a massive gym, it was the one time of year that parents, teachers, priests, nuns, and students all congregated under the same roof.

Lorelai stopped by the table and whispered in my ear, "Mack Daddy seems to be the main attraction. Even a couple of the nuns are getting in on it."

I glared at her in an attempt to warn her to shut up before Victor overheard.

In the distance, I could see Mack's wet, white T-shirt stuck to his abs as he ran his hands along his drenched hair. His muscular body looked obscenely hot through the wet clothing. I tried my best not to look too long in that direction.

Victor hadn't mentioned anything but finally turned to me. "That's him in the dunking tank, right?"

I nodded. "Yes." Even though I was trying to sound calm and nonchalant, in reality my nerves were shot. I was sure my face was probably red.

Victor was onto me, and I truly didn't know how to handle it.

"The line seems to be getting a little shorter. Mind if I have a try at it?" he asked.

"What?"

"I want to dunk him. When else will I get this opportunity?" He got up without waiting for my approval.

Oh, no.

My heart was beating out of control as I raced to follow Victor over there. Mack hadn't spotted us yet as he continued to clap his hands and heckle the people in line—mostly women, of course—who were trying to hit the target.

When Mack noticed that Victor and I were among the crowd, the expression on his face changed dramatically. His eyes met Victor's, and his body stilled.

When it was finally Victor's turn, Mack was no longer joking around. Tension filled the air as his eyes seared into mine before moving over to meet Victor's incendiary stare. A full thirty seconds must have passed, and it felt like forever. Mack's body remained still as he just sat there waiting for what he knew good and well was coming.

Victor grabbed the ball and in a sudden and swift movement, whipped it toward the target, hitting it smack dab in the middle in one shot. It surprised me that the contraption didn't break from the impact. Mack plunged into the water below.

When he came up, he looked even more pissed than before. All of the noise in the gymnasium seemed to fade away. At least, that was my perception as my ears throbbed louder with each second that I stood there gauging Mack's reaction. He stared at Victor with daggers in his eyes.

Victor turned to me. "Are you going to be alright handling that table alone if I go home and catch some shut eye? The jet lag seems to be catching up to me all of a sudden." He didn't acknowledge what he'd just done; he didn't have to.

I swallowed, barely able to speak. "Of course."

He simply walked away without saying anything further. I opted to let him go because I knew there was nothing I could say that would make it better, especially given the realization I had this morning.

My heart felt like it was breaking as I looked over at Mack, who was still staring at me. The next woman in line was already trying her hand at dunking him, but he wasn't paying attention. He just kept looking straight at me like he wanted to say something.

"I'm sorry," I mouthed, not really even sure what I was apologizing for. Before he could respond, his body dropped down into the water; someone had managed to hit the target.

It was then that I spotted Jonah sitting alone on a corner bench nearby.

Mack had mentioned Torrie was supposed to be at the event; I wondered where she was. Most of the kids were just running around, playing with each other while the parents mingled at the various display tables. But as was typical, Jonah had separated himself from the crowd. I'd wanted to go talk to him but realized I needed to get back to the pastry table.

Some time later, I noticed a few boys surrounding Jonah. While I couldn't hear what they were saying, it seemed like they were trying to stir up trouble. When I spotted one of them grabbing a fistful of Jonah's curls and yanking his hair, I flew up out of my seat.

Before I could get to him, I noticed Mack charging toward his son. He was soaking wet, his hair dripping. He must have noticed what was going on from the dunk tank and jumped out. When the kids saw him coming, they scurried away like bats out of hell.

He knelt down, placing his palms around Jonah's face. Mack's hands were shaking. "Are you okay, son?"

Noticing a crowd of bystanders starting to congregate, he grabbed Jonah by the hand. "Come on." He whisked him away down a hallway into an empty function room. I followed them but stayed in the doorway to give them space.

"What happened, Jonah?"

The boy sniffled as he answered his father. "They were calling me ugly and making fun of my hair. They started pulling on it. My head hurts."

Mack closed his eyes momentarily in an attempt to gather his thoughts before blowing out a breath. "You have to understand something. Those boys were picking on you because they know it affects you. Mean people won't change. The only thing you have control over is your reaction to them. I promise you, if you don't let them see you're upset, or if you act like you don't care, they won't want to pick on you anymore."

"But I *do* care."

"I know. I know, son. But you have to try to pretend like it doesn't bother you, even if it does. It's not easy. You know what I want you to do next time something like that happens?"

"What?"

"I want you to walk away."

"What if they run after me?"

"They won't. You just walk away and pretend you don't care about what they have to say. Just trust me on that, okay? And if by some chance anyone ever hurts you, Jonah, they'll have to deal with me. I have one job now and that's to protect you. I'm not gonna let anyone hurt you. I promise." He pulled his son into a hug. "You trust me?"

Jonah nodded.

"I love you, son."

My ovaries nearly exploded, and my heart felt like it was ready to burst. What an amazing feeling to witness what a loving father he was. I was almost envious of Jonah for getting to experience the love of a father like Mack. Then, it hit me that I, too, got to experience what it was like to be loved by this man—in a different way.

I reminded myself that he'd told me he loved me just a couple of days ago.

Mack finally noticed me standing there. I suddenly felt like an imposter.

Taking a few steps inside the room, I asked, "Are you okay, Jonah?"

"Yeah."

Addressing Mack, I said, "I want you to know I'm going to be calling those kids' parents to let them know what happened."

"Thank you," he said without looking at me.

Then came a very unwelcome interruption when Clarissa McIntyre and her son, Ethan, walked in.

Great.

"Sorry to intrude. We heard there was a little scene out there and wanted to make sure Jonah was okay."

"Hey, Jonah," the boy said.

Jonah's face perked up a bit. "Hi, Ethan."

Ethan was actually a very good kid, shy in his own right and seemed to be Jonah's only friend. His mother, on the other hand, was the opposite of shy and couldn't have been more obvious in her intentions.

Clarissa batted her eyes at Mack. "How are you holding up, Dad?"

"I was rattled, jumped out of the dunking cage when I saw those little punks messing with him." He squeezed Jonah's shoulder. "But we had a talk about ignoring bullies, didn't we?"

"Ethan had the same problem with that group of boys." She cleared her throat. "Anyway, I saw Kyle

McDonough took your place in the dunk tank. So, I think you're off the hook."

"Good. I'm in no mood to go back there."

"I'm kind of bummed I didn't get one shot at it, though," Clarissa said as her gaze wandered along Mack's wet physique in admiration. "We were wondering if you guys wanted to join us for dinner tonight."

Mack looked pensive. "What do you think, Jonah? You want to go over to Ethan's for dinner?"

Jonah nodded.

"Okay. Thank you. I'll call you later to find out what we can bring," Mack said.

Clarissa looked like she'd won the lottery. "No need to bring anything. I'm gonna cook up a bunch of different things for us. Come hungry."

Mack glanced over at me before he replied, "I will."

He was totally fucking with me because he knew I was jealous. I couldn't blame him for being pissed after what Victor pulled. Mack had every right to be frustrated.

"Can't wait. We'll see you boys later, then." She looked over in my direction, acknowledging me for the first time on her way out. "Bye, Francesca."

Almost as soon as Clarissa and Ethan exited the room, things took a dramatic turn for the worse when Torrie appeared at the doorway. It was like a game of Whac-A-Mole, one down, and an even worse one appears.

A look of alarm shone on her face. "What the heck is going on, Mack? I asked around looking for you, and they told me something happened with Jonah."

"I didn't think you were going to show."

She knelt down and kissed her son. "I'm so sorry, honey." Turning to Mack, she said, "I didn't expect to get called into the office on a Saturday. But I'm here now." She gave her ex a once over. "Why are you drenched?"

"I was volunteering in the dunk tank but left when I noticed some boys picking on Jonah."

"What were they doing exactly?"

"Pulling his hair and making fun of him."

"Are you serious? You shouldn't have left him alone."

She was such a bitch to him.

Torrie finally acknowledged me. "Miss O'Hara.

"Hello, Miss Hightower. Good to see you again."

She addressed me, "Did you see what happened?"

"I did see them taunting him and pulling his hair. Mack interrupted it. They're a group of boys who are known for making trouble. I'll be contacting their parents."

"I'd like their parents' names and contact information, as well," she said before turning her attention to Mack. "I'm going to get him out of here, take him home with me for a little bit."

"He's fine, Torrie. He needs to learn to be strong. He should stay."

"He doesn't look fine to me. I'm just around the corner anyway. You can come get him later."

Mack seemed upset that Torrie insisted on cutting into his scheduled time with Jonah, but he let Jonah decide. "Do you want to go to Mom's?"

When the boy nodded yes, Mack said, "Okay...well, it's my night, Torrie. We have dinner plans with some friends, so I'll come get him at five."

I inwardly cringed at the thought of Mack going over to Clarissa's tonight.

"Fine," she said curtly before holding out her hand. "Come on, honey." She looked at me. "Good to see you, Miss O'Hara."

I faked a grin. "Same."

After they disappeared, Mack and I were left alone for the first time.

A long moment of silence followed until he bitterly bit out, "Where's your boyfriend?"

"He went home."

"That was real funny what he did. Pretty juvenile for an old fucking man."

"I'm sorry. I didn't know he was going to be mean about it. I think he just finally snapped."

"I can relate. I can feel myself snapping at this very moment, in fact." He wrung the water out of his shirt. "What was supposed to be a good day has turned into a real shitty one. I'm so done."

"You need a drink."

His reply took me aback.

"I need a fuck is what I need, Frankie. Want to volunteer? If not, I bet Clarissa would be down for that."

That burned.

He was mad and intentionally trying to get a rise out of me. But I took it without dishing anything back because I felt like I somehow deserved it after this morning. I could see right through him. More than anything, he looked hurt.

Still completely soaking wet, he got up suddenly and exited the room without saying goodbye. All eyes seemed to be on him as he walked through the gymnasium and eventually out into the parking lot. I watched as he got into his truck and sped away.

I stood there frozen at the entrance, unsure of what to do. Lorelai had taken over manning the pastry table. The right thing would have been to stay and figure out another way to help. But I was so done with going against my own happiness to do the right thing.

As I escaped into my car, I decided I was going straight home to face Victor, to tell him I would be moving out. It was the right decision, even if things didn't work out with Mack. My having such intense feelings for another person wasn't fair to him. So, I told myself I was heading to our condo on Beacon Hill. But the reality was, I was driving down Route Nine toward Framingham.

When I arrived at his house, Mack's truck was parked outside.

He was home.

I nervously knocked on the door, thankful that Mrs. M. was nowhere in sight.

After about a minute, he opened, still looking angry as hell. "What are you doing here?"

All of our time together seemed to flash before me as I looked into his pained and exhausted eyes. It had all come down to this moment.

Say something.

"I'm still her, Mack—that, awkward, unsure girl who's just in awe of you. I've been enamored with you for many different reasons over the years, but today, seeing you with your son, well, I've never loved you more. I *love* you. And I *see* you. I see how hard you try. I see all the love you have to give."

He closed his eyes briefly. "You should go home."

Not this time.

"I've been lost and scared, but I'm pretty sure this *is* home."

Grabbing onto the wet material of his shirt, I stood on my toes and pressed my lips against his. For a split second, it seemed like he was going to resist, but then I felt his tongue slip into my mouth, and a deep groan of concession escape him.

"Fuck," he muttered over my lips as he gripped my ass before pulling me into the house and kicking the door shut. I knew the second I heard it slam that there was no turning back.

Mack bumped into some furniture as he walked backwards while he kissed me harder. He unwound the paisley scarf that had been wrapped around my neck and threw it carelessly onto the ground. Refusing to detach ourselves long enough to see around us, we stumbled down the hall, practically glued at the mouth until we were finally in his bedroom.

The shades were drawn, but there was just enough light coming in for me to be able see him. Running my fingers through his damp hair, I could taste beer on his breath. He must have opened a bottle the second he got home, certainly not expecting that I would follow him here. More than the beer, though, I could taste him. For the first time in my life, I got to taste the man of my dreams and become intoxicated by his indescribable, yet addictive, flavor. Breathless, wet, and shaking, nothing else mattered in the world anymore. Reaching up as high as I could on my tippy toes, I refused to come up for air as we consumed each other, our tongues colliding in a desperate struggle for more.

He growled over my lips, "You'd better leave right now if you have any intention of going back to him, because I don't plan to leave an inch of you unmarked. I'll give you ten seconds to walk away." He started to count, kissing me in between each number he recited. "Ten...nine...eight...seven..." He lowered his mouth to gently bite my neck. "Six...five...four...three...two..." He kissed upward then whispered over my mouth, "One."

I hadn't budged.

Mack took hold of my wrists, locking them behind my back before flipping me around toward his bedroom wall. "You've always belonged to me, haven't you, Frankie?" His kiss was no longer gentle as he sucked voraciously on the skin at the back of my neck. The heat of his breath was making me crazy. My entire body went limp, completely submitting to him. "I need you...now," he panted in my ear. "Need to fuck you hard. Please don't tell me to stop."

"I won't." My nipples stiffened. "Don't stop. Please."

He slid his hands up my sides then began to unbutton my blouse before practically ripping it off of me and tossing it aside.

My cheek was pressed gently against the wall as he slowly kissed a line down my back.

His hands moved to my waist, where he pulled the fabric of my skirt down just low enough to see the tattoo on my lower back.

I closed my eyes and waited. Ten seconds felt like a minute.

Then, I felt his lips tenderly kissing the area of my skin where the lotus flower was inked. He gripped my hips and continued to kiss over my tattoo, grazing me with his tongue. Having his mouth on my body was making me so incredibly wet with an urgent need to feel him inside of me.

Suddenly, I felt my underwear sliding down.

"They're so freaking wet," he muttered. "I need to taste it."

This time, when he resumed his worship of that spot on my back, he kissed lower and lower before spreading my ass cheeks. Without warning. I felt his hot mouth between my legs, under me, devouring my pussy from behind. Kneeling, he continued to take ownership of my body in a way I'd never experienced before. It was seriously like a symphony of movements and sounds: his tongue thrusting in and out of me with rhythmic precision in sync with the motion of his mouth while he worked his fingertips over my clit. And fuck me...he was hitting *all* the right notes. Nothing had ever felt this good. *Nothing.*

He flipped me around and gazed up at me with hazy eyes that reflected the highest threshold of hunger and desire. Returning his mouth to my swollen clit, he began to suck on my clit with renewed enthusiasm. His sexy moan vibrated between my thighs. No one else had ever seemed to take such pleasure in going down on me.

As my fingers raked harder through his hair, he must have sensed I was about to lose control. He suddenly stopped and slowly stood up. "I want to feel you come against my mouth, but I'd rather you come with me inside of you." Placing his forehead against mine, he said, "Remember all those things you wished I could do to you? I'm about to make all your wishes come true if you let me."

"I've wanted you for so long," I whispered, unable to contain the desperation in my voice.

Mack's hair was a mess. His shirt was still damp from earlier and clinging to his chest. When I looked down and saw his hard cock straining through his jeans,

I couldn't help but place my palm against the heat of his erection. He hissed at the contact then removed my hand before pulling me into a firm embrace. The muscles in my back nearly cracked. I realized in that moment how strong Mack was, and I wanted nothing more than to feel all of his weight on top of me, to let him ravage my body. I desperately needed him to fuck me.

His eyes were penetrating as he slowly lifted the wet T-shirt off of his perfect body. I could have watched that over and over again.

I licked my lips at the sight of his sculpted chest in the flesh. It had been a long time since I'd seen him completely shirtless. He had even more definition now and a true six-pack. To this day, I still felt undeserving of this beautiful man.

Running my palm in a line down his chest to the happy trail of hair at the base of his abs, I whispered, "I love your body."

"You're all it needs right now."

He unsnapped my bra from the front, letting it fall. His chest was rising and falling as he stared down at my breasts before leaning in to suck on my nipples one by one. He was sucking so hard that I knew it would hurt tomorrow; but I didn't care. The harder, the more painful, the more intense...the better.

I pulled away from him. He thought it was because I was uncomfortable.

"Am I hurting you?" he asked.

"No." Without further explanation, I dropped to my knees.

He got the picture fast and didn't hesitate to facilitate. Mack unzipped his jeans and took his beautifully thick cock out.

Wrapping both of my hands around it, I marveled at the hot, veiny, shaft before slowly swirling my tongue around his crown. Tasting the salty arousal as he throbbed in my mouth was probably the single biggest turn-on of my life. I circled my tongue faster around his tip before lowering my mouth down over almost the entire length. Feeling him at the back of my throat, I intentionally moaned so he could feel it.

"Fuck. Are you trying to kill me?" he rasped.

I began to take him faster, rubbing the precum all over his dick with my hand. The sounds of pleasure coming from him made me want to suck him completely dry.

He bent his head back, willfully taking everything I had to give. "You're amazing at this. Best fucking head ever," he said before suddenly pulling my hair. "But you need to stop."

Grabbing my hand, he lifted me up and led me over to his bed before pinning me down and hovering over me on all fours. His silky sheets, which were covered in the scent of his cologne, felt smooth under my bare ass. The anticipation of finally getting to feel him inside of me caused the muscles between my legs to contract.

"You tell me if I'm hurting you, okay?" he said as he spread my legs apart wide. Those were the last words spoken before he lowered his body down and slowly pushed inside of me. The girth of his cock stretched me until he was balls deep. What started out as almost painful eased into a fast and intense rhythm.

"I love you." His words were soft in my ear, almost apologetic, considering the forceful way he was rocking into me. I couldn't get enough. At one point, I started to buck my hips, and he stopped his own movement in order to feel me riding him from underneath his body. "Fuck, that feels good," he groaned before he resumed pounding into me hard.

Mack wrapped my legs around his back so he could go even deeper as he fucked me. The bed was creaking. His balls slapped against my ass as he hit all of the right angles, making it so hard not to come. I didn't want it to end. Sweat was pouring off of us as our eyes stayed glued to one another. We were connected in both mind and body in that moment. It amazed me how sex with him could feel so primal—animalistic—and yet it was still the most tender, emotional experience of my life.

As I dug into his muscular back with my nails, grasping onto him for dear life, I knew that no other man would ever satisfy me again. No other man *had* satisfied me in this way. I was more certain than ever that Mack was the only one for me. There was no way this feeling could ever be replicated...because it had been years in the making.

His pace became more frantic, matched by his ragged breathing. I knew he was going to come.

"Look at me, Frankie. Look at me, and tell me when you want me to come inside of you. I'm gonna come so hard. I want you to feel every bit of what you do to me."

When I felt myself climaxing, I couldn't find the words to say it. My eyes simply rolled to the back of my head. But he knew. His body then came crashing down in a series of thunderous thrusts as his orgasm tore through both of us, his warm cum shooting inside of me.

Mack swore as he came. "Oh, fuck...fuck...fuck... yes...fuck." It seemed to last a long time, his hips moving in and out as he savored his orgasm. He eventually collapsed on top of me. "Excuse my language...but fuck!"

"Fuck, yes." I panted and laughed, trying to catch my breath. "Please tell me we can do that again."

"Best sex of my damn life. Screw that. Single. Best. Moment."

"Are you serious?"

He smiled. "Yeah. I swear on my life. That right there was it. Took thirty years, but it *was* the single best moment. Bar none."

Closing my eyes, I pondered that. "Mine, too," I said, honestly.

He ravaged me with a kiss then said, "Good to know you're not allergic to me anymore, Frankie Jane."

"Well...your injection worked." I laughed.

When he slowly withdrew from me, it was like a gravitational pull had been unnaturally interrupted. I felt empty, immediately wanting to be filled again. He wrapped his palms around my face and devoured my lips.

"My beautiful, quirky, girl. I can't believe I finally had you. Do you have any idea how long I've dreamt of this?" He kissed me long and hard again before he said, "Now, I can fucking die in peace."

"Please don't die on me now. Things are just getting good."

"Not a chance. I need to live to be able to do that to you again many times over. You're stuck with me."

Hands interlocked, we lay in a blissful state for several minutes before loud banging shook us to our core.

I jumped up. "What's that?"

"I don't know. Stay here." Mack threw his jeans on before bolting out of the room.

Wrapping my naked body in his comforter, I nervously waited.

That was when I heard a woman's voice say, "Jonah, go back into the car right now, please."

Torrie.

Oh, no.

No!

A rush of adrenaline hit me. I hopped up and began frantically putting my clothes back on. I could feel his cum dripping down my thigh as I hid inside the closet and listened to every word of their altercation

"I told you I was going to pick him up later."

"Yeah, well, he wanted to come back. Whose car is that parked in your driveway, Mack?"

"That's none of your concern. Please take Jonah back to your place, and I'll come get him soon."

"Who's here? Who are you fucking?"

Please, Jesus. Make her leave.

Then, I heard her say, "That scarf on the ground. That looks like the same one Jonah's teacher had on."

"Torrie, you need to leave."

"Where is she?"

Footsteps approached. I could hear Mack frantically trying to stop her.

"Don't touch me!" she spewed.

The bedroom door burst open, banging against the wall.

She slid the closet open next. Torrie's eyes were filled with venom as we came face to face. My chest was rising and falling. I had no words. I could only imagine how this looked to her, given that she had no inkling of our history.

Mack braced for her reaction. I knew I should have said something, but the words wouldn't come.

She was shaking in anger. "Isn't your son already fucked-up as it is? This is what you do to him? Fuck his teacher? You're a despicable human being."

Despite the seriousness of this, Mack remained relatively calm. "No, Torrie. There's a lot more than you think you know going on here, and we need to talk about it."

She pointed her index finger at me. "As for you, I'll be reporting you to school officials tomorrow."

I wanted to cry, but the tears wouldn't come.

No.

"You don't understand," Mack said.

"Oh, I understand just fine, and you're gonna pay for this. Don't even think about picking up your son tonight."

"You can't do that!"

"I can do a lot more than that. Believe me."

Torrie ran out of the house, and the next sound was that of her tires screeching.

Finally unleashing the tears I'd been holding back, I said, "What do we do now?"

"I'm not gonna let her go to the school. I need to go over there tonight and explain everything."

"I'll lose my job, Mack. St. Matthew's has a strict anti-fraternization policy that prohibits any kind of relationship between faculty and parents. She goes to them, and I'm toast. But honestly, I'm more concerned about Jonah finding out about this than anything else."

"I'll talk to him, too. He already knows we knew each other. But I want him to the know the full truth." He pulled me into his chest. His heart was pounding against mine when he spoke into my hair, "I'm gonna fix this, Frankie. I promise."

The evening only got worse as I returned to Victor's brownstone. Not that I should have expected anything to the contrary, considering I hadn't even contacted him all day, and it was now nightfall. I knew I would be breaking up with him tonight and suspected he already knew that. In an effort to avoid the inevitable confrontation, I'd driven around for hours.

As soon as I walked in the door, he took one look at me and nipped any plans I had of explaining myself in the bud. Feeling like a teenager who'd gotten caught sneaking out of the house, I was sure I reeked of sex and guilt.

"You don't have to say it, Francesca. I know you. I know what's happening here. Just spare me the agony, okay?"

"I'm so sorry, Victor."

Without looking at me, he said, "You can stay as long as you need to find a new place and figure out how to move your things. I've made up the guest room upstairs for you. There's plenty of room here to give us space from each other."

"Victor..."

He cut me off. "Please...there really is nothing left to explain. I don't want to hear how you'll always love me, how you never expected this, how you never meant to hurt me. It is what it is. I've been hurt before, and I survived. I'll be okay. I'd like to end this with some dignity. Maybe I can at least convince myself I had some control over it."

Fair enough.

"Okay..."

Choosing to respect his wishes, I had no energy to argue with him on that anyway—not after this day. His letting me stay in his house was beyond gracious.

Sleep evaded me that night. As I tossed and turned, a text from Mack came in shortly after midnight. I reached for my phone on the nightstand.

Mack: Are you awake?

Francesca: What happened? I've been waiting to hear from you.

Mack: I'm sorry. I've been at Torrie's all night. I told her everything.

Francesca: What do you mean by everything?

Mack: Can I call you?

Francesca: Yes.

My phone buzzed, and I answered it.

"Hi."

"So, I was brutally honest," he said. "I told her that I've been in love with you for years. She needed to know that I didn't risk my son's well-being for some tawdry affair. I'm done living a dishonest life. Fucking done, Frankie."

"Did Jonah overhear any of this?"

"I'm pretty sure he might have, even though he was in his room playing with his videogames. I have to have another talk with him separately. I promised her I wouldn't mention anything to him about you yet."

"What now? Where do we go from here?"

"Where are you?"

"I'm at Victor's. He ended it."

"*He* ended it?"

"I was going to tell him everything as soon as I got home. But he already deduced what I was going to say. Not to mention, I'm pretty sure what happened between us was written all over my face. He's set me up in a bedroom on the second floor until I can find another place. It seriously feels surreal."

"You're not staying there. Come home. I want you to live with me."

"It's really late. And honestly, I don't think that's a good idea because of Jonah. I can't move in with you yet."

He sighed into the phone. "I guess you're right, but I really don't want you with Victor. I'll pay for a hotel if you leave sooner."

"I promise it will be soon. I'll start looking for a place tomorrow."

He changed topics. "Listen, I got her to agree not to go to school officials."

"How did you do that?"

"She's pulling him out of St. Matthew's. It was either that, or she was going to report you. Agreeing to take him out of your school was the lesser of the evils."

I felt so badly for Jonah.

"That's not in his best interest."

"I realize that, but Frankie, he'll be fine. You need that job, and you're damn good at what you do. It's the only choice right now. She's pissed and capable of making serious trouble for you."

"Where's he gonna go to school?"

"I'm not sure yet. He might be home for a couple of weeks. But I'll make it my priority to find a good placement for him. Don't worry about that."

"This is like the worst day of my life," I muttered.

"Really? Because I'm still certain it was the best day of mine."

"How can you still mean that after what happened?"

"Because I'm free. I don't have to hide anything anymore. I don't have to pretend that the woman who matters to me more than any other doesn't exist. But mostly, it was the best day of my life because I finally made love to the girl of my dreams."

"That really happened, didn't it?"

"It did. Nothing and no one can take that away from us. It was fucking amazing. I can still practically taste you. I need more, Frankie. I'm sitting here in bed like a fucking animal in heat. Please let me come get you. I want you in my bed tonight."

"Believe me, I want to, but I can't. I think I need to face Victor in the morning and try to talk it out a little, even though he told me he'd rather not."

"Okay. I guess you owe him that. I should try to be more understanding, but I'm selfish when it comes to you. Promise me I'll get to see you tomorrow night."

"I promise."

"Seriously, I should be so upset after everything that went down today, but I just can't be. I'm delirious. I can still smell you all over my sheets. It's heaven."

"I can still feel you between my legs."

"That was what you wanted."

"It was way better than I ever imagined, though."

"Things are gonna be shitty for a while, Frankie, but there's nothing that can wipe this damn smile off my face."

CHAPTER EIGHTEEN

Mack

I should've known she wasn't going to let me off that easy. Being happy without my entire world turning upside down soon after was apparently too much to ask.

A few days after Torrie caught Frankie and me together, I showed up at my ex's place to find her standing outside with a realtor. A vinyl sign had been planted into her front lawn.

Jonah was out of school. He was supposed to be starting in the public school system the following week until we could find him a suitable private school fairly close to her house. At least, I'd thought that was supposed to be the plan.

"What's going on, Torrie? Where's Jonah?"

"The sitter took him to Target." She spoke to the agent, "Can you excuse us?"

As soon as we stepped inside of the house for privacy, Torrie dropped her bomb. "I'm putting my house on the market."

"Why?"

"I've requested to be let out of my contract."

"I don't understand."

"Okay, let me spell it out for you. My life has been miserable ever since moving to Boston. And after what I discovered about you, it's even worse. I don't want to be here anymore. So, we're moving back to D.C."

"When exactly were you gonna tell me that you're planning on leaving with my son?" I yelled it, not giving a shit if the realtor overheard.

"It's in his best interest. He was never happy here. And quite honestly, you didn't show me any respect when you started fucking his teacher, so why should I consult you on this? *You* clearly don't have his best interests in mind."

Fisting my hands, I tried to compose myself before I did something stupid— like trash her house. Taking a deep breath, I said, "I get that you're upset that I never told you about her, but you can't take it out on our son."

"I'm doing what's best for Jonah. He doesn't need to see you with her. Now I know why you were so gung ho about moving to Boston. I should've known it had nothing to do with us."

"Seeing me with her is not going to disturb him. Jonah knows about my friendship with Frankie. I'll explain it to him properly. She won't even be his teacher anymore."

"That doesn't matter. She's the entire reason for the demise of his parents' relationship."

"That's not true."

"You told me yourself that you were in love with her even as far back as when Jonah was conceived. I never stood a chance. You were probably thinking of her while you were fucking me back then."

Now was definitely not the time to admit that she was right about that.

"She's not the cause of the demise of our relationship, and you know it. If it weren't for Jonah, we wouldn't have lasted as long as we did. We tried, Torrie, but it was never going to work out between us."

"I tried. You didn't."

"I *did* try...for over seven years."

"The seven-year itch. Just wonderful. You'd told me once that you never really loved me. Now, I know why." Her stare was icy. "If you'll excuse me, I need to get back to the realtor."

Following her out the door, I shouted, "You're not going anywhere until we settle this. This is a reckless decision. Do you even have a job lined up?"

"I'll be working for your father again."

I should've known.

I stopped in my tracks. "You told him about this?"

"Yes. I told him everything."

"It's none of his fucking business, Torrie."

"You *are* his business. And I needed to know I had a position lined up before leaving this one. I had to tell him why I felt the need to come home to D.C. It made no sense otherwise. Needless to say, he's not happy."

"Please don't do this."

"Why? Because you don't want to leave your girlfriend? Stay here, then. No one is stopping you."

"You know I can't live away from Jonah. That's why you're doing this. You're doing it to spite me because you're blaming her for what happened with us."

"I'm moving home with my son. If you have a problem with that, I suggest you get a lawyer."

Feeling completely deflated, I drove straight over to St. Matthew's. I remembered that Frankie mentioned she'd be working late.

When I showed up to her room, she looked concerned to see me there at that time of day. "What are you doing here?"

"I needed to see you."

"Is everything okay?"

"No. No, it's not."

She pulled me into the room. "Come. I don't want anyone to see you." She then led me into a supply closet that was right off of her classroom before locking the door. "What happened?"

"She's taking him back to Virginia."

"What?"

"Yeah. She's taking her old job back...working for my father. They'll be gone in a matter of days."

"Can you stop her?"

"No. Unfortunately, I can't do anything legally to stop her." I took both of her hands in mine. "I always knew that this would happen eventually...that she would move back and that I would have to go, but I expected a couple of years here at the very least."

Fear filled her eyes. "What does this mean?"

"It means I have to leave, too."

"I don't get it. She pulled a total one-eighty. I thought you said Jonah was enrolling in the Newton Public Schools."

"She basically lied about that, probably so I would let my guard down. Now she doesn't even want him to start school until they get back down to Virginia. She's not waiting until the house here sells. She's leaving with him in the next week."

Frankie looked like she was starting to panic. "What about your house?"

"I'll have to put it on the market, even though it pains me to do it."

"Oh, my God." She squeezed my hands, which were still enveloping hers. "How is Jonah taking it?"

"Well, that's the thing. He's happy. Jonah never wanted to be here. He's close to Torrie's mother and my sister, and I don't have any doubt that he'll actually be much happier there."

She nodded silently. Lost in thought, Frankie looked down for a moment then said, "We can still make it work."

"You mean that?"

"Virginia is not that far away. We'll figure something out."

Squeezing her hands tighter, I said, "I don't want to be away from you again. This fucking feels like déjà vu."

"It does."

"Tell me what to do, and I'll do it, Frankie. Tell me how we can make this work."

"I want to finish out the school year here, but maybe I can start looking into my teaching certification out there in the meantime."

Hope seemed to rise from the ashes inside of me.

"You'd do that? You'd really move for me?"

"How else are we gonna be together?"

She'd said it as if long-term separation wasn't even an option. The fact that she would not only relocate for me, but that she would accept me with all of my baggage made me love her even more. Even though it should have been obvious, it was the first time it really hit me that she'd made her choice.

She'd chosen me.

I took her face in my hands and kissed her so hard before whispering over her lips, "I don't want to leave you."

"I'm here now," she whispered back before wrapping her arms around my neck and pressing her body into me.

It was as if a switch went off inside of me, one that made me forget where I even was. We became lost in our kiss. Neither of us seemed to care that we were technically still in her classroom, albeit locked in a closet.

Lifting her skirt, I flipped her around and unzipped my pants. My cock was fully erect and throbbing. I slid her panties down and couldn't enter her quickly enough. I sunk into her, marveling at how wet and ready for me she was.

Slow movements in and out quickly turned fast and frantic.

I lowered my hands to her waist and fucked her desperately, unsure if this would be the last chance I would have to be inside of her for a while. Her pussy wrapped around my dick felt hotter and wetter with each thrust.

I could have come anytime but willed myself to hold off because it felt so damn good. Her low whimpers of pleasure only egged me on even more. There was also that slight thrill of possibly getting caught, although I sure as hell hoped that wouldn't actually happen.

Lifting her skirt up farther, I focused on the blue lotus flower on her lower back, which ignited a feeling of possession. My gaze then travelled down even lower. There was nothing hotter than this view, being able to watch myself moving in and out of her.

The sight of her wet arousal all over my dick caused me to lose control fast.

She moved her ass faster until I could feel her orgasm shudder against me. "Shit." I slammed into her harder, tightly shutting my eyes as I shot my load and filled her with my cum until there was nothing left.

My movements slowed to a halt as I softly kissed her neck. My greatest desire was just to be able to end every single day this way. I knew it would be a while before that wish was granted.

Tucking my shirt back in, I grabbed some paper towels and handed them to her. She turned around to face me. Frankie's hair was all messed up, and her face was pink. She looked thoroughly fucked, and the fact that I was the one who caused it was enough to make me want to fuck her all over again.

Needing to taste her lips one more time, I bore my mouth down onto hers before saying, "The next few weeks aren't going to be easy."

"We'll get through it."

"I need to be down in Virginia, making sure she's not manipulating things or feeding him false information. Not to mention, I have to once again find a place to live."

"We both need to work on getting our lives in order. You do what you need to for Jonah. That's the priority. In the meantime, I'll focus on moving out of Victor's and finding a place of my own."

"I hate the idea of you still living with him. It seriously drives me mad."

"It's been okay. We've been cordial. I really don't see him much, since he's mostly on a totally different floor. I'll be out soon."

"If I wasn't leaving, I would be moving your shit into my house myself."

"I'm a big girl. I can handle things."

Those words would come back to haunt her.

I couldn't shake the bad feeling that followed me all the way back to Virginia. Soon, I'd realize it was warranted.

It shouldn't have surprised me that my father would be at the root of it all.

Two weeks later, I was moving into an apartment I'd rented in Alexandria just outside of D.C.

It was small and cold, but it would have to do, because I didn't plan on buying a new house until the property in Massachusetts sold. Winter was tough for the housing market. Patience was going to be necessary until it picked up in the spring.

One of the hardest parts of leaving the Boston area was having to move away from Mrs. Migillicutty. She'd come to depend on me for certain things, and I'd come to depend on her sound advice. We made a pact to keep in touch over the phone, and I promised to visit her whenever I came back to see Frankie. But saying goodbye sucked. I would have lived in that house next to her forever if I could have.

Now, surrounded by boxes in my new place, I cracked open a bottle of beer and sat down for the first time in hours after a long day of moving.

Exhausted, the last thing I wanted was to hear a knock at the door.

When I opened it, my father was standing there, dressed in a three-piece suit, and holding a large envelope.

"What are you doing here?"

"That's not exactly a warm welcome, son," he said as he moved past me, barging his way into my apartment.

"Well, it's been a long day. I can do without an interrogation. You should've called first."

"I have something important to talk to you about, and it couldn't wait."

"Why can't it wait?"

He took a seat. "You know I'm very fond of Torrie. She's worked extremely hard for me, and I've never understood why you've chosen to abandon her and your son."

"I don't have to justify anything to you. I'm a better father to Jonah than you ever were to me. I'm present in his life, at least. In no way have I abandoned him. I don't appreciate you walking in here and judging me in my own house."

He looked around. "This is supposed to be a house?"

"It's temporary."

"Torrie told me about this other woman—Francesca O'Hara. It pains me to see the mother of your child so upset and feeling betrayed."

"You don't need to know anything about Frankie. It's none of your concern."

"Frankie?" He furrowed his brow. "Cute name. Anyway, I'm afraid Torrie and my grandson *are* my business. So, I do need to know about anything that destroys their happiness. When someone comes along and disrupts my family structure, hurts the people who are important to me, it does matter greatly to me."

"Since when is your family important to you? You're just getting involved in this to fuck with me because you're disappointed that you can't control me anymore. And Frankie's done nothing to hurt anyone. My relationship with Torrie wouldn't have lasted. My happiness with someone else is none of anyone's concern."

"You think you really know this woman? You've turned your entire life upside down for someone you know nothing about."

"Not that it's any of your business, but I know everything there is to know about her. She's a kind, beautiful human being and a phenomenal teacher. And I knew her years before any of you ever found out about her."

"What if I told you that I have proof that you have no real clue whom you've been getting involved with all of this time?"

Anger was penetrating my bones. "What the hell are you talking about?"

"I did a little research on her."

That was code for a thorough investigation.

"You had no right to do that."

I seriously wanted to injure my own father. His connections meant that he could get access to almost anyone's most personal information very easily. I knew he was full of shit, though. There was absolutely nothing he could have dug up on Frankie that would have come as a surprise to me. But the very fact that he even tried to do that was disturbing, to say the least.

"You might want to take a look at this." He handed me a manila envelope.

I snatched it and looked inside, finding a series of articles from a Philadelphia newspaper. The dates were all from the 1990s. One headline read: *Freddie Higgins Charged in McCabe Murder*.

"What the fuck is this? What does it have to do with her?"

"It's your girlfriend's family album."

I sat down, staring at the papers. "What are you talking about?"

"Francesca O'Hara is the illegitimate child of Karen O'Hara and Freddie Higgins, a convicted felon currently serving life in a Philadelphia penitentiary for murder."

"Frankie doesn't know who her father is. She doesn't even know his name."

"There's a copy of her birth certificate there as well. You can see Frederick Higgins is listed."

"She was born in Boston not Philly. How do you know this is the same Francesca O'Hara? There are probably many people with that name."

"Do you really need to question my ability to verify information, Mackenzie? You know I have my ways. This has been authenticated by multiple sources. I can tell you everything you need to know about this girl, whom you've thrown away your family for. She currently lives on Cambridge Street in Boston, went to South Boston High School, graduated from Boston University. What else do you want to know? I'll tell you."

Filled with dread, I now suspected that there could be truth to this; I just didn't want to believe it.

"Okay, so what if this guy is her actual birth father? She's had nothing to do with him. What's your point? What are you gonna do?"

"I'll do nothing if you do the right thing, do right by your family. This will stay between us."

"You're blackmailing me?"

"If you continue to see her, continue to live your life separately from your family, this could go public—that you're dating the daughter of a reputed mobster. He's a convicted murderer, Mack. These people are dangerous."

"You're lying. You wouldn't let this get out. You wouldn't allow something like this to come out and ruin your precious reputation."

"You're missing the point. It's not my reputation that would be at stake if this came out. It's Frankie's life. Do you realize how many people Freddie Higgins must have pissed off? Karen O'Hara had to flee Pennsylvania with her family to protect, not only them, but the life of her newborn child. I don't think you want to take the risk of this getting out. If these people find out that he has a daughter and figure out her whereabouts, she immediately becomes a target. The crime family of Freddie's victim is still very much active today. It's a huge criminal network, spanning from southern New Jersey to northern Philly. In fact, it's larger today than it was back then. You talk to anyone on the streets there, and they know who Freddie Higgins and Timothy McCabe are. All the information is in that envelope. I wish I could say I was making it up, but I'm not." He pointed his finger at me. "No one will find out about her connection to Higgins if you stop seeing her and focus on your family."

"That's not an option."

"Then, I do nothing to protect this information."

"Boy...I always knew you didn't really give two shits about my well-being, but out of all of the nasty things you've ever said or done, this has got to be the lowest."

"Sorry to be the bearer of bad news, Mackenzie. I didn't bring this into our lives. You did. So, I'll let you figure out how you'd like to handle it."

After my father left, the panic started to really set in. Speechless, I just sat in my kitchen for an indeterminate amount of time. I had no idea what to do. I couldn't keep this information from Frankie, but at the same time, I felt the need to protect her from it all. I didn't know if I believed that my father would actually go public with it. It could have been an empty threat, but there was no way to be certain.

On one hand, he was far too vain to let something like this tarnish his reputation. On the other hand, if he didn't go public with it, he could've still let dangerous people know her whereabouts.

Aside from the day I found out Torrie was pregnant, I'd never felt more helpless in my life. I couldn't even ask anyone for advice, since I didn't want a single soul to know about this.

Paralyzed by shock, I was still sitting in the same spot in my kitchen nearly an hour later. The only difference was that the small amount of daylight that had been peeking through the window was now replaced by sheer darkness.

When my phone rang, I picked it up, not knowing how to react to her.

"Hi, Frankie."

"Are you okay?" It amazed me that she could sense that something was off, even though I'd only said two words.

"This move back has been tougher than I thought. I miss you."

"I miss you, too. I went to visit Mrs. M. today."

"You did?"

"Yeah. I know you can't look out for her anymore. So, I stopped by to see if she needed anything."

"Thank you. That was really nice of you. I appreciate it."

"She sends you her love and a virtual rum and Coke."

I thought my life had been difficult before. I would've given anything to just go back a month or two, lamenting to Mrs. M. about getting Frankie back. Anything was better than the current dilemma.

"I keep fantasizing about our time in the supply closet," Frankie said.

I closed my eyes. I would've given anything to go back to *that* moment in time right now, too.

"I've been holding onto that," I said. "And holding onto myself for that matter." I'd tried to joke around so she wouldn't suspect something was seriously off with me.

"Not for long. I was thinking of coming there next weekend."

Oh, shit.

"Really?"

"Is that not gonna work?"

"Believe me, I want to see you more than anything. I just want to make sure I'm prepared. This apartment is not very homey."

"It'll feel like the old days. Is there a dingy basement where we could do laundry?"

"Actually, I don't even have a washing machine in this temporary housing. I will have to go to the laundromat."

"We can go together."

I couldn't tell her not to come.

"It doesn't matter where we are. As long as I'm with you, that's all that matters, Frankie."

"Soon. Okay?"

After we hung up, the sickness in my stomach kicked in. I knew I couldn't keep the information about her father from her. I'd promised myself I would tell her in person the next chance I got. Unfortunately, that day would be coming faster than I was ready for.

CHAPTER NINETEEN

Francesca

My flight was booked for my weekend trip to D.C., and I was going to see an apartment after work tomorrow. Things were finally moving forward.

Amazingly, Victor and I were getting along pretty well. He'd begun joining me for breakfast again in the mornings. We kept our separate ways at the end of each day overall, but it was comforting to know we weren't going to be ending things on horrible terms. We were speaking, at least.

Wednesday evening, Vic and I crossed paths when he walked in the door from work. I was in the kitchen about to make some tea.

"You got a FedEx package," he said.

"Really? I didn't see it on the way in."

"Sometimes they deliver late in the day. They must have just left it at the door."

"Thank you," I said, taking the package from him.

Included in the envelope was a letter and a series of Xeroxed newspaper articles. The letterhead said *From the Office of Senator Michael J. Morrison* at the top. My heart began to palpitate.

Dear Francesca,

My reason for writing you is two-fold. As Senator Morrison gears up for re-election and the possibility of a future run for president, it's my job as one of his top advisers to see to the well-being of his career, in addition the well-being of his family—which happens to also be my family. Given your inappropriate relationship with the father of my child, as due practice, it's extremely important that we fully investigate any associates of Senator Morrison or any associates of the Morrison family.

A thorough investigation into your birth records and family history has uncovered a troubling finding regarding the identity of your father.

You are the only child of Frederick Higgins, an inmate currently serving a life sentence for extortion, narcotics, illegal gambling, murder, and conspiracy to commit murder. He was a member of Philadelphia's Irish mob. Your mother, Karen O'Hara, fled Philadelphia shortly after you were born. Included in this package is a copy of your birth certificate with Frederick Higgins named as the father. Also included are numerous press articles in regards to his trial and subsequent conviction.

This information is troubling to me on many levels, namely the fact that if your identity ever becomes known publicly, there is a very serious chance that you could be in danger. This in turn would put my family in danger so long as you are associating with Mackenzie.

While Senator Morrison has no intention of bringing this news to light, he cannot control what information his political rivals may uncover. It didn't take much for us to dig up this information, which disturbing as it may be, is par for the course in this day and age. It therefore wouldn't take long for someone else to uncover it, as well. When that happens, it will not only put your life in danger, but the lives of my loved ones, including my son. And I cannot stand for that.

Mackenzie has known about the identity of your father for several days now. I'm sure he, too, is weighing what this means for his relationship with you in the long-term. I trust he will eventually draw the right conclusion, one that will be in the best interest of his child.

Do what you may with this information. But if you care for Mackenzie or care at all for my son, I hope you make the right decision.

Sincerely,

Torrie Hightower

My head was throbbing so hard, and my vision felt blurry. I could barely make out the sound of Victor's voice.

He sounded muffled, as if he were talking through a cup even though he was right in front of me. "Francesca, what's wrong?"

My hands were shaking as I handed him the letter.

After reading it and sifting through the articles, he pulled me into his arms and held onto me tightly.

"It's going to be okay."

"I can't breathe," I said, practically wheezing.

"Try. Try to breathe. We're gonna handle this. We'll confirm whether it's true. And if it is, we will deal with it."

Too afraid to see my supposed father's face, I hadn't even been able to look at the newspaper clippings.

"First step...we need to get your mother over here. Only she can confirm what's true and what's not."

"I can't face her right now."

"You have to, Francesca. Will you be able to sleep tonight if you don't?

Letting out a long, shaky breath, I said, "Probably not."

"I'm going to call her. Okay? Can I do that? I won't divulge the reason...just that we need her to come by, to discuss something with her."

Hanging onto a chair for balance, I nodded. "Yes."

Victor retreated to the den to call my mother. I couldn't fathom the possibility that the person I had trusted most in this world had lied to me all these years. This news was just devastating on so many different levels.

After Victor returned to the kitchen, he came up behind me and massaged my shoulders slowly. "Take a deep breath. I'm gonna make you some tea. I want you to drink it down and try to clear your mind until she gets here."

Vic went over to the stove to boil water and prepared two steaming mugs.

He then sat with me as we drank the tea in silence while he rubbed my back.

"If you can't speak, I'll do the talking for you, okay?" he said, reaching over and taking my hand in his.

It was the first time tears started to fill my eyes. The fact that after everything I'd done, Victor was so comforting to me touched me beyond words. I didn't know what I would have done if I were alone when that envelope arrived. His being there for me was like being thrown a life raft after getting suddenly tossed overboard.

When the doorbell rang, I jumped. Victor placed his hand on my shoulder. "You stay here. I'll let her in."

My mother's dark hair looked windblown, and her nose was red from the cold. She was wearing her typical bright, neon pink lipstick. I knew she had no clue why we'd called her here. She was probably even more confused by the fact that Victor was involved when we were supposedly broken up.

"What's going on? Why have you been crying?" She approached me. "Are you pregnant?"

"Please sit, Karen," Victor said.

He handed my mother the envelope, the contents of which said it all.

Her lips quivered as she closed her eyes and collapsed down onto one of our kitchen chairs. "Oh, God," she whispered, covering her mouth and repeated, "Oh, my God."

My body was starting to tremble. "So, it's true?"

She just kept nodding for a while before she finally said, "Yes."

Tears were now pouring down my cheeks in a steady flow. "How could you have kept this from me?"

"There's so much to explain, Francesca. But please know...it's all been to protect you. I don't even know where to begin."

"You can start from the beginning," I cried.

Victor put his arm around me for support as my mother began to speak.

"I know I've led you to believe that you were born in Boston, that my family is from here, but I actually grew up in a section of Philadelphia called Kensington. My grandfather, Patrick, was involved in the local Irish mob."

She rubbed her eyes and continued, "When I met Freddie, he was one of your granddad's acquaintances. He was much younger and better looking than most of the men who'd come around, but he was older than me by five years. I was seventeen. He was twenty-two. He really wanted to change, get out of the mob, but he was in too deep. It was the only world he'd ever known. I do believe that deep down he was a good person, but he got caught up in it with no way out. He was forced to do some terrible things."

I just shook my head and muttered, "I can't believe this."

She went on. "His own life would've been on the line if he didn't adhere to what he was told to do. That didn't make it right, but that was the way it was. I almost didn't tell him I was pregnant, but I couldn't live with the guilt. He wanted to be a part of your life, but by the time you were born, it was just too dangerous. Someone would have killed us—you and me. My parents did what they felt they had to. They moved to Boston and took us with them. We were lucky that no one had really caught on to my pregnancy. No one ever followed us to Boston. Freddie didn't tell anyone about you being born because he knew that it would put you in danger.

I chose not to tell you who your father was for your own safety. I was afraid you'd go against me someday and try to see him. Even though he's in jail, those people have ways of finding certain things out. There are a lot of informants in prison. So, telling you was just too big of a risk because if anyone were to know about you, they could try to come after you to get back at Freddie."

"So, my father is alive. He's in prison. Have you ever contacted him?"

"No, I haven't. He's in jail, but if he weren't, he'd be dead, Francesca. It's actually a good thing he's in there. There are still people out there to this day looking to enact revenge in some way for what Freddie and his partners did."

"You could've told me. I would've heeded your advice and stayed away. But I've spent my entire life thinking that my father was some standup person who simply wanted nothing to do with me. That's not exactly the case."

"I know. And I've felt extremely guilty about that. It was always the worst part of keeping this from you. I still feel like it was the only choice I had."

Feeling utterly floored, I said, "I honestly don't even know where to go from here. I think I'm just still in shock."

"I always knew there was a chance that you could find out, but never did I imagine it would happen in such a horrible way. These people should be ashamed of themselves for putting you in this position. Have you talked to Mack? Does he know about this package?"

"I only got this a couple of hours ago. I was supposed to fly to D.C. this weekend. I don't know exactly what he knows."

Victor interrupted, "I don't want you going anywhere near there. Anyone who would put you in this kind of position is pure evil. This woman is blackmailing you and putting everyone else involved in danger."

I turned to my mother. "Not only am I grappling with the fact that you've kept this from me all of these years, but I can't believe that Mack knew about this and didn't tell me."

"Well, I'm sure he probably didn't know how to go about it."

"I really think you should consider cancelling your trip," Victor said.

Looking down at one of the newspaper articles, I allowed myself to see what he looked like for the first time. Although the ink was black and white, I could tell he had red hair like me. We had the same small pudgy nose and bone structure. There was no doubt.

"I do look like him."

"That part was never a lie," my mother admitted.

"I need some time alone. I'm gonna take all of this upstairs and read every word in private."

"Please promise me you'll call me when you're ready to talk about it again. I need you to work on forgiving me."

It hurt my brain to even think about how to go about doing that. "I understand why you thought you were doing the right thing. It's just going to take me a lot of time to absorb this."

"Okay." My mother wiped tears from her eyes. "I understand. I love you, honey. Take all the time you need."

After an hour alone sifting through all of the contents of that envelope, I decided that I couldn't face Mack this weekend. I couldn't bear to see him, knowing that he knew about this and didn't tell me. At the same time, a part of me felt like it needed him more than ever.

When my phone rang and I saw that it was him, I debated whether or not to even pick up before I finally answered.

"Mack..."

"I've called you twice." He sounded upset. "How come you didn't call me back?"

"I'm sorry. I haven't been feeling well."

"No need to apologize. I just wanted to hear your voice, make sure everything was okay."

"I don't think I'm going to be able to come this weekend."

"Are you serious? I really needed to see you."

"I'm sorry." I kept my words to a minimum because I didn't know how to hide how upset I was.

Simply unable to pretend that I wasn't devastated, I ended up cutting the phone call short. I couldn't get over the fact that—at least according to Torrie—he knew about my father and still hadn't mentioned anything.

The rest of that week had flown by in a fog. I'd gone through the motions at school, barely getting by.

Still unable to deal with talking to my mother, I'd spent most of my time in my room at Victor's. He was being a true friend, joining me for dinners and offering his ear but not forcing me to talk about it, either. He'd also rounded me up the names of some therapists in the event I needed to see someone. Talking to a professional about my daddy issues was long overdue, but now the need seemed urgent.

Saturday afternoon, I remained holed up in my bedroom when the phone rang. It was Mack.

I picked up. "Hi."

"I'm outside. Can you come down, or are you too sick to be out in the cold?"

"You're here?"

"Yes. I just flew in."

He was here?

"How come you didn't tell me you were coming?"

"I didn't want to hear you tell me not to come. I'm getting a vibe from you, and I haven't been able to sleep. I needed to see you. I'm here until tomorrow night. Jonah's with my sister."

"Where are you staying?"

"I couldn't go back to my house because the realtor is showing it this weekend. So, I rented a room at the Beacon Hill Hotel around the corner from here. Grab a bag of your things and meet me out front."

Hesitating for a moment, I realized there was really no way out of dealing with this. "Okay...I'll be right down."

I'd nearly forgotten how much I missed him. Mack was leaning against a car that was parked out front. He was wearing a navy wool coat and rugged boots under his jeans. His hair had grown out a bit longer, and his stubble was more shadowy than usual.

His warm kiss was a welcome contrast to the cold air. It was desperate and forceful. He took my hand as we walked in silence to the hotel just a few blocks away.

The room at the historic hotel was small but comfortable with windows that let in a lot of light. Mack sat down on the edge of the bed and pulled me close, resting his head on my stomach as I stood before him.

Immediately, I started to cry. It was impossible to hide anything from him.

He looked up at me, and his eyes slowly widened. "You know?"

I nodded, unable to form the words.

"I knew it." He stood up and pulled me into him.

As much as it had been comforting to have Victor's support this past week, nothing felt better than being in Mack's arms, even if I still didn't understand why he'd kept the news about my father from me.

He whispered into my hair, "I know you, Frankie. You're inside my fucking heart, and when something's bothering you, I can literally feel it. Tell me how it happened. How did you find out?" He pulled back so he could look at me.

Wiping my nose with my arm, I said, "It was Torrie. She sent me a package with a letter and all of the articles."

He froze for a moment and just blinked repeatedly to let that sink in. "Fuck. What?"

"Yes. It was a horrible way to find out."

"I suspected she was in on it, but I just can't believe she would do that and that he let her do the dirty work."

"Mack, how could you have known about this and not told me the second you found out?"

"I've been sick over it," he pleaded. "I've only known for a few days. I was trying to figure out how to do it in a way that would hurt you the least...if that was even possible. I'd planned to tell you this weekend when you came to visit. Then you canceled, so I had to come here. I would've never kept this from you, Frankie. You have to know that."

"I know this isn't your fault. I just don't know how to handle it."

"This is typical of my father. This is the type of shit I've seen him do to people my entire life. Back when you and I first met, I'd always feared that something like this might happen someday, that if I loved you openly, somehow my father would do something to hurt you.

277

More recently, I had myself convinced that I could protect you from anything even if that did happen. This time around with you, I'd stopped obsessing about it, choosing to just enjoy life. I let my guard down. I wanted to just love you without worrying about all of that. But out of all the possible things he could've done, I never could've predicted this scenario."

"My mother confirmed everything. She never planned to tell me, but it's all true. Freddie Higgins is my father."

"Are you okay?" He rested his forehead against mine. "I know that seems like a dumb question."

"I'm just in shock. This feels like a dream. I can't even explain what I'm feeling because it hasn't sunk in yet."

"I hate that I caused this."

"You didn't cause it."

"Not directly. But if I hadn't come back into your life, this never would've happened. I'd never forgive myself if I ever put you in any kind of danger. What did Torrie say to you?"

I reached into my bag and took out the folded piece of paper. "I have the letter here."

Mack's ears were turning red as he read it. He looked like he was burning up in anger. "I can't believe this. I just can't believe she would threaten you like that. This is the fucking mother of my child acting like this." Running his hand through his hair in frustration, he looked down at the floor and then up at me. "I swear to God, if it weren't for my son, I'd take you away and hope we never came back. I just wish I knew the best way to handle this. I truly feel helpless."

"I don't think the answer is going to come overnight."

"What do we do in the meantime?"

"Honestly? I just want you to hold me tonight. That's all. I don't want to think. I just want to be with you."

"I can do that."

Mack closed the curtains, shutting out most of the light. He rolled down the bedding before taking off his shirt. As he enveloped me in his arms, I curled into his warm body. For a few moments, I was able to forget the past week.

His heart was thumping against my back. I knew his mind was racing.

He finally spoke. "All these years, you thought your father didn't want you. He was just fucked-up."

"I'm glad I know the truth. I just wish I knew what to do with it."

"Do you think you'll ever contact him?"

"I honestly don't know."

"I think it's better if you don't. It's not worth the risk."

"Do you really think someone would come after me after all this time?"

"I don't want to find out, Frankie. The thought of something happening to you because of what my father pulled is unfathomable."

He held me tighter. I felt tiny in Mack's big arms.

We eventually both drifted off to sleep. It was the first good sleep either of us had gotten in days.

After he returned to Virginia, during the days that followed, things would change again and not for the better.

This time period reminded me so much of how it felt years ago when he'd left our apartment in Boston and went home for the summer only to come back and break my heart.

Mack was once again distancing himself much like he'd done back then. Whenever I questioned him, he'd tell me he was trying to figure out what the best step was moving forward.

I couldn't help but worry that he'd come to the conclusion that it was safer for everyone if we went our separate ways.

For the first time, I doubted whether we would be able to recover.

CHAPTER TWENTY

Francesca

As I waited in front of Mrs. Migillicutty's, the sight of Mack's empty house next door made me melancholy. The windows were dark, and the *for sale* sign still sat out front on the dried-up, ice-coated grass. It was a terrible time to have a house on the market in the middle of winter, so he hadn't gotten any bites on the property.

I longed to be back inside the warmth of that house with him. More than that, I missed that time when things seemed complicated, but in retrospect weren't complicated at all compared to the present.

She opened the door. "I got the water boiling for the hot chocolate, Frankie Jane. I'm gonna spike it real good."

"Thank you. That sounds like exactly what I need." Kicking the snow off my boots, I asked, "Have you heard from Mack?"

"No, honey. But I sure do miss him."

"Me too."

"Why do you ask? Is something wrong?"

"I'm getting concerned because he hasn't called me in a couple of days. That's really unlike him. His texts have been short and vague, too. I'm really scared I'm losing him."

"What in the hell?" She poured the hot water into two mugs.

Mrs. Migillicutty didn't know anything about the blackmail or my father. I felt like I needed to tell her everything. In fact, I was bursting at the seams to get her opinion because, not only was she straightforward, but she always seemed to make a lot of sense.

"Can you keep a secret? It's kind of a long story, but I really need to get it off my chest."

She pointed to her round stomach. "See this belly? I'm pretty sure it's full of secrets. Well, maybe it's full of Tim Tam cookies, but in any case, keeping secrets is what I'm best at."

I trusted her. Since I hadn't been to see a professional, she was probably the next best thing. I needed someone unbiased to talk to who was far removed from the equation. Over the next forty minutes, I recounted everything that had happened since Mack moved back to Virginia.

"Wow, what a guttersnipe," she said, referring to Torrie. "I'd like to snap her neck."

I sighed. "Yeah."

"Don't worry. Karma is a bigger bitch than that cunt ever could be."

Her dirty mouth always made me laugh.

She noticed my amusement. "What?"

"Nothing. Your looks don't always match your mouth. I just don't expect you to say certain things, but I should know better by now."

"Mack used to say the same thing. What's up with you people?"

"Thank you for making me laugh."

She sighed, and her expression turned serious. "Okay. Let's try to work this out. What's at the root of your fears now?"

I stopped to really think for a moment, swirling my hot chocolate around. "Honestly, I don't even care about that bitch or anything she or his father have done to try to hurt me. I'm concerned about Mack and Jonah. I'm also worried that he's decided that it's safer for him to distance himself from me, even if that's not what his heart wants. But more than anything, what's bothering me is my own doubt, that inner voice that's telling me that they would be better off without me."

"Bullshit. Mack wasn't living until you came back into his life. I refuse to accept the two of you letting fear rule your worlds." She added a bit more peppermint Schnapps to my hot cocoa. "What was the last thing he said to you?"

"He said he needed some time to figure out a solution."

She blew on her drink before taking a sip. "Okay. You have to trust that he knows what he's doing. I don't see how he could possibly be considering a life apart from you. He will figure it out."

"Well, Jonah really has to be his top priority. What if he feels that being with me could potentially put his son in danger?"

"Do you really think that senator is going to do anything to endanger the life of his grandchild? He won't go public with this, Frankie."

"But like Torrie's letter stated, what if someone else, like a political rival, uncovers my background?"

"People only go after people who give them a reason to. If you don't want to have to worry about that, then you may have to keep things under the radar until this blows over."

"You mean pretend not to be with Mack? Sneak around?"

"Whatever it takes. But I will say this. I do not believe that dirty politician or that nasty witch would ever do anything to put that little boy in harm's way. If you and Mack are together, that means you'll be around Jonah, and they know that. They are trying to scare you away from him."

"I hope it's just that. I really hope you're right."

"Like I used to say to Mack...I *am* always right."

While my evening with Mrs. M. had served to reassure me a bit, doubt would always set in most when I was alone at night. The physical and now emotional distance from Mack was taking its toll. Something had changed since his return to Virginia, and I was afraid to push him for answers. I was afraid of the truth. More and more, it was feeling like he'd decided that our being together was just not worth the risk. It seemed like he was pushing me away with actions because he didn't have the guts to say what he was thinking.

I'd signed a lease on a new apartment in Brookline but couldn't move in for another few weeks. Victor never made me feel like I was overstaying my welcome. A part of me felt that he was secretly hoping my relationship with Mack wouldn't recover from this.

Whenever I thought about keeping Vic around as a safety net, I had to remind myself how unfair it was to even think like that. But with Mack keeping his distance, it was easy to see why my mind was veering in that direction. I was at a crossroads with no sense of direction.

My state of confusion was disrupted in a big way one afternoon after school when I received a knock on the door of my classroom. I'd been correcting papers but got up to answer, expecting to see that Lorelai had returned because she'd forgotten something.

Instead, two very well-dressed women stood before me. One looked about thirty years older than the other, but she was nonetheless striking. I didn't recognize them as being related to any of my students.

"Can I help you?"

"Are you Francesca O'Hara?" the younger woman said.

"Yes."

"I'm Michaela Morrison, Mackenzie's sister. And this is my mother, Vivienne."

Oh, my God.

Michaela had the same hazel eyes and bone structure as Mack. And they both looked like their mother.

"Wow. Oh, my goodness. Come in. Please." I led them over to one of the student tables where we each took a seat.

"You look really nervous. Please don't be," Michaela said.

Vivienne looked morose. "We didn't come to make trouble for you. I have to first apologize immensely for what has happened recently. Mackenzie made me aware of the letter you received and the information that was dug up on your father. That was very unfortunate, and I'm terribly sorry for my husband's actions."

It was a really inopportune time to lose my cool. Nevertheless, a tear sprang free and fell down my cheek.

Mack's sister reached out and placed her hand on my arm. "I'm sorry if we're upsetting you."

"No. Not at all. It's just really good to meet you. I never knew what to expect when it came to you both. This is a bit of a relief, actually."

"Meeting you seems long overdue," his sister said.

"I know."

"My brother once told me about you years ago when Jonah was about three years old. It was Christmas Eve.

Mack and I were sitting by the tree talking. I asked him if he planned on marrying Torrie, and he was honest with me. He told me he couldn't bring himself to take that final step because he was still in love with someone else. And that was when he told me the whole story of how he'd met you and how he'd left things with you back in Boston. I'll never forget the look of longing and regret in his eyes. I'd never seen that side of Mack. It broke my heart."

"Really?"

"Yes. I remember thinking it was so romantic yet tragic. And I've thought about you a lot after that, even though I never knew you, because I'd just felt so terrible for my brother. At the time, I had just met my now fiancé, and I remember wishing so badly that Mackenzie could find the same happiness I did."

Vivienne interrupted, "I'm afraid apologizing on behalf of my husband is only half of the reason why we needed to travel here to see you."

"My brother is in a really bad place."

My stomach dropped. "I knew something was wrong. He hasn't been opening up to me."

"Something new has happened."

My heartbeat accelerated. "Is he okay?"

"He's physically okay, yes. I'm sorry if I scared you."

"What's going on?"

"My brother and I have been used to dealing with my father's crooked ways our entire lives. But when I found out about what Dad had done to you, I decided that I'd had enough."

My heart was pounding in fear. I had no clue what else they could have possibly come here to tell me.

She continued, "I started investigating my father. One of the things I did was break into his private office. A long time ago, I'd watched him open a safe. He didn't realize I was mentally taking note of the combination. I never thought I would actually use it someday." Michaela held onto her mother's hand for support. "So, recently, I used the code to open it. I was thinking that maybe I would find something in there that I could use to blackmail him in the same way he'd done to you, except my one condition would be for him to leave my brother alone. I never expected to find what I did."

Vivenne closed her eyes and seemed to be gearing herself up for what would come next.

Michaela took a deep breath then said, "I found pictures of Torrie...and a video on a thumb drive."

"Torrie?"

"Yes. Naked photos...and a sex tape."

I couldn't grasp it. "What? Naked?"

"I know. It's a shock. My father had apparently been having an affair with her for years."

Mack's mother finally spoke. "Deep down, I think I knew that Michael had been unfaithful to me at some point in our marriage. But the level of betrayal that this has brought upon our family is beyond comprehension."

"Did you confront him?"

Michaela nodded. "We confronted them both. They didn't deny it. They claimed it's been over for a long time."

"Does Mack know?"

"Yes. After my mother and I confronted my father and Torrie, we went to Mack's and told him everything. He basically went into shock. He's having a very hard time accepting this. He's given up a huge chunk of his life for that woman, only to be burned in the worst possible way. Not to mention being betrayed like that by your own father."

For some reason, it hadn't dawned on me before, but when the thought entered my consciousness, it hit me like a ton of bricks.

Oh, no.

No.

No.

No.

"Is there a chance that..." I couldn't even say the words.

She finished my sentence. "That Jonah is my father's son? We believe there is a chance, yes. But we just don't know."

Oh, dear God.

"How long has Mack known all of this?"

"We told him when he got home from his last visit with you, the one where I was watching Jonah."

That explained the bizarre behavior soon after he left me.

"He's been acting strangely toward me," I said. "I thought it had to do with my own situation. He obviously chose not to tell me any of this."

"As you can imagine, he's not handling it well. Knowing that there's a possibility that Jonah could be our father's is causing him a lot of mental anguish. He's been shutting us out, too. In some ways, I feel terrible for having uncovered this, but I suppose it's better to know than to be kept in the dark about something so significant."

I turned to Mack's mother. "How are you handling it?"

Her voice was barely audible. "Not well, I'm afraid."

"How long are you both here in town?"

Michaela looked down at her phone to check the time. "We're heading right back to D.C. in a few hours. The purpose of this trip was to meet you and to let you know how sorry we are for everything that happened but mostly to make you aware of what's happening now."

CHAPTER TWENTY-ONE

Mack

There's nothing harder than trying to keep a brave face in front of your kid when it feels like your world is crumbling around you.

"Want some more sauce?"

Jonah nodded. I lifted the ladle, pouring the marinara over his spaghetti and frozen meatballs. I was a suckass cook before, but with everything going on lately, the cuisine around here was even more sub par than usual.

He twirled the noodles around with his fork. I hated that I obsessively stared at his face now every chance I got, looking for signs of my father. This was *my* son, and nothing was ever going to change that.

I wondered if Jonah thought about why my beard was almost fully grown. I also wondered if he could somehow sense the pain that was now constantly squeezing at my heart.

Making matters worse, I couldn't even bear to look at Torrie. I'd been staying in the car whenever I would pick him up or bring him back. Since the day my mother and sister dropped the bomb, Torrie and I had barely spoken. During one conversation that took place while Jonah was at school, I'd demanded that she come clean as to whether my father could technically be Jonah's biological father. When she admitted that it was a possibility, I flew off the handle. She kept apologizing, using her age at the time and naivety as an excuse, pinning it on my father as the seducer. She kept emphasizing that the affair was brief and had ended years ago. She even tried to place the blame on me, saying she felt vulnerable to his charms because of my lack of affection toward her.

In addition to smashing some of her possessions, I made a number of empty threats I knew I would never follow through with. Filing for full custody was one of them. That wasn't an option because Jonah loved his mother too much despite her faults. As vile as I now realized she was, I didn't want to put my son through another major transition; it wouldn't have been fair.

My son.

As for my father, I couldn't get myself to confront him out of fear that I would've wanted to physically annihilate him. I couldn't ever lay a hand on Torrie despite my anger; the idea of physically harming Dad, however, didn't seem that far-fetched. So, I stayed away for my own good.

He hadn't reached out to me once since everything came out. That didn't surprise me; he was a fucking coward. And honestly, there was nothing to say that would have changed this situation or made it better.

I was done with him. It didn't matter if I never spoke to him again as long as I lived.

When Jonah put down his fork, I asked, "You're not hungry?"

"Not really." He stared off then suddenly said, "Mom's been crying a lot."

I didn't know how to respond. What I wanted to say—"Good"—wouldn't have exactly been the right answer.

"I'm sorry to hear that." *I wasn't*. The only thing I was sorry about was that Jonah had to witness it. "Has she told you why she's upset?"

"She told me not to worry."

"That's right. Sometimes, people get sad and cry, but it always passes. It'll be okay." I hated that I had no energy to even pretend that I cared about why his mother was crying. My inclination was just to drop the subject as fast as possible, so that he couldn't sense anything on my end. Telling him the truth wasn't an option.

I knew that Torrie had no intention of confirming Jonah's paternity, unless I somehow forced it. I still wasn't sure what I wanted, often going back and forth between demanding a blood test for peace of mind and never wanting to know.

My mind was just one jumbled mess, intercepted every so often by flashes of red hair, flashes of light, flashes of Frankie. I couldn't even begin to imagine what she was thinking about my virtual absence from her life. I couldn't bear to break this news to her, to explain that my breaking her heart all those years ago may have all been in vain.

Then, there was the issue of her safety. I was even more far removed from my father's antics now. What if he was still planning on causing trouble for her? He was probably more angry and disillusioned with me after being outed for his affair with Torrie. I just didn't know what to do. It felt selfish to be bringing Frankie into the mess that was my life right now. In my darkest moments, I'd have myself convinced that she would be better off with that old man, who could take care of her and keep her hidden and safe, away from my fucked-up family.

That evening as I pulled up to Torrie's, Jonah finally called me out on my actions.

"How come you don't walk me inside anymore?"

"It just has to be like this for a little while. I promise it won't be forever."

"What did Mommy do?"

"Adults fight from time to time, okay? Everything is going to turn out alright. I promise. You don't need to worry. When people have a disagreement, sometimes it's best if they just keep their distance until time passes. Mommy and I both love you very much, and that's all you need to remember."

I hugged him extra tight before watching him walk from the car to make sure he entered the house safely.

My mind was racing on the way home. Distracted, I almost crashed into another car in the opposite lane. That was a wake-up call. I thought about all of the regrets I would have had if my life were to have ended just then. It was a needed reminder of my will to get past this dark time. I just needed help.

Once back at my cold and empty apartment, I grabbed a beer and sat on the kitchen floor with my back against the refrigerator. There was no energy left in me to move from that spot. It was such a random place and moment to hit rock bottom, but I truly felt that was it; I'd hit my lowest point.

"Please."

I wasn't even sure at first who I was talking to. It must have been God.

I whispered again, "Please."

It proved that I did believe someone was listening despite my never really having taught Jonah about religion. Even though St. Matthew's happened to be a Catholic school, my son hadn't really grown up with any kind of faith before that nor had my parents ever taken me to church growing up. Despite not knowing what my God looked like, I just felt a spiritual presence in that moment. So, I continued to beg this higher power for guidance. I prayed to God to help me figure out my next steps, how to move on with my life. It was the first time I'd ever acknowledged a true belief.

I went to sleep that night vying to leave everything in God's hands, because it didn't feel like my own were capable of handling this situation any longer. I'd hit rock bottom, and there was nowhere to go but up.

The next morning, I was still wearing the same clothes from the day before. The only thing that had changed was that my beard had gotten even longer.

A knock on the door startled me. It was way too early to deal with anyone. It better not have been my father.

When I opened the door, I blinked a few times to make sure I wasn't hallucinating. Anything was possible given my lack of sleep lately.

Frankie was standing there with a gigantic suitcase.

She seemed shocked to see me looking like this. "What on Earth, Mack..."

Blinking repeatedly, I said, "Frankie?"

I still couldn't believe she was here.

Abandoning her luggage, she leapt into my arms. Until I was actually holding her, I hadn't realized just how badly I'd needed her. With the distance between us, I'd somehow been able to convince myself that I could live without her. But now, it felt like I was breathing again for the first time in weeks.

What she said to me next truly threw me for a loop.

"I know, Mack."

"What?"

"I know about the discovery your sister made. Your mother and Michaela came to see me in Boston. They were worried about you and told me everything. We don't have to talk about it right now. But I just wanted to let you know that I know and that you don't need to rehash it. You don't owe me any explanations. I'm just here to do what I can to make it better, because I love you so much."

I just broke apart in her arms, crying like a baby for the first time since Jonah was born. How I ever thought I could get through this without her was beyond me. God had sent me exactly what I needed: her.

Once I'd calmed down, I wiped my eyes and asked, "How long can you stay?"

"How long do you want me?"

"Forever," I said without hesitation. "I don't *want* you forever. I *need* you forever."

"Then, I'm here."

"What about your job?"

"I took a leave of absence. I don't know that I'm ever going back."

"What about...him?"

"Things truly ended with Victor a long time ago. The only difference now is that I finally left. It was the right thing to do. Even before you and I got physical, my heart was yours. I'd just been afraid to admit it. Victor is a smart man. I think he never really held out true hope for a reconciliation even when things seemed bad between you and me in recent weeks. From the moment he found out about you, he could see how consumed I was. After your mother and sister came to see me, I was a wreck. I told Victor that night that I planned to leave for Virginia as soon as I could get my affairs in order."

"What about the stuff with your father?"

"What about it? I have to accept it. But I feel very far removed from it all, to be honest. I don't know him and probably never will. It has nothing to do with us... aside from your father and Torrie's threats. Anyway, I think I have a plan for how to handle that situation. But I don't want to get into it now. I don't want to talk about anything upsetting today. I just want to spend time with you, get you feeling strong again so that we have the energy to deal with all that."

I kept running my fingers through her long hair. "I can't believe you're really here. Last night, after I dropped Jonah off, I felt hopeless. I prayed for the first time that I could ever remember and asked God to help me. He sent me you. I'm pretty sure that was more than I could've hoped for."

Frankie was overcome with emotion. "When we first met, you saw something in me that other people didn't. You were the first man to come into my life and make me feel special. Life got in the way of our plans. But I want to take it back. Who says we can't? When you left Boston all those years ago, you were supposed to come back to me. That wasn't our time, but that doesn't mean we weren't still meant to be together. So, this is me coming back to *you*. Let this be the moment that it was supposed to be all those years ago, the start of a new beginning."

"You make it sound so simple."

"Why can't it be? We're not going to let fear rule our lives. We'll figure it all out in good time."

I gave into the sudden urge to lift her into my arms. "As long as you're with me, I feel like I can handle anything."

She wrapped her legs around my waist. "We just need to take it one day at a time. And today...we have only one mission."

"What's that?"

"It's to get you cleaned up and shaved."

"Are you saying I'm a beast?"

"I'm saying if I had gotten here two days later, I would be sleeping with Chewbacca."

My laughter roared throughout the apartment as I put her down. "God, it feels good to laugh again."

"When was the last time?"

I slid my hands slowly down her back. "It was with you."

Frankie took my hand. I led her into the bathroom before turning on the faucet. She removed all of my clothes then took hers off until we were both stark naked.

She sat across from me in the small bathtub that was filled to the rim with suds and gently shaved my beard. I closed my eyes, so thankful to have her with me. When she finished, she softly kissed my face.

Wrapping my arms around her, I lifted her onto my cock as she straddled me. We fucked under the water until we both came. If last night was hell, this was my light after darkness.

I realized that this wasn't the naïve girl I first fell in love with. This was my woman taking care of me, taking control of my life when I'd completely lost it. I'd asked God for help, and He sent my angel.

Looking up toward the bathroom ceiling, I silently thanked him.

You did good.

Frankie and I stayed holed up inside my apartment for a few days. I was slowly coming out of my funk with a renewed determination to get my life—our lives—in order.

We finally ended up venturing out to go shopping for the apartment. Cleaning out HomeGoods, we purchased lamps, pillows, candles, artwork and other household items.

After spending the entire afternoon sprucing up the place, my cold apartment was finally looking like a home. I realized it had never really been terrible; it had only seemed that way because it was empty, a reflection of how I was feeling. Suddenly, it was a warm, inviting place. I also wanted to christen every room with her in the worst way.

That night, we took our dirty clothing to the laundromat just down the road. It was situated on the first floor of a small housing complex.

We were both standing side by side with our arms crossed, watching the clothes flying around the dryer. It was dark out, and we were lucky to have the entire joint to ourselves.

"After all these years...how did we end up in this place, doing laundry together again?" I asked.

"It's pretty amazing, isn't it? So much time can go by, so much has changed, and yet here we are. The exact same situation."

"Except back then, we'd go upstairs to our separate rooms, and I would have to jerk away all of my sexual frustration. Tonight, I get to take you home and have my way with you. I much prefer Laundry 2.0."

"I wanted you so badly back then," she said.

"That thought makes me crazy. I'm getting horny just thinking about how it used to feel wanting you and feeling as though I would never have you. It was unbearable sometimes. You seemed so inexperienced and innocent back then. I remember just wanting to lift you up against the washer, wrap your legs around me, and fuck you until you couldn't talk."

"Or walk." She winked.

"That, too." I moved in to suck on her bottom lip, slowly releasing it. "But we were too good. We never gave in to our feelings."

"I had it so badly for you that I used to get off from just being near you, talking to you, listening to your voice. Any contact at all would make me wet. We would just be hanging out down in that basement, and my panties would be soaked."

Damn.

"I'm glad I didn't know that at the time." Pressing my erection into her, I said, "Tell me more though."

"Actually, I have a confession. I think you'll appreciate it," she said.

"Is this gonna require us having to abandon our shit to head to my car?"

"Maybe."

"I can only hope so." I kissed her then spoke low over her mouth, "Say what you were gonna say."

She bit her lip. "One time...I stole a pair of your boxers and put them on. I masturbated in them until I came."

"Are you screwing with me?"

"No."

"That's fucking hot. What else did you do, you little deviant?"

"I'd touch myself in your bed when you'd go away to D.C."

"No shit? I could've sworn I smelled you on my sheets sometimes."

"Yup. That was me. I would get off just from your scent. I'd pretend you were with me, and I'd come, sometimes multiple times rolling around in your sheets."

"You're killing me right now. Tell me more."

"One time, we were watching TV, and you fell asleep next to me. Your shoulder was only barely touching mine. But I started to rub my clit right next to you while you were sleeping."

"Holy shit. And I had no clue. Damn girl, you were like a chronic masturbator back then."

Her cheeks were turning pink. "I was."

"I missed all of that. We need to rectify it. I want to live out that boxer fantasy."

"Maybe later we will."

Looking around before placing my hands on her ass and squeezing it hard, I said, "No. I don't think it can wait."

Frankie's eyes practically bugged out of her head. "Here?"

I kissed her neck then reached for a pair of my underwear that was in the batch already folded in our basket. "Yes. I want you to put on my boxers, and I want to watch you getting yourself off right next to me. Except I'm not gonna be asleep like a fool. I'm gonna watch every second while I rub one off and come right along with you."

"And where are we supposed to do that here?"

"We're pretty good at making due in supply closets. That one right over there is open. The dude who's working is too busy playing on his phone. He won't even notice us in there."

She was adamant. "I can't."

"I'll tell you what, if it has a lock, then we do it. If it doesn't, we wait until we get home."

I walked over to check and found that it did have a lock. With a goofy smile on my face, I gave her a thumbs-up.

Returning to her, I smiled. "Bingo!"

"He's looking right over at us. I can't do it."

Scratching my chin, I said, "Hang on."

She watched as I walked over to the attendant and had a brief conversation with him.

"What did you just do?" she asked upon my return.

"I slipped him a fifty. He agreed to let us go upstairs to his apartment."

"You're crazy."

"I'm helping the economy."

"You're helping the economy by watching me masturbate in your underwear in some strange man's bed?"

"I told him we'd been apart for eight years and needed a place to be alone so that we could have sex for the first time."

"He thinks we haven't had sex yet?"

"It's just a minor detail. I figured he'd be more likely to go for it."

I grabbed a towel before leading her up a steep stairwell to the stranger's apartment. We walked through the dated kitchen until we found the bedroom. I placed the towel down over the bed, knowing that would make her feel better.

"Take off your pants." I playfully threw the gray boxers at her. "Show me how you used to get off in these."

She slowly removed her underwear, showcasing the pussy I'd shaved bare just last night. My mouth watered as she then slipped my boxers up her slim thighs.

"Lie back on the bed."

Frankie bent her head back and closed her eyes as she slipped her two fingers through the crotch opening and began to move them around in a small circular motion. Wanting to just soak it in for a few minutes, I pretended to be a voyeur looking in on an act that I wasn't meant to witness. I'd taken off my shirt but just stood there with my jeans still covering my full erection. My hands were on my waist as I specifically forced myself to resist the need to interfere. The reward would be so much greater that way.

When I started to notice the wetness seeping through the fabric of the boxers she was wearing, it became impossible to restrain myself. Unbuckling, I let my pants fall to the ground before stepping out of them and walking slowly toward her.

She wriggled her hips as she continued to get herself off. Standing at the edge of the bed, I began to stroke my slick cock just inches away from her, my gaze fixated on the motion of her fingers and the slight whimpers of pleasure coming from her mouth.

As she watched me jerking off, she licked her lips and rubbed herself even faster. Feeling like I was going to come, I let go of my cock and walked over to the foot of the bed before crawling toward her. The only thing better than the site of her pleasuring herself in my underwear was being able to slide them down her legs and taste the fruit of her arousal.

My tongue lashed out as my mouth devoured her swollen clit. With the towel still under her, she pulled on my hair to guide my face over her.

I groaned over her skin, "Take off your shirt, because after you come on my face, I want to come all over your tits."

After she quickly did as I said, she gripped my hair tighter and pushed her hips into my mouth as she climaxed. My tongue swirled around her delicious mound, enjoying every last drop of her.

I waited for her breathing to slow down before moving up to hover over her. Enjoying the view of her glassy eyes for a moment, I smiled before lowering my mouth to hers, so turned on knowing that she could taste herself on my tongue.

Needing to come, I placed my cock in between her gorgeous teardrop-shaped breasts and began to fuck them. She squeezed her tits over my dick as I slid back and forth. I could tell she was getting anxious about getting out of the strange apartment, so I let go, releasing my hot load all over her creamy skin. She was covered in my cum when I lowered my chest down onto hers and kissed her with all my might.

We did our best to hide the evidence before putting our clothes back on.

When we reemerged downstairs, the laundromat employee gave us a knowing nod. I returned it with a thankful smile. It felt so good to feel human again.

Pulling Frankie into a kiss, I said, "Thank you for bringing me back to Earth. I was starting to get sucked into a very bad place. I'd forgotten just how amazing life can be when you have someone who loves you by your side, even in the midst of a difficult time. I know we haven't dealt with the tough stuff yet, but you've managed to make me forget about it for a few days. And I really needed to recharge before handling it all."

"I'm here for the long haul, you know—the good days and the bad days."

"The fact that you're willing to take this chance with me despite everything that's happened means everything."

"We're gonna fix this," she said, wrapping her palms around my face and scratching the stubble. "Are you ready to hear my plan about how to deal with your father?"

My beautiful woman had such a determined look on her face. I was curious about what she had cooked up in that pretty little head.

"Yeah."

"We're gonna give him some of his own medicine, and we need everyone to be involved." She looked so confident as she took a shirt out of the dirty pile and sniffed it.

"Did you just smell my dirty shirt?"

"Maybe." She smiled impishly.

Some things never change, and I was damn grateful for that right now.

CHAPTER TWENTY-TWO

Francesca

"Are you ready?" I asked.

"As ready as I'll ever be."

Mack and I were standing in front of his father's D.C. office building. We had called an urgent family meeting which also included Torrie.

Torrie was the last to arrive. Mack's mother, Vivienne, and sister, Michaela, kept their distance and wouldn't even look in her direction.

"Looks like we're all here," Mack said. "We should head inside."

Michael Morrison was sitting behind his large wooden desk and swiveled the chair around to face us. He was expecting a meeting with Mack and me but wasn't expecting to see his wife, daughter, and Torrie.

"What is this...an intervention?"

Mack answered, "It's the final meeting you'll ever have to have with me."

Mack's father was more fair-skinned than his son; Mack definitely looked more like his mother.

He turned to me. "It's good to meet you, Miss O'Hara."

"I would say it's nice to meet you, too, but I'm sorry it's going to take a lot more than one day to warm up to you, sir."

"I'm glad you finally decided to see me, son. I can imagine what you've been thinking."

Mack put his arm around me. "I'm only here because of her. I don't want to hear what you have to say, your excuses. I'm not here to talk about those horrible images that my mother had to witness. I'm just here to tell you where things stand with us—with all of us."

"Alright."

"I think there's no disputing that your number one priority has always been your reputation...the public's perception of you. That's never going to change. If there's one thing I've learned in my life, it's that you can't change people. You're a selfish man. You take whatever you want regardless of what it means for others."

He said nothing as Mack's attention turned toward Torrie.

"Torrie, I don't really know what to make of you. Jonah's been saying you've been crying. You obviously have some regret. I don't think you're a horrible person deep down nor do I believe you're totally at fault for what happened. You're partly right when you say I never gave you the affection that you needed. I was in love with someone else, and I guess I didn't do a very good job of hiding the fact that my heart wasn't in it with you. In the meantime, you fell under the spell of a powerful yet corrupt man, who happens to be my father. He manipulated you. Since I can't detach myself from you because you're my son's mother, I want to try to learn to forgive you, provided we come to an understanding today."

With tears forming in her eyes, Torrie simply nodded.

"Let me just make one thing very clear off the bat. I don't want to have to pursue a paternity test. Jonah is my son. I'm the only father he knows. I don't want him ever doubting my love for him. If I ever decide to tell him about the possibility that his grandfather is actually his father, it will ideally be when he's much older, unless you force me to do it sooner."

Mack didn't really have any intention of putting Jonah through a test, but we wanted his father to believe he did. So, we were counting on this threat working.

"What does that mean?" his father asked.

Michaela intercepted, "I have the video and naked photos of Torrie. I will go to the press with them if you don't agree to our terms. Your political career will be over. The press will have a field day with the fact that you had a torrid affair with your son's girlfriend and that you could potentially be the father of your own grandson."

Not really seeming surprised by the threat, Michael asked, "What are your terms?"

"First, you give Mother whatever she asks for in the divorce," Michaela said.

Vivenne spoke for the first time. "By the way, I'm filing for divorce." Apparently, she hadn't announced that until now.

Michaela held her mother's hand and continued, "She keeps the family house, and you make sure everything is handled as quickly and seamlessly as possible."

Michael tapped his pen against the desk. "I suppose there's more?"

"Yes, there is," Mack said. "The information you uncovered about Frankie's biological father will be concealed. You will do everything in your power to protect her and to keep that information as private as possible, which, in turn, protects Jonah because Frankie's going to be living with us. You keep the three of us out of your political endeavors altogether. We want nothing to do with any of it."

Torrie spoke up for the first time. "What exactly do you mean when you say Jonah's going to be living with you? You're not taking him away from me."

"Nothing will change in terms of our custody arrangement during the week, but I don't want him with nannies anymore during the day. I will pick him up after school and keep him with me until you get home from work."

She didn't argue with that.

"Are there any more conditions?" his father asked.

"Yes. You keep your distance from my son, and you accept that I have no intention of questioning my role as his father."

Michael nodded once then said, "Are we finished?"

"There is one more condition," Mack's sister said. "You seek therapy. I don't know how you will go about keeping it private, but figure out a way. You're a narcissist, and you need help."

After a long silence that seemed to go on forever, the stern politician rubbed his eyes and said, "I agree to these terms."

"Good," Michaela said. "I hope you can heal yourself. I really do. Your career will come to an end someday, and then what will you have left? Mom and us kids will have each other, and what will you have?"

Everyone waited with bated breath for his answer until he finally said, "I hope to have your forgiveness someday."

"That will depend on your actions moving forward," she said.

He looked his daughter in the eyes. "Understood."

Mack had enough. He stood up from his seat. "Goodbye, Dad."

I followed him outside.

He had paused at the front steps. The wind was blowing through his hair.

I came up behind him and said, "Are you okay?"

"Yeah. I feel amazingly free." He smiled. "Welcome to my crazy family."

"Hey, you're forgetting. I come from crazy stock, too, apparently. So, I'll fit right in."

"Good. Maybe together we can cancel the crazy out." Mack gave me a chaste kiss.

The sight of Torrie's long legs approaching us interrupted our moment. We both turned to face her.

She cleared her throat. "I just wanted to say that I'm deeply sorry for how everything has turned out."

"Everything has turned out great, actually." Mack said. "I couldn't be happier with how things have turned out."

She addressed me. "I guess what I'm trying to say is that I'm sorry for what I did to you with the letter. I understand what it feels like now to be on the receiving end of blackmail, and it's not fun. I was feeling desperate when I sent you that correspondence. I know I have a lot of work to do, and while I don't expect you to forgive me, I just need you to know that I'm sorry for any pain I've caused."

Looking over at Mack, she said, "Please come inside to the house when you drop Jonah off from now on. That's all I ask. I want him to believe that things are going to be okay, even if we have a long way to go. I know you think I'm pure evil at this point, but I do truly care about my son's perception of the situation."

Oddly, I believed that she did.

"I can do that...for him," Mack said.

"And I'm not going to make trouble for you, Francesca. If you're going to be around Jonah, then we need to at least be cordial, even if you and Mack both hate me deep down. I really do want him to see us all getting along, even if it's an illusion."

Mack didn't even try to argue with her assertion of hate. He simply said, "Have a nice day, Torrie."

Torrie stayed true to her word. Mack and I would pick Jonah up from school every day and bring him back to our place until she got home from work.

As I looked for teaching jobs in the area, I started to think that maybe my time was better spent helping to take care of Jonah so that Mack could concentrate on work and didn't have to hire help. Even though Jonah was in school most of the day, being out of work made it possible to pick him up in the afternoons. He hated the bus, and we didn't force him to take it.

Since I'd moved in, we'd noticed that Jonah's behaviors had worsened. He seemed more withdrawn and anxious, which was strange, since he'd probably never had more attention.

I'd always seen a lot of my younger self in him, but one afternoon, I discovered something that really proved how true that was.

Cleaning his room while he was in school one day, I came across a notebook hidden under his bed. I opened it and found the same two sentences written over and over in Jonah's handwriting.

I will not kill my dad.

I'm a good person.

I wasn't sure what to think at first. I was afraid to go to Mack and more afraid of Jonah's reaction if he found out that I had. I decided that I was going to take Jonah for a ride after school so that we could discuss it before telling his father. I didn't think Mack would handle this very well. He was such a strong person, but when it came to his son, he worried a lot and often felt helpless.

That afternoon, Jonah sat quietly in the backseat of my RAV4. He was looking out the window as I drove us to a playground near our apartment.

When we arrived, I asked him to join me on a bench that overlooked the wooden jungle gym. The sun was shining into his hazel eyes.

"So, I found something in your room today, and before I show it to you, I want you to know that I have not told your dad. This is just between you and me for now. I also want you to know that you can tell me absolutely anything, and I will never ever judge you. Sometimes, it's nice to have someone to talk to besides our parents, someone we can open up to. I want to be that person for you, Jonah. Okay?"

Fear filled his eyes as I took his notebook out of my bag.

"I found this notebook in your room." When he began to tremble, I took his hand in mine. "Everything is going to be fine, but I want you to tell me why you wrote these two sentences repeatedly."

A tear fell down his cheek. This was painful, but I knew it had to be done.

"It's okay. Take all the time you need. I only want to help you."

He finally looked at me and said, "Please don't tell my dad. Please."

"Your daddy loves you, Jonah. There is nothing you can ever say, do, or think that will change that."

After a long silence, he admitted, "I have these scary thoughts. I can't stop them." He closed his eyelids tightly to ward off more tears.

"How long have you had them?"

"For a long time."

"As long as I've known you?"

He nodded yes.

"Tell me about them."

"Sometimes, I can see myself hurting my dad, sometimes it's my mom, but mostly Dad."

"You know thoughts are just thoughts, right? They don't mean anything."

"I hate them. I'm afraid." The look of fear on his face was palpable.

A light bulb went off in my mind. This sounded awfully familiar.

"When you get the thoughts...what do you do?"

"I have to go over them in my head over and over until I feel better...until I know I won't do it. Then, they come back worse, and I have to do the same thing. It never stops."

"Jonah...I know this is going to sound strange, but I think we were meant to meet, that I was meant to be in your life."

"Why?"

"This is a lot like the same thing that used to happen to me when I was your age. It's called OCD."

"OCD?"

I had to stop myself to think about how to best explain it to him. While I wasn't a doctor and couldn't diagnose him, I suspected what Jonah was suffering from was a case of really bad intrusive thoughts, otherwise known as Pure O—the very same thing I suffered with for years. He was performing never-ending mental rituals to ease his fear.

"When I was younger, I used to have visions of stabbing my grandmother. She used to watch me while my mother worked. Deep down, I knew I would never do that, but the thoughts scared me. The more they scared me, the more they would reappear."

"You never hurt your grandmother?"

"No. No, I didn't. But you know what? These thoughts...they tend to focus on the people you love the most. So, if you're having them about your dad, then that's probably why."

"How do you make them stop?"

"That's the thing. You really can't make them stop. You have to accept that they are just thoughts. As long as they scare you, and as long as you focus on them, they will always be there. But if you recognize them for what they are...just junk that your imagination comes up with...they eventually stop bothering you."

"What do I do when I get one?"

"You stop, and you say, 'Okay, here are those thoughts again. I know they're just thoughts. I'm gonna let them be there and go play something I enjoy or have a snack.'"

"That sounds really hard."

"It is...at first. But it takes time and practice. I'm gonna get you help, okay? You need to let me tell your dad, though."

He suddenly placed his little hand on my knee. "No, you can't!"

"I promise he'll understand. His insurance might be able to pay for a special doctor who will help you understand that what you have is OCD and doesn't mean anything bad. The doctor will do exercises with you that help you deal with this."

"That's what you did?"

"Yes. I went to a specialist who helped me. He saw people every day with the same exact scary thoughts that we have. And I promise you, Jonah, it will get better. You can learn to live with it. You should never be ashamed to tell me anything, okay?"

After a long pause, he said, "Okay, Frankie Four Eyes."

When he smiled, it warmed my heart. I knew the pain and suffering he must have been enduring in keeping this to himself. Between his eyesight and OCD, Jonah truly reminded me of my younger self. Forget teaching, I felt my place right now was to help this little boy come out of his own mind.

I had no doubt that I was exactly where I was meant to be.

CHAPTER TWENTY-THREE

Mack

We had taken Jonah to a professional who'd officially diagnosed him with Obsessive Compulsive Disorder. The doctor described it as a thinking disease that feeds on self-doubt.

Apparently, my son had been suffering from it for at least a couple of years. The OCD, in conjunction with his generalized anxiety, had been making his life a living hell.

We had no way of knowing about the scary thoughts inside of his head. If it weren't for Frankie, we probably wouldn't have discovered it at all. I'd always known that her presence in my life was a blessing, but I could never repay her for what she did for my son. Even though he still struggled with his OCD, Jonah no longer felt ashamed.

My house in Massachusetts had finally sold. We'd just moved out of the apartment and into a brand new townhouse in Alexandria. Surrounded by boxes, our lives seemed to be in chaos. But despite the physical clutter, I'd never felt more at peace.

Frankie was getting dressed for our first night out since the move. She was looking at herself in the full-length mirror and had no idea I'd been watching her. She turned around to look at her ass in the dress, and all I could think about was how I couldn't wait to see that beautiful body pregnant with my baby some day. Experiencing that with her would seem like going through it for the first time, since I'd been in denial up until Jonah's birth. I couldn't wait to experience life with her and continued to be so grateful for the second chance.

"I really want to knock you up."

Startled, she shook at the sound of my voice.

"Well, I can't say anyone else has ever greeted me that way before."

"Did I say that out loud?"

"You didn't mean to?"

Wrapping my arms around her from the back, I said, "I was just thinking about how much I love you and how badly I want us to have our own baby someday."

"Someday...or now?"

"I would knock you up now if you'd let me."

Frankie turned around to face me. "Really?"

"Why does that surprise you?"

"I don't know. We've never discussed it. I guess, I just always assumed that you wanted to focus on Jonah for a while."

"That will always be the case, won't it? There's nothing more that I want in this world than to make a little human with you. I think a baby would be exactly the glue that this broken family needs right now. A sibling might also give Jonah something positive to focus on. But I would never expect you to agree to it until you're ready, whether that's next year or five years from now. I was just thinking out loud." I kissed her on the forehead. "You look shocked."

"Actually...this might sound crazy, but lately, I've been thinking about how much I really want a baby with you, too. I was afraid to tell you how badly I wanted it, because I'd assumed it was too soon."

"Don't ever be afraid to ask me for what you want. Chances are, I'll want it even more, especially if it makes you happy. And especially if the process to get there involves lots of sex with you." I looped by finger under the strap of her dress. "So, should we get started, then?"

"Isn't this a little ass backwards?" She laughed.

"What do you mean?"

"Shouldn't we get engaged first or something?"

"Oh...sure." My heart started to pound as I reached into my back pocket. "Hang on." I took out the small velvet pouch I'd been carrying around with me every day for weeks.

"Is that what I think it is?"

"It is, Frankie. I'm not gonna be pulling a pendant out. That would suck."

Her eyes widened. "You were going to propose tonight?"

"Not sure. I've carried it around every day in case the right moment comes up."

"Now? Now is the right moment?"

"You just told me you're gonna let me knock you up. I would say the right moment was probably a year ago. I'm late."

She covered her mouth in shock. "Oh, my God. Is this really happening?"

Getting down on one knee, I looked up at her. "Frankie Jane...thank you for giving me joy. You were the first person to ever bring it into my life. True joy left me when we were apart. But it's back. Will you marry me and let me knock you up...whichever comes first?"

She waved her hands in excitement. "Yes!!"

After I slipped the one-and-a-half carat diamond on her finger, she looked down at her hand and shook her head in apparent disbelief. "Part one and part two are a lot different, aren't they?"

Looping her fingers in mine, I said, "What are you talking about?"

"I feel like our relationship can be divided into two parts. Our time in college is like part one. It was fun and about self-discovery. It was even innocent...aside from the fact that you had a girlfriend. Part two has been challenging. We had to reacquaint ourselves with each other to find that old connection again but also had to deal with new obstacles."

"You chose the more difficult road when you picked me. That's for sure."

"Sometimes, the more difficult road leads to the greatest destination. Part two is a lot harder, but the rewards have been greater than I could've ever imagined. Easier isn't always better. I would choose part two with you and Jonah any day."

I suddenly lifted her up and carried her over to the bed.

"What are you doing?" She laughed.

"I'd like to get started on part three."

ONE YEAR LATER

I couldn't sleep for shit. The excitement of what was going to be happening tomorrow was keeping me up. I impulsively grabbed a pen and paper from my nightstand and began writing something that I'd been debating for a while.

Dear Freddie,

You don't know me, and I'm not even going to tell you my name. But I've felt compelled to write you for a very long time now.

I know that you know you have a daughter. What you likely don't know is the kind of person she is or what's become of her. Your daughter is a beautiful human being and the woman I love. You might be wondering how someone good and kindhearted could have come from you. I anticipate you have had a lot of time over the years to think about your past actions, and maybe you regret everything you did in your youth. Maybe you don't. But, in any case, I'm writing to let you know that you did do one thing right in your life; you brought a selfless, compassionate person into this world.

Your daughter grew up thinking that her father abandoned her, that you didn't want her. I know the truth wasn't as simple as that. You were young and got yourself into some shit that you can never take back. She knows now. She was recently told the story about you, and even though she's decided not to meet you, she's come to terms with it. My almost nine-year-old son had asked her a long time ago whether she forgave you. That was before she knew the truth. At the time, she told him she needed to get back to him on that question. Last night, she fulfilled her promise to him. She told him that, even though her father had made some mistakes, she did forgive him and used it as a lesson to teach my son forgiveness. She's a better person than I am, because I'm still working on forgiving my own father for his indiscretions. Anyway, I thought that maybe knowing this might help you sleep better at night, whether you think you deserve that forgiveness or not.

As I sit here writing this, I'm preparing to marry her tomorrow in a small ceremony with just our closest family and friends. You won't be there to walk her down the aisle. Instead, she's going to be walking toward me alone. That's her choice and representative of the strong, independent spirit she's always had.

I'm not sure if writing this letter is a mistake or not. I'm not even sure what has prompted me to write you tonight. Maybe it's because, as a father, I truly understand that no matter how many times we fuck up, the one constant is our love for our children.

I want you to know that you don't need to worry about your daughter's well-being. She will always be taken care of and will never want for anything ever again—especially love from a man.

Take care of yourself, and I hope this letter brings you even an ounce of the peace that your daughter has brought to me.

Sincerely, M.M.

EPILOGUE

Mack

THREE YEARS LATER

"Remember those stories you used to tell...the ones about Frankie? How come you don't write those anymore?"

I love that my son called her Frankie, too.

"I guess real life is more exciting than any adventures that Frankie Four Eyes could possibly have. Frankie Four Eyes married Mackenzie Magic, and they lived happily ever after. The End."

"You should dig them up and read them to Joy when she can understand," Jonah said.

"That's a good idea. Maybe we can bring them back when she's old enough to comprehend."

Despite my having boasted about my plans to knock Frankie up, it took us a while to actually conceive. I was scared that it wouldn't be in the cards for us. But our little miracle was born a little over two years after we got married.

I'd always dreamt that I'd have a daughter with the same red hair as her mother. Turned out, my beautiful baby girl was meant to look just like me instead. She did have Frankie's pudgy nose, though. It made me laugh to see my wife's cute nose on a little human who otherwise looked like me. It was like our own special version of Face Swap.

Joy Elena had just turned one and was starting to walk. Jonah was holding his sister's hands and stood behind her to make sure she wouldn't fall. Having a little sister to watch over and protect had given my son a new purpose and helped take his mind off of himself. Jonah still struggled with his anxiety disorder but had made a lot of progress in the past few years.

I'd come up with the name Joy for obvious reasons. I would always thank Frankie for bringing Joy into my life, and having our daughter gave new meaning to that. Her middle name, Elena, was after Mrs. Migillicutty, who'd passed away suddenly around the time Joy was born. My former neighbor had elected to have her ashes distributed amongst the various people she cared about. Some time after her death, we received a notice from her family that we were one of the recipients of some of those ashes. When the small urn was delivered to our house, it was clear that even in death, Mrs. M. could manage to make us laugh. There was a note included that said, *Keep me somewhere at the bar. Just don't mistake me for margarita salt.* We decided to keep her ashes inside a bottle of her favorite rum in a special spot.

On this particular night, I was in my glory. I had my wife, mother, son, and daughter with me. We were celebrating Joy's first birthday. Earlier, we'd watched as she smashed her little chubby hand repeatedly into her very own special cake, making a huge mess.

Frankie was loving being a stay-at-home mother. Even though she never returned to teaching full-time, she tutored on the side in the evenings and planned to go back to graduate school eventually to become an OCD therapist.

We were still estranged from my father, who'd just been re-elected to public office. While his political career thrived, his personal life remained a mess as we continued to live our lives separated from him. To the best of my knowledge, he'd followed through with all of his promises, including discreetly seeking therapy. Torrie still worked for him, but overall, my relationship with her had turned into a cordial but distant one. After the intervention at my father's office, the question of Jonah's paternity was never brought up again.

Joy inched her way toward me with wobbly legs. Jonah was right behind her every step of the way, leading his sister straight into my arms. I lifted my daughter up and kissed her chubby, rosy cheeks that still smelled like sugary frosting. She'd taught me that I had an even greater capacity to love than I'd ever thought possible.

Frankie plopped down onto the couch next to us. She looked over at my mother. "Did you notice that Joy has the same twin toes as Jonah?"

"You mean webbed feet?" my mother asked.

"Yes. Just the two toes but the same two." Frankie lifted our daughter's foot. "Look at the way these two toes look like they're sewn together. Jonah's are the exact same way."

"Just like their grandma," my mother noted.

"You mean...you?" I asked. "You have twin toes?"

Mom pointed to her feet. "Yes, I have them, too."

My eyes widened. "How did I never know that?"

"I'm not sure. Maybe I never pointed it out, or you just didn't care to look at your mother's feet. It's genetic, you know. My mother and sister had them, too. Many of the Mackenzies did. It can skip a generation, which is why you were spared, Mack."

My world seemed to stop in that moment as I processed what she'd just told me.

"You mean to tell me that my kids inherited these twin toes from *you*? Joy inherited them from you? And Jonah...Jonah...inherited them from you, too? So, it's a Mackenzie trait, not a Morrison trait. You see what I'm getting at?"

My mother beamed. "I can't believe we never figured this out before. I never once noticed Jonah's toes. Otherwise, I would've said something."

Frankie's expression brightened, and tears began to form in her eyes. She had figured out exactly what I was getting at. If webbed feet were genetic and ran in my mother's family, then there was a damn good chance Jonah had inherited his from me. Not from my father. *From me.*

I reached over to him and planted a huge kiss on his face. He was completely taken aback and perplexed. "Dad, what are you doing? Gross!"

"Nothing, son. Nothing. It doesn't matter."

But it did. It mattered so much—more than I ever thought it did.

We didn't need the damn test.

He was my son.

Jonah walked away oblivious as he helped Joy take her wobbly baby steps to the other side of the room.

My wife, who understood the magnitude of this discovery, leapt into my arms and whispered, "Congratulations, Mack Daddy."

ACKNOWLEDGEMENTS

Thank you first and foremost to every single reader who continues to support and promote my books. Your enthusiasm and hunger for my stories is what motivates me every day. To all of the book bloggers and authors who support me, I wouldn't be here without you.

To Vi – Each time I thank you in a book, I am more at a loss for words than the time before, because you become even more important to me as a friend and partner in crime as time moves on. I couldn't do this without you. I'm so glad we took a "chance" on the writing partnership, but I also know that if all the books went away tomorrow, I would still have an amazing friend, and that, to me, is more valuable than anything.

To Julie – You kicked ass this year and took names. Thank you for your friendship and for always inspiring me with your amazing writing, attitude, and strength.

To Luna –Thank you for your love and support, day in and day out. I so look forward to getting to see you this year. This is the year of Luna, and I can't wait to celebrate you, Mamacita!

To Erika – We met because of my words. But *your* words of kindness and encouragement on a daily basis mean more to me than you know. Love and Larry for life.

To my Facebook fan group, Penelope's Peeps – I love you all. Your excitement motivates me every day.

To Queen Peep Amy – Thank you for serving as the Peeps admin. and for supporting me from the very beginning. More lunches to come!

To Mia – Thank you, my friend, for always making me laugh. I know you're going to bring us some phenomenal words this year, and I can't wait for more from Arsen's momma!

To my publicist, Dani, at InkSlinger P.R. – Thank you for taking some of the weight off my shoulders and for guiding this release. It's a pleasure working with you.

To Elaine of Allusion Book Formatting and Publishing – Thank you for being the best proofreader and formatter a girl could ask for.

To Letitia of RBA Designs – The best cover designer ever! Thank you for always working with me until the cover is exactly how I want it.

To Lisa of TRSoR and Milasy Mugnolo – Thank you for your unwavering support throughout the years.

To my agent, Kimberly Brower – Here's to coming full circle. Thank you for believing in me long before you were my agent, back when you were a blogger and I was a first-time author.

To my husband – Thank you for always taking on so much more than you should have to so that I am able to write. I love you so much.

To the best parents in the world – I'm so lucky to have you! Thank you for everything you have ever done for me and for always being there.

To my besties: Allison, Angela, Tarah and Sonia – Thank you for putting up with that friend who suddenly became a nutty writer.

Last but not least, to my daughter and son – Mommy loves you. You are my motivation and inspiration!

OTHER STANDALONES

ROOMHATE
New York Times, USA TODAY and #1 Wall Street Journal Bestseller

STEPBROTHER DEAREST
New York Times, USA TODAY and Wall Street Journal Bestseller

NEIGHBOR DEAREST
New York Times, USA TODAY and Wall Street Journal Bestseller

SINS OF SEVIN
USA TODAY Bestseller

COCKY BASTARD
(co-written with Vi Keeland)
New York Times and USA TODAY Bestseller

STUCK-UP SUIT (co-written with Vi Keeland)
New York Times, USA TODAY and Wall Street Journal Bestseller

PLAYBOY PILOT (co-written with Vi Keeland)
New York Times and USA TODAY Bestseller

JAKE UNDONE (Jake #1)

JAKE UNDERSTOOD (Jake #2)

MY SKYLAR
USA TODAY Bestseller

GEMINI

ABOUT THE AUTHOR

Penelope Ward is a *New York Times, USA Today* and #1 *Wall Street Journal* Bestselling author of thirteen novels. She is a fifteen-time *New York Times* Bestseller (hitting at the #2 spot on three separate occasions). Several of her books have been translated into foreign languages and can be found in bookstores around the world.

Penelope spent most of her twenties as a television news anchor before switching to a more family-friendly career. She grew up in Boston with five older brothers. She lives for reading books in the new adult genre, coffee, messaging with her buddy and sometimes co-author Vi Keeland as well as hanging out with her friends and family on weekends.

She is the proud mother of a beautiful 12-year-old girl with autism (the inspiration for the character Callie in Gemini) and a 10-year-old boy, both of whom are the lights of her life.

Penelope, her husband, and kids reside in Rhode Island.

Email Penelope at: penelopewardauthor@gmail.com
Newsletter Signup: http://bit.ly/1X725rj
Facebook Author Page: https://www.facebook.com/penelopewardauthor
Facebook Fan Group (Request to join!) https://www.facebook.com/groups/PenelopesPeeps/
Instagram: https://instagram.com/PenelopeWardAuthor
Twitter: https://twitter.com/PenelopeAuthor
Website: www.penelopewardauthor.com

CPSIA information can be obtained
at www.ICGtesting.com
Printed in the USA
BVHW032130040319
541790BV00001B/5/P